# THE INITIATE

*The Tales of Zhava: Book 1*

## H. Dean Fisher

The Initiate: The Tales of Zhava: Book 1 Copyright © 2019 by H. Dean Fisher. All Rights Reserved.

All rights reserved. No part of this book may be reproduced in any form or by any electronic or mechanical means including information storage and retrieval systems, without permission in writing from the author. The only exception is by a reviewer, who may quote short excerpts in a review.

Cover art by Carrie Kingsbury, Promiseland Art – PromiselandArt.com
Author photo by John Kilker – JohnJKilker.com

This book is a work of fiction. Names, characters, places, and incidents either are products of the author's imagination or are used fictitiously. Any resemblance to actual persons, living or dead, events, or locales is entirely coincidental.

H. Dean Fisher
Visit my website and sign up for my email newsletter:
Website: www.HDeanFisher.com

Follow me on social media:
Facebook: www.facebook.com/SeventhBattlePublishing
Twitter: @HDeanFisher1
Instagram: HDeanFisher

Printed in the United States of America

First Paperback Printing: Sept 2019
Seventh Battle Publishing

ISBN-9781072980513
Library of Congress Control Number:2019907283

*For Freyja: Pursue your passion*

# CONTENTS

Author's notes ........................................................................................ 7
Chapter 1 .............................................................................................. 8
Chapter 2 ............................................................................................ 18
Chapter 3 ............................................................................................ 28
Chapter 4 ............................................................................................ 37
Chapter 5 ............................................................................................ 45
Chapter 6 ............................................................................................ 62
Chapter 7 ............................................................................................ 76
Chapter 8 ............................................................................................ 92
Chapter 9 .......................................................................................... 110
Chapter 10 ........................................................................................ 118
Chapter 11 ........................................................................................ 129
Chapter 12 ........................................................................................ 142
Chapter 13 ........................................................................................ 149
Chapter 14 ........................................................................................ 164
Chapter 15 ........................................................................................ 172
Chapter 16 ........................................................................................ 185
Chapter 17 ........................................................................................ 192
Chapter 18 ........................................................................................ 209
Chapter 19 ........................................................................................ 216
Chapter 20 ........................................................................................ 224
Chapter 21 ........................................................................................ 234
Chapter 22 ........................................................................................ 247

# AUTHOR'S NOTES

Though this debut novel is my first in print, I have been crafting stories since I was 5 and writing novels since I was 13. My passion has always been to tell an engaging story with a powerful message, and I created characters and plots to do just that.

This story, however, came to me in a dream, one of those 3 a.m. moments that shone with such clarity I had to sit up and take notice. Zhava and Plishka introduced themselves to me in a dramatic scene that became the heart of this book. They live in a harsh world that barely cares they exist, surrounded by people as likely to strike at them as to speak with them – and Gods who seem to find pleasure in toying with them.

Actually, that sounds a lot like the world of today....

Special thanks to my wife, Suzanne; my parents, Ken & Geri; my editor, Julee C. Meketa, @littlecityjulee; trauma advisor, Dr. Mark Hall; publishing advisor, Ann Lavendar, www.AnnLavendar.com; fighting advisor, Robert Thomas of Tsunami Self-Defense Academy, www.TsunamiSelfDefense.com; and my most critical first reader, my daughter.

For those so inclined, the soundtrack to The Initiate is:
    Lana Del Rey, "Born to Die (the Paradise Edition)"
    Audra Mae and the Almighty Sound
    Rachael Yamagata, "Elephants...Teeth Sinking Into"

# CHAPTER 1

*Seven thousand years ago, in the land of Remmli, on the northern border of Go'aab, on the edge of the Sineise Desert, and two days east of the Purneese Mountains....*

Everything began to change the morning Zhava met her future husband. He came with his family to their small farmstead on the edge of the Goodspring. They reclined beneath the cover of the noonday court, he and his family eating dates and pomegranates as if Zhava's family owned an entire orchard instead of just the little grove alongside their home. His name was Ooleng – as if she was supposed to say that funny little name for the rest of her life. He brought his two older brothers, and his mama and papa were there to negotiate the bride price, the silver and the livestock that they would pay for Zhava to leave with them and to never return, to become wife to this little Ooleng and his hungry family. His eyes were too wide, though. And his brothers never stopped babbling at each other, critiquing the courtyard and the shade trees and the state of her papa's tent awning and the way that papa's shirt had been resewn at the hem and....

She did not like them.

Of course, she had not yet spoken to them. To any of them. She peaked around the heavy curtain blocking her path to the courtyard in the center of their square home. She watched them from around the cover of her hiding spot, critiquing their eating and their drinking and their talking and their lack of any manners. And she was supposed to go with them? She was supposed to keep home for this little Ooleng? What kind of a name was Ooleng, anyway? It meant "third" in their language, but third of what? The third child born? That would be a stupid way to name children. "First and Second, meet Third." It showed a lack of imagination...or education. And she was supposed to do what with a "Third"?

Ooleng's parents sat quietly and ate and let their older sons jabber. They had the same too-wide eyes as their third son, and those eyes took in everything without betraying thoughts that seemed to spill from their children's mouths. They nodded appropriately when their children found the smallest thing to praise – which was not often – but otherwise they sat and listened without commenting anything of their own.

Of course, none of this was obvious to Zhava's Papa because he could not speak their tongue. Papa tended the livestock and he cared for the grove of trees on the land alongside their home, but he never found the purpose in learning the other tongues. He knew Remmliit, and that was sufficient for most anything he did in the village and dealings in the desert markets. He rarely ever traveled east, and he never crossed the Purneese Mountains, so learning the tongues of the Purneesites was a luxury of his time that he could little afford. All of that meant that the babbling of little Ooleng's brothers was a noise to his ears, a noise that meant little to him beyond the excited sounds of their voices. That excitement, however, betrayed their true feelings for Zhava's family as they mocked the lack of wealth and the lack of luxury and the lack of soft, colorful clothing on Papa's back. These people, this little Ooleng and his brothers and his papa and mama, these people were jackals dining in the pit of their own laughter.

"Zhava," came Marmaran's voice gently from the kitchen table behind her.

Zhava let the curtain fall shut and rushed back to Marmaran's side. Old and blind and frail, Marmaran was the wisest person Zhava had ever met, a former priestess of the land and the person with more education than anyone else within several moons' walk, and if she asked anything in the world, then Zhava would do it for her.

"Yes, Marmaran," she said at the old woman's side.

"Zhava, you hear it too?"

"Yes, Marmaran."

"And you do not approve?"

"No, Marmaran."

Marmaran let out a quiet hum from the back of her throat as she leaned against the far wall. Zhava could see through the open doorway Mama returning across the yard with a bucket of water from the well, probably for the evening stew. She looked cross as she strode purposefully and scattered the chickens from her path.

Marmaran set her hand to the table and flicked a small stone to its center. "Again," she whispered.

"But," Zhava said, glancing out the door again. "Mama is coming."

"Then quickly."

Zhava rested her hand against the cool stone of the tabletop, spread her fingers wide, and flicked her wrist. The stone bounced across the table and fell to the floor.

"No, Zhava, no," Marmaran said, scowling and taking another stone from her shawl's pocket and setting it near the center of the table. "Gently. With control."

Zhava sighed, glanced nervously at her approaching Mama again, who would reach the kitchen in a few seconds. She looked back at the rock, spread her fingers wide, and gently twirled her wrist over and under and over again. The rock sat up from its spot in the table's center and lightly bounced and rolled across the table.

"Kindle it," Marmaran whispered.

Zhava sighed again, but did as she was told. She closed her hand and began rubbing the tips of her fingers together, feeling the dust and dirt grip as she gently motioned as if she kindled the remnants of an evening's fire. The stone balanced on the edge of the table, gently whirling and spinning as if her fingers actually touched it, as if she was sliding the rock back and forth and spinning it on its edge–

And then it was gone, scooped up in her Mama's hand.

"You stop!" her Mama hissed in her ear, slopping water from the edge of the pail and onto the kitchen floor. "And you, Marmaran, you know better. Do not let them see!"

"That family would no sooner step foot in this kitchen," Marmaran said with a growl, "than they would stoop to wash the shit from their boots."

"They are willing to take our Zhava," Mama said, "and that is reason enough to allow them into our home."

"You do not know the value of your Zhava," Marmaran said.

Zhava started backing away, but Marmaran reached out with one swift hand and clapped Zhava's wrist to the table. She was going nowhere during this conversation. She never liked this conversation, though, and she had heard it 20 times in the past several moons. Mama would say that Zhava was of no use to the household now that Marmaran had arrived and begun instructing Zhava in the ways of the Kandor; and then Marmaran would say that she had received a vision that Zhava must be taught the ways of the Kandor if the people of Remmli were to survive; and then Mama would say that the vision – if there had even been a vision, because Mama was a blasphemer who did not believe in the visions of the Gods – was given when Marmaran was no longer healthy but had grown old and feeble and her last student was a dozen years moved away and probably dead and that Marmaran was just trying to relive the glory days of her youth. That's when Mama would say that Zhava's monthly period was the only gift that the family needed because now she could be bartered away for supplies the family truly needed – not for having dirty rocks cleared from the kitchen table.

And that was what it truly came down to, Zhava thought. Since she had reached her maturity and was no longer a child but now capable of having a child of her own, her value had increased – even though that had happened only a few moons ago. It now meant that Papa could entertain offers such as this one from Ooleng and his brothers and his parents to accept the bride price and to relieve Mama and Papa of the burden of a daughter who could contribute nothing more to the family.

She listened to the conversation play out between her Mama and Marmaran, and it transpired exactly as she had predicted...exactly as it had the previous time they argued...and the time before that...and the time before that. Marmaran's days of Godly visions were long over, and Zhava's days of being a burden to her family had just begun. As the argument wound down once again, Marmaran eased her grip on Zhava's wrist, and Zhava slowly edged out the kitchen door and into the late afternoon shade of their little home.

She sat in the dirt, though she knew her Mama would be mad for grubbing her dress, and she opened her hand before her. She could still hear the voices of Ooleng and his family drifting from the open courtyard in the center of the home, and the argument between Mama and Marmaran continued as if Zhava had never left, and so she knew she could remain alone and undisturbed for a while yet. She blew into the center of her palm, and the little flame flickered to life. She rolled her fingers, and the flame danced across her palm. She held out her other hand and tilted the flame until he slipped gently between them, and like that she played with the little dancing flame, rolling him around and sliding him back and forth between her hands and laughing at his tickle across her palm.

This was something she had not even shared with Marmaran. She had simply been cold one morning and blew into her hands to warm them, and this little flame had appeared, and ever since that one morning she had kept him her own little secret. She would bring him out to play when she was alone, and she would whisper to him all of her life's deepest secrets, and he would listen and tell no one else. She was not sure what Marmaran would even say if she knew Zhava could do this, but she certainly knew what her Mama and her Papa would say: they would tell her that such foolishness only made her less desirable in the eyes of any future husband, and that she should stop such nonsense and better prepare herself for the duties required in the running of a household with a dozen children, because that would be her life. The King might want people who had been given the Abilities of the Gods, but those Abilities were a curse on the far edge of the frontier, where the only Gods that mattered were the ones that brought the spring rains and helped the cattle and sheep to birth strong, healthy young.

***

Later that night, after the first day's bartering and the evening meal and the cleanup and the more mindless chatter in the evening court, Zhava had asked permission to retire early to her room. Of course Mama had wanted her to remain so that Ooleng and his brothers could continue staring at her and snickering at their little jokes about her hair and her eyes – and her rounded chest – but those were all conversations that Mama could not understand because they were in another tongue. Marmaran had taught those tongues to Zhava only, much to Mama and Papa's disapproval. And now she almost wished that Marmaran had never come and taught her those tongues because she was not sure which was worse, to sit in ignorance and smile along with the foolish men and their foolish laughter, or to sit in knowledge and to know that those smiles and that laughter came only at Zhava's expense.

So she lay on her bed and stared out the open window with the heavy cloth blowing in the evening breeze, and she watched the stars twinkle in the heavens. The stories of the stars swirled in her head, conflicting with each other but coming together in one beautiful, Godly tapestry. The stories her parents had told her, of the snake-eyed Nastor and his fight with the three lions; of Coredor, the eater of the dead, and his vengeance upon the women of his youth; of the water nymph Preizhavan and the garland of grapeseed vines wrapped elegantly about her hips. Preizhavan had always been her favorite – and only somewhat because the goddess' name was so similar to Zhava's own, a fortunate happenstance that her Mama assured her had not been planned when they began the naming ceremony in the week after Zhava's birth. No, she thought Preizhavan was the most beautiful woman that Zhava had ever seen, no matter that the other Gods and Goddesses found her comely, and no matter that Erinian, the Goddess of Beauty herself, would curse Zhava with ugliness and barrenness if she were to ever say that thought aloud. There was just a certain elegance in the life that Preizhavan brought forth from the earth, that she could ripple the life-sustaining beauty of the red and purple irises that Zhava and Mama tended along the morning side of the home, and yet she could rise the bounty of harvest from the ground every fall, enough to sustain all of the family through the coldest of the midwinter nights. Zhava found that kind of beauty...engaging...fulfilling in a way that Erinian's golden hair and sumptuous smile and perfectly rounded body could never be for her. Preizhavan's beauty as the bearer of bountiful life was far more stunning to Zhava than she could ever express aloud, both because of her fear of Erinian's curse but also because she simply lacked the words, in any language, to truly express those thoughts.

And she had believed all of that long before Marmaran had even arrived and begun to share new and different stories of the Gods and Goddesses. Zhava quickly found Luliuh, the god of the eternal fountain, within the stars above; Marmaran had said that he provided the waters of life that even Preizhavan used to bring forth her bountiful harvest – but of course Zhava had never heard of this god before Marmaran arrived. She counted in the stars all of the other Gods and Goddesses that Marmaran had shared with her until she had reached their complete number: 28. She was quite pleased with herself for finding them in the midnight sky, and for correctly naming them all. When Marmaran first arrived at their home only a few seasons ago, that was the first thing she had taught to Zhava, the names and places of all the Gods and Goddesses in the heavens above, and their places upon the earth below. Zhava had never forgotten.

The sky began to darken even more, and Zhava knew it was truly the mid-night hour as the little town in the valley snuffed out most of the evening torches. Of course Zhava could not see it happen because the valley and its little town were on the other side of the house, away from Zhava's view, but the snuffing of the lights always provided Zhava with a grander view of the stars of the Gods and Goddesses.

This night, however, there was something different on the horizon. A set of lights weaved and bobbed in the near-far distance. She silently counted five individual lights. They each swayed back and forth on their own individual paths, not connected, and they dimmed and brightened as they moved, as if small clouds swirled around them. She guessed they were lanterns atop camels, something Marmaran had described to her in a story once, long ago, but as she had never before seen such a sight, she was left only to guess.

The swaying lanterns slowly grew brighter, as if they approached Zhava's home.  She remembered something Marmaran had taught her about distance, and she thought this a good chance to practice.  She looked at one light, the one farthest to the desert, and then she sighted along a straight line until her eyes reached a little mound of rocks – she knew them as Fountain Rocks, though Mama had never let her run that far, so she had no idea the significance of the name.  Then she started counting, just as Marmaran had taught her.  When she reached the number 10, she sighted a straight line back toward the lights...and saw that the lights were now quite a bit closer.  They were approaching Zhava's home, and they were approaching rather quickly.

"Iya!" she heard the evening watch cry out from the roof.  So, he had only now seen the lights himself.  It made Zhava feel good to know that she had seen them so much sooner than he, though he was the one dutied to stand watch upon the early night.

There were stirrings from within the home as Zhava heard her father arise from his bed.  Her brothers, in the homes of their own scattered along the valley would be arising as well – but again, her bedroom window did not face in the directions of any of their homes.

Papa woke the two servants, and she heard them all gathering weapons.  Ooleng and his family began asking questions in the hallway outside her bedroom door, but Papa assured them all would be fine and to return to their beds.  That was the polite thing for him to do.  They were guests, and their protection fell upon Papa and his household.  It would also be polite for the guests, Ooleng and his brothers and their own papa, to decline the offer of safety when a potential threat existed against the entire household, and they would quickly arise to accompany him.  She heard Ooleng's papa instruct his two sons to accompany Papa, though, while he and Ooleng returned to their nighttime rest.  Zhava would not have thought it possible, but she now liked them even less.

By now the lantern lights were much closer, and Zhava could see that the clouds drifting through the air were dust, and they were caused by the stamping of the feet of at least a dozen soldiers marching alongside five camels.  Four men and a woman rode atop those camels, all five of them dressed in the deep blacks and reds of the King's advisors.  Zhava had seen a King's advisor only once before, when she was a small girl. The man had come through their little town on his way to report on the border patrol at the Purneese Mountains, and she had never forgotten the strength and beauty of that man as he stopped at the town center and watered his camel and talked with the city elders. But to see five of them at one time? And accompanied by soldiers in their black and red armor and their swords? Zhava never would have expected such a thing in all of her days.

As the King's people rode closer, they slowed to a stop some distance from the home. Papa and Ooleng's two brothers and Papa's two servants walked slowly across the yard, their own swords strapped to their belts and their arms open wide – both in caution and in greeting. Visitors would never be turned away, especially visitors from the King, but visitors should also have the politeness to appear while the sun still shone and when hiding in the bushes would be that much more difficult.

"Peace to you," Papa called out.

"And peace to you," the one woman called back. She lightly dropped down from the camel's mount and stepped slowly forward, her arms held wide and away from her own sword. The dozen soldiers stood back, their own hands loose at their sides. The lanterns swayed gently on their tall hooks, the mounts set securely against the camel's saddles.

"You honor us with your presence," Papa said, folding his hands and bowing forward.

"And you honor us with your patience upon this late night journey," the woman replied, her own bow echoing that of Papa.

"Won't you please step inside?" Papa asked.

"Again, you honor us," the woman said. "But you must know the nature of our journey before we can accept your gracious offer."

Papa stiffened a bit, something the woman probably did not notice, but Zhava knew it right away. He did that when things did not go his way, when he expected to have to strike out at something, either with his words or with his weapon.

"Please," he said, standing straight and stiff, "tell me the nature of your journey."

"I seek the one trained in Kandor."

"You seek...Priestess Marmaran?" Papa asked.

"Priestess Marmaran?" the woman said. She turned to glance at the men still seated on their camels. They only shrugged and looked at each other. The woman turned back to Papa. "Priestess Marmaran resides with you?"

"Yes, of course," Papa said. "The priestess trained in Kandor, the one of whom you speak."

"We would, of course, be honored to have an audience with the Priestess Marmaran," the woman said, waving a hand quickly through the air. "But she is not the one we seek. We are here because of the Candidate of Kandor, your daughter, Zhava."

# CHAPTER 2

Things became very busy and very loud at the woman's announcement. Papa called for Priestess Marmaran to be awakened and brought to the home's center courtyard, Ooleng and his brothers went to re-awaken their own papa, a servant was dispatched to bring Zhava's three brothers quickly from their own homes – though that would take some time, with them living far down the valley – the King's soldiers were directed to the near pasture to tend their mounts, and the four King's men and the one King's woman were ushered into the home, two of the soldiers following close behind. Weapons were left with the camels or placed within the front entry hall. The courtyard would be crowded tonight, but people would be civil.

Zhava threw on her nearest dress and padded down the steep steps and through the narrow passage to the kitchen with its single oil lamp on the table where Mama was already preparing a plate of small fruits. Zhava recognized it immediately as most of the extra foods that her family had kept aside for the final day of Ooleng and his family visiting – the feast food they would use to celebrate the final negotiations of her bride price. The King's servants, of course, would receive this fine fruit, but now Zhava wondered what they would serve to Ooleng and his family. Troubles for another day, she thought.

"No, no, no," Mama said, glancing up from the meal preparation. She waved at Zhava's dress. "Change now. Quickly! Your shepherding clothes, wear those."

"But why?" she asked, aghast at the suggestion she would wear such filthy rags in the presence of the King's servants.

"Do not ask questions." She shooed away Zhava with a curt wave. "Go now. Quickly!"

Zhava turned and trudged back up the steep, narrow steps. She went to the cleaning room, braced herself against the heavy, wooden door, and pushed with all her strength. Her feet slid across the dusty floor, and the door opened with an agonizing creak of old hinges. The midnight stars lit the tiny room through the long hole in the roof, the hole that let the stinky air escape and the clean rainwater pour down into the large catch-basins set around the corners of the room. She stepped around the washbasin set in the center of the floor, grabbed her shepherding clothes from the washing pile and rushed back out of the smelly room as quickly as she could. She pulled on the heavy door but could only get it halfway closed again. She had no time to try harder, what with Mama's instructions to move "Quickly!" She pressed the bunch of clothes to her nose and breathed in, squinting at the odor of sheep that was embedded into the fabric. She had worn these only two days before when she had been told to tend her brother Caleb's sheep while he was away at market, and between Mama's instructions for preparing for Ooleng's arrival and Marmaran's instructions on playing with rocks and learning meditations and reading the histories, Zhava had not yet had the time to thoroughly clean her shepherding dress. But of course Mama knew that, and she had insisted on it anyway. Was Zhava to go tend sheep while the King's servants were entertained in the moonlit courtyard?

She changed clothes, left her pretty dress in her room, and ran back downstairs to the kitchen. It was empty, and it looked especially so in the glow of that single oil lamp Mama had left burning at the kitchen table. Zhava went to the doorway, slipped a finger across the blanket's heavy edge, and peered into the bustling courtyard. Mama was there with a servant, and they were offering the King's woman and her men those delicious fruits, which they were graciously accepting; Ooleng and his brothers and his mama and papa were there also, looking quite unhappy with their eyes squinting in the dim light of the rising moon and the dozen lamps lit across the walls; Papa was seated at the head of the low table, reclining with a smile on his face that Zhava was certain was not as happy of a smile as he normally would be giving for such honored guests; and

Marmaran was seated at the opposite end of the table, pleasantly bowing to the King's servants and quietly asking after the goings-on at the Hibaro – whatever that was.

Zhava could not hear everything the King's servants said, what with Ooleng's mama and papa hissing their whispers to each other, but she heard enough to know that things were not good at the Hibaro. Someone had fallen, and someone else had been lost, and another someone had been found with a knife in her back; the work had been slow, but now it was hardly progressing at all, and the King was most displeased; the keepers were asking everyone, and a Salient was interviewing people with little notice. Though she understand little of what they were discussing, it sounded to Zhava as if this Hibaro was one of the worst kinds of places anyone could imagine.

She had little time for more thought, however, as Mama rushed back through the curtained door, gripped Zhava by the arm and pulled her through the kitchen only to shove her outside into the cold night's air.

"What did you do?" Mama asked in a harsh whisper.

"I did only what you said," Zhava replied, her arm tingling in her Mama's grip. "I changed into my shepherding dress. But I did not have time to clean it, and so it smells bad and it looks bad."

"No!" Mama said, pushing Zhava further from the kitchen doorway. "What did you and that evil Marmaran do to bring the King's Ios here?"

"I don't know, Mama."

Mama squeezed harder. "Do not lie to me! Did you send for them? Huh? Did you pass a message to them from the town? Tell me!"

"Mama, please," Zhava said, beginning to cry. "You're hurting me. I did nothing – Marmaran did nothing. She has only taught me the words in her books-"

"Yes, the words in her books," Mama said, and she turned to spit upon the ground. "The words of the faithful. The words that mean the end of all peace."

"I do not know, Mama," Zhava said, not sure what she could say that would make her Mama pleased. She tried to wipe the tears from her eyes, but Mama swatted her hand away. Then Mama reached to the ground, came up with a handful of dirt, and spread it across Zhava's face. It quickly caked to mud where the tears streaked down.

"You listen," Mama said, kneeling down and looking Zhava in the eyes. "Your Papa and I have worked hard to attract a good husband for you. Today's negotiations went well, and Papa believes we can double our herd by the time you are sent away to marry Ooleng. But that will not happen – none of it will happen – if you are taken away by the King's Ios. Do you understand?"

"Yes, Mama." But she did not want a dirty face. She did not like Ooleng.

"So you will listen to what we say, and you will do as we say to do."

"Yes, Mama." She was, in fact, quite certain she did not care what her Mama said. She did not like Ooleng or his brothers or his parents, she did not want to stand before the King's Ios in her dirty shepherding dress, and she was more certain than ever that she did not want to go with her "husband" and his oafish family back to wherever they lived across the Purneese Mountains.

"Your Papa will talk these Ios away from here, and he will tell them that the bride price has already been paid – and Ooleng will agree to this, just to get these Ios to go away. And then Ooleng will give us even more because he will see how valuable you are."

"Yes, Mama." But Zhava did not hear. She had already decided within her heart that she would not obey.

Mama led Zhava back into the kitchen and directed her to sit at the kitchen table and wait. So that is what she did. She sat, and she waited. She clenched her fists tight in her lap, and she felt her little flame friend rolling in her palm. He would know what to do. He would see her through this. He had been with her for so many moons, her own little secret from her Mama and her Papa and her brothers – even from Marmaran – but tonight they would all see what he could do. They would all see, and they would feel his heat. She would let loose her little friend of flame, and she would set him upon the little bushes of the courtyard, and upon the tall trees that sat at the corners and provided shade from the noonday sun, and upon the very finery that Mama had worked so hard to embroider upon the windows of the courtyard. Her little flame that she held so tightly would burn so bright in the chilled night....

But Zhava realized he was not alone. She felt more little flaming feet dancing within her fist, prancing upon the skin of her palm, and she looked down to see, to assure herself that she was not simply imagining this. What she saw, however, made the breath stop within her body. Between the fingers of not only one hand but of the other also, she saw the flickering, dancing light of many little flaming men. Their red and orange light flickered out from between her fingers. Their little heads popped out from around her thumbs, and then they ducked back within. They threw out stones of flames from between her fingers, and they laughed as the flames spun out and fizzled into the darkness.

Zhava looked up. She stared at the curtain across the room, the barrier that separated her from the King's Ios and from Ooleng and his family of pigs and from her Papa who would see her off to the richest man he could find and to her Mama who could not wait to be rid of one more unproductive mouth to feed – and of Marmaran. Marmaran who had been Zhava's friend and teacher and guide for these long moons...and likely visited this terrible night upon her now. It must have been Marmaran who passed word to the King's Ios – no one else in her home would have done such a thing. It must have been Marmaran who had sent word to the King himself – probably spoke about her directly with that King's man who appeared in the village all those years ago. That man had looked directly at Zhava even back then, and he had winked at her and smiled. She had thought it something he did only because she was a little girl and waving at him, but it must have been because Marmaran knew – even back then, before she arrived – that Zhava would be trained in the Kandor, and she had made certain that the King's Ios knew of her and that they would return to collect her one day.

Mama burst through the curtain, the oil lamp flickering upon the table in the wind of her passing.

Zhava slipped her hands within the folds of her dress, squeezing her fists tight to hide her men of flames.

Mama set the plate of grapes upon the counter, turned and knelt before Zhava. "They have requested your presence," she said.

"Remember: You are betrothed today, and the bride price has been paid. You leave with Ooleng at first dawn."

"Yes, Mama," she whispered. The flaming men clawed at her palms.

"Good." Mama stood and pointed. "Now go."

Zhava stood. She stepped slowly forward, the curtain looming before her. What she would do, there was no returning from. What she would do, it could never be undone. She would be cast out of her home for this thing she would do, and she would never see her Papa or her Mama again…but she was uncertain how much sadness she would really have at such an end, for she would never again have to look upon another Ooleng. She would miss her brothers, most especially the youngest brother, Caleb, but she would never again endure another indignity at her Mama's hand. She would never again find herself being bartered for a few dozen cattle and sheep.

She nudged aside the thick cloth and stepped into the nighttime courtyard. She glanced up at the sky and saw the stars blinking between the curtains of palm branches and tightly closed flowers…and she imagined the sight of a hundred little dancing men climbing those trees and devouring those petals.

She heard her name being spoken, and she looked back down at the circle of people within the courtyard, her Papa and the King's Ios and Ooleng and his brothers and his own papa…and at Marmaran. She heard her name spoken again, and she stepped forward. She removed her tight fists from the folds of her shepherding dress. Again, her name was spoken aloud, but she spread her fingers wide and prepared to release her army of flaming men upon the ground at her feet. Someone was yelling her name, but she would not stop-

Marmaran's face suddenly appeared before her, yelling out Zhava's name with her fog-filled eyes wild and her hair blowing in a storming wind. "Zhava!" Marmaran screamed.

Zhava stopped. The silence echoed through her mind, but her vision cleared. The night was chilled. The people around the midnight courtyard all smiled at her and watched her – even Marmaran, still at her place at the end of the low table. She turned to look straight at Zhava from across the courtyard, and Zhava could feel the old woman's blind eyes upon her. She had never moved, so how had Marmaran appeared before Zhava? More of her Gods'-given Abilities? Something she had not yet taught, something that would be saved for another day's lesson? If that day would even come?

Zhava looked down, and she saw that the flaming men had all vanished, dissolved when her concentration had been broken.

"My child," Marmaran gently said from her place at the table's far end. "Come here."

Zhava shuffled forward and leaned into Marmaran side. Tears escaped, and Zhava hid her face in Marmaran's sleeve.

"This is her?" the King's woman said. "This is Zhava?"

Marmaran did not answer, but instead cupped her hand around Zhava's head and leaned closer, petting Zhava's hair and making quiet little shushing sounds into her ear.

"Yes," Papa said sadly. "This is our Zhava. We shall all miss her when she leaves us in the morning. But that is the delight of every young girl, to find a good husband and to be at his side for all the days to come."

Marmaran gently guided Zhava back up and began smoothing the shepherding dress. She used the back of her hand to wipe the muddy tears from Zhava's face.

"You are still so dirty?" Marmaran asked.

"I'm sorry," Zhava said, "but yes. I should have cleaned myself better."

"It is not a well-kept secret," Marmaran whispered, pulling Zhava close again, "that the dirt upon a woman's face is no more permanent than the pebbles upon the ground."

"Priestess Marmaran," the King's woman said. "We would meet Zhava now, and judge her for ourselves."

"As you wish," Marmaran said. She bowed her head and gently pushed Zhava away.

Zhava turned to the King's Ios. The five sat stiffly at the low table, their backs straight and their arms resting before them. The woman sat nearest Zhava, and she had a hard, weathered face – though the smaller ears of a much younger woman. She was not old, but Zhava could tell this woman had traveled far and experienced much. Her short black hair and deep brown eyes made her face appear fierce in the dark night. She stared intently at Zhava, obviously appraising her. The four men at her side were watching Zhava also, but none so intently as this woman. The man farthest away actually seemed more intent on Papa than on Zhava, as he slowly plucked a grape from the table with one hand and clenched his other hand into fist.

Zhava looked around the rest of the courtyard and noticed for the first time that the one Io was not the only tense person. Papa was moving slowly, deliberately, his jaw clenched and his eyes wide and alert. Ooleng and one of his brothers sat forward on their heels, ready to jump up from the ground. Many of the people seated at this table expected violence, and they were prepared to meet violence with even more violence at the slightest hint of it from someone else. Had Zhava set loose her flaming men, someone might very well have struck her down.

With a little gasp, she turned back to Marmaran, but the woman's head was still bowed. She had inclined an ear in their direction, however, to better follow the conversation.

"You are Zhava," the King's woman said. It was a statement, not a question, but Zhava turned back to her and nodded an ascent. "I am Liori, Fist of the King's Third Salient, stationed at Hibaro Reverie and charged with the protection of the divine knowledge contained within."

"It is good to meet you," Zhava said. Though she had no idea what all of those titles really meant, Zhava was impressed that this young, weathered woman had accumulated them all to her name.

"It has been brought to our attention that you claim to be an Initiate of Kandor."

"Um...." She glanced at Marmaran, but the old woman gave no sign of how to respond. "I am being taught how to read and write," she said, turning back to Liori.

"And the ways of the Kandor?"

"I...don't know." She turned to Papa, who was scowling at her. That was the wrong answer. She should have said 'No.'

Liori sighed and looked at the other Ios, the men seated next to her. Only one looked back, and he simply shrugged his shoulders. Liori turned back. "Look into my eyes."

Zhava looked at Liori. The woman's eyes were so dark that Zhava had trouble seeing any of the brown color within them, but the intensity with which Liori stared back at Zhava made her uncomfortable. Zhava fidgeted with her feet. She blinked. She tried to look away, but Liori gripped her chin and made her face forward again. She tried to wipe away the dirt and mud with the back of her hand, but Liori swatted aside that hand. Finally, Liori sat back and sighed. She turned to the men again.

"This girl is no Initiate," she said. "I doubt she would even last a full moon as a Candidate. We have wasted our time. Let her go and be married."

"Zhava," Marmaran said. "The First of the King's Third Salient...is having trouble seeing past the dirty girl before her. Clean your face."

"Yes, Marmaran," she said, and she turned to leave.

"No!" Marmaran said, and Zhava, startled, spun back. "Stay here, and clean that face."

"Marmaran?" Zhava asked. The King's Ios also turned to stare at Marmaran, and though she could not see them, Zhava was certain that her Papa and Ooleng's family stared at her as well.

"You have no water," Marmaran said. "You have no clean cloth, what with that shepherd's dress your Mama made you wear. How would you wipe away the dirt of a day's labor?"

"I...do not know."

Marmaran sat back and smiled. And waited.

Zhava turned and saw that everyone was now staring at her, at her dirty face, at the mud that had caked beneath her eyes and at the dust that Mama had slapped upon her cheeks – and then Zhava looked back at Marmaran. She returned the old woman's smile. This was a far better way to prove Mama wrong. This was a far better way to display her value than to set the trees and the flowers to her dancing flames. She would show this Liori and her other Ios what a girl trained by the wonderful Priestess Marmaran could do, and it would show Mama that nothing she could do could hide Zhava's true value from the world.

Zhava reached up with one hand and gently, slowly, swiped at the air before her face – and let the little stones of dust and mud roll away just as swiftly as she had rolled away the stone from atop Mama's kitchen table. Her face was now clean.

Liori stared much more intently at Zhava now, and the King's men all gaped at her from their places at the table.

Liori held out a hand to Zhava, palm up. "Set your hand above mine," she said.

Zhava set her hand on Liori's.

"No," Liori said, lifting Zhava's hand higher. "Above mine, not on mine."

"I'm sorry," Zhava whispered.

"I believe it will be I who owes you an apology," Liori whispered. Her eyes lit with a blue flame, and Zhava felt that flame travel through Liori's hand, across the distance of air between them, into Zhava's own hand, and up through her body. The world suddenly swam in the blazing blue of midnight lightning. In that moment, the air stood still. The wind ceased its blowing. The bodies at the table were held in the stony stillness of death's very grip – all, that is, except for Liori. The woman was bathed in the radiant blue of a nighttime moon, and she smiled at Zhava. The words that came from Liori were not from her lips, but Zhava heard them travel across the infinite distance between them in the very moment they appeared as a thought within Liori's mind: *You are, indeed, an Initiate of Kandor.*

And then the light was gone. The air moved again, and the people stirred at the table, and Liori was as stern as she had been all night long.

"Zhava will come with us," Liori said.

# CHAPTER 3

At Liori's announcement that Zhava would leave with the King's Ios, several things happened at once: The first, and loudest, was that Mama began screaming from within the kitchen; Ooleng and his brothers jumped up, their fists raised and angry looks upon their faces; Ooleng's Papa and Mama were up very quickly, pulling back their sons before they could strike out; Liori grabbed and tossed aside Zhava, who landed in Marmaran's outstretched arms, and Liori jumped to her feet, her own fists raised and ready to strike; her nearest three men jumped up and placed themselves between Io Liori and Ooleng and his family; and the King's man nearest Papa grabbed him in a headlock – but did not follow through on the attack. Papa sat very still, the man's arm snug at his throat. The only sound was Mama's continued screaming as she ran from the kitchen and out into the nighttime air, and that quickly faded.

Liori turned toward Papa. "You will, of course, as master of this household be compensated appropriately for your daughter."

Papa smiled and shifted slowly back in his seat and away from the Io's grip. "Then we should discuss such a proposal," he quietly replied.

People backed away and slowly lowered their arms and opened their fists. A servant stepped forward, pried Zhava from Marmaran's grip, and rushed her from the courtyard, through the dark kitchen, up the narrow stairwell, and back into her room. He ran out again without looking back, and she heard his footsteps retreat down those narrow stairs.

Zhava stood in the silence of her dark room, unsure what to do next. The morning had begun with her meeting her future husband, Ooleng, whom she had grown to despise in the course of only one day. But the day had ended with her being visited by the King's Ios and being told that she would be traveling with them – and Papa seemed willing to discuss just such a possibility, for the right payment, of course. With a threat at his neck and violence a moment away in the courtyard, however, he had few choices in the matter. And Mama was somewhere outside, in the night and screaming about the situation. Was she truly sad that Zhava was leaving with the King's Ios? No, that made little sense. Far more likely that she screamed in anger because she did not get her way, because now the bride price would not be paid, and that Zhava would be taken from home and that Mama and Papa would not have any more cattle or sheep or even silver to go to the town and buy new things. Mama was mad, not because Zhava was leaving, but because Zhava out of the house would make Mama happy.

    That thought startled Zhava. She had never before considered Mama in just that way, that she would be happier to have more cattle for Papa and sheep for Zhava's brothers than to have Zhava at home. Mama had not heard Liori tell Papa that a bride price would be paid for Zhava, just as Ooleng and his family would have paid, and so Mama must have believed that the King's Ios were simply taking her away. And that had made Mama angry. Angry enough to run screaming out into the night, probably screaming for Zhava's brothers to rush to Papa's aid and with swords drawn as quickly as possible.

    But Papa changed his mind so quickly – certainly quickly because of the Io at his throat, but still, he did not hesitate when the King's Io told him that she would compensate him for the taking of his daughter. Zhava knew that Papa was negotiating a good bride price for her, and she knew that Mama was excited for the additional wealth those negotiations would bring to the family, but she never truly considered the price itself was their larger concern. She thought that they would be negotiating for a good husband long before the bride price. She thought they might tell her future husband that he had to provide the meat on the table, as Papa did for the family, and to make sure that Zhava had the wool she needed to sew the clothing, just as Papa did for Mama, and to make sure that Zhava would always have a good roof above her head, just as Papa did for Mama and Zhava and her three brothers before they moved to their own homes farther up the valley. She had thought those things would be part of the negotiations, but now she was not so sure. She was more certain those things were far less likely to be discussed if the number of cattle and sheep and silver and gold was sufficient for Mama and Papa.

Zhava did not like that thought.

The servant rushed up the stairs, down the little hallway, and burst breathlessly into Zhava's room.

"Come!" he said. "You are to leave now, with the King's Ios."

"What?" she asked, turning to him. His face was dark in the close room, but she knew him well enough to know that he would have large drops of sweat running down his cheeks from that little bit of work running up and down the stairs. "I am to leave now, in the middle of the night? And what of my preparations?"

"Your papa said there is no time, that you are to leave now, before your mama returns with your brothers and their servants and their swords. And the King's Ios say that you have no need of anything, that you will be given a room and a uniform. So now you must come!"

Zhava turned slowly and looked around her small room. At the little bed with its straw mattress that she worked so diligently to straighten every couple nights so it was not so itchy. At the open window where she sat most nights and stared into the sky, counting the stars and reciting the stories of the Gods and Goddesses, of the heroes of old who went on great adventures and slew hideous monsters. At the little table beside the wall, the one that held her folded clothes beneath it and her little wood carvings atop it – the little wooden boat, the old man carved into bark, the carved Marmaran that Zhava had spent most of a day whittling into just the perfect form of her old, weathered teacher.

"Zhava," the servant said, wiping sweat from his cheek. "It is time – now!"

"Leave," she whispered.

"No, you do not–"

"Leave." She turned to him and gripped the shoulder sash of her shepherding dress, twisting loose the knot. "I will change clothes and be down."

He bowed quickly, turned, and rushed from the room.

Zhava twisted open the sash and let the shepherding dress slip to the floor. She took her favorite dress from the shelf, the pretty blue one with the embroidered chicken along the bottom hem, and she slipped it over her head and secured it at her shoulder and waist. She started to walk from the room but stopped. She looked back down at that shepherding dress once more, retrieved it from the floor and laid it out neatly across the bed. It was stained from the dirt and mud of the fields as well as from her own sweat while she had been tending her brother Caleb's sheep, but Marmaran's words slowly drifted to her mind once more: The dirt upon a woman's face is nothing more than the dirt upon the ground. She wondered if it would work as well on cloth as it had on her face.

She leaned down, held her hand above the dress, and imagined the little pebbles of dirt rolling swiftly away. She brushed her hand through the air, and a puff of dust scattered into the room. One clean swipe spread across the length of the dress, obvious even in the midnight glow of moonlight through the open window. Where her hand had brushed through the air, she had, once again, wiped away the dust and dirt. Zhava smiled.

She left everything behind, though it wasn't much, her clothes and her carvings on the little table, her scratchy mattress, and the moonlit glow outside her window, and she slowly walked the darkened hall and the narrow staircase and the empty kitchen with the oil lamp casting flickering shadows upon the wall. She plucked a handful of dates from a half-emptied bowl on the counter, then stepped out the kitchen door and into the chilled night air. The King's soldiers were organizing their equipment down the dirt path a ways. The black-and-red clad Ios were arrayed around the yard, two of the men already mounted on their camels, another two standing near the back door, and the woman, Liori, standing apart from them all and handing over several small, clinking bags to Papa. Zhava gaped at that sight. No cattle or sheep had been exchanged, but she counted five of the tiny bags filled with coins. She had no idea that she was worth so much to anyone, certainly not to the King.

With an aching wheeze, Marmaran stepped slowly down the back steps of the home, and Zhava turned to bid her farewell. She stopped, however, when she saw the little bag slung across Marmaran's back. One of the Io men strode toward Marmaran and relieved her of the bag.

"Is that for me?" Zhava asked.

"Maybe," she whispered, her voice sounding harsh in the night's air. "For now, however, it remains with me."

"So...you will not continue here?"

"With your Mama and Papa?" she said, with a laugh. "No, my place is with you."

"No," Zhava said, gripping Marmaran's arms. "You mustn't come with me. I do not know where they will take me, but it cannot be any place good."

Marmaran chuckled, then pulled Zhava in close for a hug. "Child, you honor me," she said. "But I know where you are going. The King's Ios will take you to the Hibaro."

Zhava felt a chill down her back at the sound of the name. Marmaran and the woman, Liori, had spoken in the courtyard about the Hibaro, and it had sounded like the worst possible of places. People had fallen there and died, or they had been taken away in the middle of the night and were never seen again, or they had been found stabbed – all of this Zhava had heard from her hiding place in the kitchen.

"Ah," Marmaran said, squeezing Zhava just a little bit harder. "So you heard." She stepped back, gripped Zhava's hand, and started leading the girl toward the camels. "Give me a date," she said, holding out her other hand.

Zhava thought for a moment that she had misheard, but then she remembered the dates she had taken from the kitchen, and she lightly set one in Marmaran's hand. Marmaran held it up to Zhava's face.

"The Hibaro looks very old," she said, "just like this date. And if you are not on your best guard...." She popped the date into her mouth and quickly chewed it up. "It will take you in, grind you down, and swallow you whole – especially once inside the Proving Cove."

This did not make Zhava feel any better about leaving, even with Marmaran at her side.

"But just as the date is sweet to the taste, the Hibaro can be sweet to your soul."

"How do you know this?"

"Child," Marmaran said with a smile. "It is where I was trained when I was even younger than you. Don't you see? You are leaving the place of your childhood. But I? No, I am returning home."

Their slow walk had taken them to the side of one of the camels kneeling upon the ground, and one of the King's Ios stepped forward. "Priestess," he said, extending a hand to Marmaran's elbow. "Allow me to assist."

She took his hand, and the Io and Zhava helped Marmaran to climb onto the wool blankets slung across the camel's back. Immediately, she began coughing into her hand, a loud, wet cough that Zhava had only heard from Marmaran on the worst of nights.

"Priestess?" the Io said.

"The chill of the night's air," Marmaran said, her voice rasping as it did each evening.

"Of course," he said, and stepped quickly away.

Zhava moved in close to Marmaran's side. She bowed her head and idly stroked the camel's hair. "I shall remain at your side," Zhava said.

"You are a good girl," Marmaran replied.

Liori and Papa bowed to each other, and Liori turned and strode away from the little home – from Zhava's home. Papa stood there, surrounded by the little bags of coins at his feet, and watched the Ios and the soldiers as they made their preparations. He turned to Zhava, and their eyes met. He smiled and bowed. Zhava returned the smile, but she did not return the bow. Papa turned away again and watched everyone else in the yard except for her. She knew because she did not turn aside. She wanted to remember this one last moment, to never forget the revelation she had received of what her Mama and her Papa had done – that they had bartered her away to the highest bidder, and that Papa stood smiling at the side of his home with the bride price scattered at his feet.

"Eeya!" Liori called out.

"Eeya!" the Ios and the soldiers yelled in return.

"Go forth!" she called.

And with that, the camels arose from their spots in the yard, the soldiers formed up along the sides of the dirt path, and the procession began.

Marmaran gripped the reins of her mount with unsteady hands, and she slipped in the woolen blankets, but she remained atop the camel. Zhava walked briskly at the camel's side as they strode off into the night. As they left the blazing light of the lanterns scattered about the yard, she chanced one last glance back at her Papa. He was carrying two of the bags into the kitchen door of their home while the servant followed with the remaining three. Neither of them turned to watch Zhava leave.

After a short while at such a quick pace, and after the brilliant light from Zhava's home was little more than a dim glow behind them, Liori ordered them to slow. The camels adjusted to a plodding pace that Zhava had no trouble keeping. They followed the trail as it wound its way through the little valley and on out to the open plains. They began walking toward the evening star, Liori leading the procession up and away from the village far to their left. This was not a direction that Zhava would usually go on her own or even with her family. They went frequently to the village, at least once a moon; her brothers had built their own homes down the valley and even farther from the village; and the family kept the sheep and cattle grazing in the fertile crescent. But nothing productive lay in this direction, away from home. Away from her old life. It was not long before Zhava did not recognize where she was, and she stopped even trying.

She looked up at Marmaran who was rocking and swaying with the movements of the camel, her eyes closed. Zhava could tell that she was not sleeping, though. Marmaran's mouth moved a little up and a little down as she either prayed or talked quietly to herself. She always said that Zhava was always welcome to speak, and so she did now.

"Marmaran," she quietly said, gripping the old woman's dress and gently tugging. "I was to be Ooleng's wife."

"Yes," Marmaran said, her eyes remaining shut.

"But now the King's Ios paid the bride price, and I am going to the Hibaro."

"Yes." She coughed a little into her hand, then continued rocking and swaying with the gentle rhythm of the camel's stride.

"So...am I to now be wife to the King?"

Marmaran burst out laughing. She hunched over and gripped the camel's neck as her laughs rang through the still night. The nearby Ios all turned to stare at Marmaran and Zhava, and several of the soldiers looked at them also. Liori scowled at Zhava, but she did not tell them to quiet, and so Marmaran continued laughing until the laughter changed to aching coughs. Marmaran then lifted her shawl and hid her mouth within the folds of cloth until the coughing subsided. She sat straighter upon the camel's back and turned in Zhava's direction.

"Oh, child," she said with a rasping wheeze. "You are a delight."

Zhava did not feel as though she was a delight. She felt foolish, and her face burned with embarrassment. Liori and the other Ios and the soldiers had all turned away again and continued their scanning of the darkness around them. Zhava stared at the ground, wishing now that she had not even spoken, that she had let Marmaran continue in her prayers or her meditation or whatever she had been doing before Zhava's foolish question. The foolish question, she thought, which Marmaran had still not answered.

"Oh, Zhava," Marmaran continued, more quietly this time, and with less of the nighttime wheeze. "You are not to become anyone's wife, at least not yet."

Zhava looked up.

"You truly do not know the honor that has been bestowed upon you?"

Zhava shook her head, but of course Marmaran could not see that, and so she said, "No, Marmaran. When I awoke this morning, I was to be pledged to Ooleng. Now I am to be pledged to the King. What more is there to know?"

"Oh, child," Marmaran whispered, and she sat up straighter on the camel's back, rubbing at her chest and grimacing at a pain. "You are...." She grunted, squeezed her chest more, then cleared her throat and continued. "You are so very honored." She coughed again and leaned forward, her hand gripping the shawl about her chest. "You are...you are...." She never finished. In the next moment she slid from the woolen blankets, tumbling toward Zhava and the ground far below.

"Marmaran!" Zhava yelled. The woman fell, and Zhava tried to hold her, tried to heft her back onto the camel, but she was so much heavier than Zhava, and the two of them tumbled to the ground. Marmaran fell across Zhava, and the breath was knocked from within her so that she couldn't even call to her teacher. Zhava tried to yell for help, and though nothing came, the Ios had already stopped, and the soldiers were already surrounding them and searching the darkness for any sign of attack.

Zhava lay spread upon the hard, cold ground, Marmaran sprawled atop her, and she had no idea if her teacher even still lived. But then Marmaran reached up one hand and coughed, and blood sprayed across her fingers and upon the ground.

Liori and the other Ios were at their side in a moment. Two of the men slipped their arms beneath Marmaran and gently lifted her, while Liori slid Zhava across the dirt and out from beneath. Marmaran continued coughing, and more blood spread upon the ground and upon the Ios' dark robes.

"What is happening?" Zhava yelled, but the Ios ignored her. "What happened? Why is there blood?"

"Ooya!" Liori yelled.

"Ooya!" the soldiers yelled back.

"Make camp," she called.

# CHAPTER 4

The Ios and the soldiers moved with swift efficiency, erecting a campsite along the side of the trail. Within moments, a small tent had been erected, and Marmaran was carried inside it, laid out upon the ground, and covered in warm blankets, several more of them wadded up for a pillow beneath her head. She continued coughing, though not as severely as she had atop the camel. Zhava never left her side, and one of the Io men, Kua, knelt on the ground at Marmaran's side, gently poking and prodding across her body. He first felt around her head and neck, then ran his hands along her shoulders and arms, across her chest and stomach, around her hips, then down along her legs and to her feet. When he had finished, he returned to her stomach, slowly poking down and up, beneath her ribs. Each time, Marmaran sucked in a breath, coughed, and grunted in pain. Kua sat back on his knees and stared sadly into Marmaran's clouded eyes.

"How long?" he asked.

"How long what?" Zhava asked.

"Just the one season," Marmaran whispered.

"One season for what?" Zhava insisted, turning from one to the other. "Please, what is happening?"

Kua sighed and dropped his head to his chest, staring at the ground. "Priestess, why would you travel with us?"

Marmaran coughed again, slower this time, but from deeper within. "I want to go home," she whispered.

Liori flipped back the tent's opening flap, stepped inside, and joined them at Marmaran's side. The morning's dawn streamed in through the opening, and Zhava noticed for the first time that the birds had awakened. It seemed important to her to take in that detail, as if she would need it now and for time to come.

"Report," Liori said.

Kua hesitated, glanced at Zhava.

"Young one," Liori said, "leave."

"No," Marmaran said, gripping Liori's wrist. "Zhava stays with me. Let her learn the truth."

"Very well," Liori said, her mouth tight. Then, again to Kua, "Report."

"She has the breathing death," he said.

The words struck Zhava with the force of her mother's slap.

Kua continued, "She claims it has been for only the one season, but I believe she is mistaken. The pain is too severe, there are too many lumps within her, and...." He gestured at his own blood-stained robes. He shrugged. "There is nothing I can do for her. There is nothing even Viekoosh could do for her. She will not last the journey home."

Liori sat back upon the ground and gently took Marmaran's hand into her own. "Priestess," Liori said, kissing Marmaran's fingers. She leaned forward and brushed her fingers through Marmarn's hair, wiped some of the blood and dirt from her face. Two tears quickly ran down Liori's cheek and fell upon the ground at Marmaran's side.

"You honor me, Io," Marmaran said.

Liori leaned forward, near Marmaran's ear, and whispered, "You know what I must do, my Priestess. Give to me your final wish, and if it is within my power...."

And with that, the tears began to slide down Marmaran's face as well, dripping from the corners of her eyes and running down through her fine hair.

"My Priestess," Liori continued. "You know my charge. You know your own."

Marmaran turned her head away, but she nodded.

"Then give to me your final wish, so that I may fulfill it."

"Leave Zhava with me," Marmaran said.

Liori nodded, then said, "Of course."

"I must give to her my final instructions."

"No," Zhava whimpered. She gripped the hem of Marmaran's shirt.

"Those instructions will include exactly what is to be done with my body."

Zhava began to weep. She fell forward and buried her face in Marmaran's shirt and blankets, trying to block out the sound of her voice – but all the while forcing herself to hear every word clearly, to be sure and understand her duty.

"You shall provide for Zhava anything she requests for my final passage, and you will not question."

"Of course, my Priestess."

Marmaran turned back to Liori. "You will not question."

Liori bowed her head. "I have never questioned you, Priestess."

Liori stood. She gestured to Kua, and Zhava saw that, even though he had been silent this entire time, his own face shown with the spread of tears. The two Ios quietly left and shut the tent flap behind them.

Zhava lay in the stillness of the dim light of the tent. She wanted to let loose her cries, to weep and proclaim to the world the unfairness of it all. That she should be torn from her home, that she should lose her Papa and Mama – no matter hard their hearts, they were still her Papa and her Mama – and then, as if the Gods piled calamity upon heartbreak, that she should lose her teacher, her mentor, her only remaining friend in all the world. The person who called the Hibaro "home." The only person who seemed to want to make this journey. It was not fair, and Zhava felt the sting of the situation within her very soul.

"Child, I am so very sorry."

Zhava wrapped her arms around Marmaran and hugged her tight, and she cried into her shoulder. Marmaran coughed a little, but she quickly returned Zhava's affection, kissing Zhava's hair and whispering soothing sounds into her ear. They lay like that for a long while, gripped in each other's arms, as the light rose against the tent walls. Neither spoke the words aloud, but their soft touches and their tears mingled together in the bond of the love that went deeper than merely student and pupil.

The air began to grow warm and stale as the sun rose through the morning, and Zhava lifted her head, suddenly afraid that Marmaran had passed without notice.

"I am here," Marmaran whispered.

"Do not go."

"The choice is not mine. I am sorry I never shared the secret of my illness, but it did not matter in the calm life of your little home. Settled there, I could have pushed this aside for...at least a couple more seasons. Out here, however, on the trail and upon that accursed animal, and with the dust in my face, well...you see."

"I wish you had stayed."

"I am so very glad that I came."

Zhava hugged her tightly again, knowing in her heart that Marmaran's journey with the soldiers and the Ios was as much for love of Zhava as for love of the Hibaro.

"But now you must listen."

"No." Zhava shut her eyes.

"I will remain with you forever, child. I promise. But for now you must listen."

Zhava nodded into Marmaran's arm, and then Marmaran began to instruct Zhava one last time. They spoke of the lessons of Kandor, of the things that Zhava had learned and of the many, many things that she still had to master. They spoke of the Hibaro, and how Zhava would come to love it as her home, just as Marmaran had done so many years before. They spoke of the family Zhava had left behind, of Papa and Mama and Zhava's three brothers, and how it was unlikely that Zhava would see them again for many more seasons to come – though Zhava found that thought far less sad than she had expected. And finally, as they knew they must, they spoke of Marmaran's passing, how Marmaran herself would choose the moment – very near to the sun's setting – and of what Zhava was to do, the order in which she was to do it, and the very words she was to speak upon Marmaran's still body. And then Marmaran spread Zhava's hand open wide and tapped her palm with one crooked finger.

"Your little friends," Marmaran whispered. "Your little dancer friends. They shall be my friends too."

***

As afternoon slowly turned toward evening, Zhava passed along a set of instructions to Liori and her people, then she returned to the tent and to Marmaran's side. She could hear the Ios issuing orders outside, the soldiers gathering wood and arranging things the way they had been told. She snuggled against Marmaran's side to wait, and she sang a soft melody to make the waiting a little easier. It was a simple song she had learned when she was a child, about the love of the Gods to their people, about the people being devoted to the Gods and doing their will no matter how confusing or how hard the cost. The song was meant as an inspiration to children, but Zhava felt it to be more of an inspiration for Marmaran at this time in her life, something to hear and to help her along this final journey.

Just as the last rays of evening began to dim, the tent flap was opened, and Liori gently said, "It is time."

Marmaran nodded, then said, "The others remain outside, but you may come."

"You honor me, my Priestess." Liori entered, shut the tent behind her, and knelt at Marmaran's other side.

Zhava sat up and rubbed at her face. She could have used her Gods'-given ability to wipe her face clean, but that did not seem to matter in this moment.

Marmaran took their hands. She held tightly and said, "Zhava, your singing is beautiful. Would you do that song just once more?"

"Yes," she said as she struggled to hold back more tears. She began the simple melody again, more softly this time, as if the moment required a tenderness.

Marmaran smiled, and she squeezed their hands. Then she took in a deep breath, silently mouthed words that Zhava could not hear...and when she exhaled, she was no longer with them.

Liori bowed her head. Zhava shut her eyes and continued singing, fighting to keep her voice steady against the sadness that threatened to overwhelm. Too soon, however, she reached the song's end, and she and Liori sat there in the silence.

"You realize," Liori said, "that Priestess Marmaran's instructions are a blasphemy."

Zhava sat up straighter and stared at Liori through her teary eyes. "They are the instructions of my Priestess, and I will do exactly what she said."

Liori stood up, opened the tent flap, and called out to the camp, "Come!"

Four of the soldiers moved into the tent and stationed themselves at Marmaran's sides. Zhava stood aside as they lifted Marmaran's body from the ground and gently carried her outdoors. The four Ios stood in a line, each chanting a solemn blessing. The remaining soldiers stood lined up along the perimeter of the campsite, their armor gleaming in the evening glow, and their swords held firmly across their chests. Zhava was amazed; though she had heard stories of the King's soldiers honoring a fallen hero – who hadn't? – she had never thought to ever see such a grand occasion.

The four soldiers carefully laid out Marmaran's body on a small pile of wood that had been set within a shallow grave in the ground, just long enough for Marmaran's frail body to fit from head to feet. They spread a blanket across her body, smoothed out the wrinkles, and backed away to join the ranks of sword-clad soldiers watching.

Zhava stepped forward, Liori close behind.

Liori leaned forward and whispered into Zhava's ear. "Let us give her a proper burial. You need not do this thing."

"I must," Zhava said, and she began to chant the prayer that Marmaran – Priestess Marmaran – had taught her just that afternoon. It was a solemn prayer. A prayer, not of redemption or of sadness or even of the rewards to come in the afterlife with the Gods. It was a prayer of survival. A prayer of victory. A prayer of finding fulfillment in the life to be led upon this very earth, and not somewhere within the Heavens. It was a prayer that would not please the Gods, a prayer of remaining behind, and Zhava had said just those words when Priestess Marmaran first recited this prayer to her. But this was Priestess Marmaran's wish, and Zhava had vowed she would fulfill it.

When she finished, she knelt at the head of the little grave, leaned forward, and gently kissed Priestess Marmaran's forehead through the blanket. She sat back and stared at the body.

"What now?" Liori quietly asked from behind. "Are we to participate in this blasphemy? Are we to bring the torch to bear?"

Zhava did not answer. She did not want to do this duty, but Priestess Marmaran had insisted that it fall to her. Had insisted that none of the King's Ios or soldiers have anything to do with this final part of her journey into the great release. Zhava clenched her fists. She whispered a welcome to her little friend, and she invited him and all of his own friends to her. Within moments she felt them prickling at her fingers and palms, felt them dancing within her fists, joyous at the chance to be set loose. They would enjoy their duty, even if Zhava could not.

She leaned forward, spread her fingers wide, and cast the little dancing flames upon Priestess Marmaran's body.

Liori gasped. The soldiers and the Ios around them shifted nervously, but they remained at their stations.

Zhava watched the little flames dance upon the blanket, work their way down to the wood at the bottom, and then begin to circle the Priestess' body within.

A hand gripped Zhava's shoulder, and she turned to see Liori leaning forward, a little clay jar in her hands. Liori passed it over, then leaned nearer to Zhava's ear.

"You are not what I was led to believe," she whispered. "What are you?"

Zhava had no answer, and so she took the jar and turned back to the flames. She would watch this through to the end. She would say her goodbyes to the last true friend she had in all the world.

***

The little flames consumed Priestess Marmaran's body far more quickly than Zhava expected – far more quickly than any natural flames would have done. The sun had barely dropped below the horizon, and the first stars twinkled to the east. The soldiers stood at attention, their swords crossed upon their chests, Liori remained seated behind Zhava, and the other four Ios stood at the corners of the smoldering grave. The dancing flames still flickered about, but they had lost some of their energy, the ones at the edges of the grave collapsing upon the ground and flickering away. Zhava's first flame, however, her little dancer, was busy within the center.  He hopped across the ashes of Priestess Marmaran's body, picking through the smoldering pieces of broken bones, sorting them into some system that Zhava could not discern.  He picked up a piece of bone, tossed it aside, then another and another – then he found one that seemed to hold his attention, danced back up the grave, and gently placed it within the clay jar that Zhava had set upon the ground.  This process he repeated many times over, slowly filling the jar.  Next he took a bead of Priestess Marmaran's shirt, which had somehow escaped the dancing flames, bound himself tightly within it, and curled up just inside the jar's narrow opening.   His flame flickered blue-white, then flashed out of breath.  The piece of shirt glowed, then cooled, and the jar was sealed tight.

Zhava sat back.  In all of her watching, she had not noticed that the other little flames had all died away long before.  Priestess Marmaran's shallow grave lay cool in the dark evening.

"Oiya!" Liori called.

"Oiya!" everyone called back.

"Commend her spirit!"

"Commend her spirit!" they replied.

Liori stood, dismissed everyone with a flick of her hand, then turned to Zhava.  "Do you know what you have done?"

Zhava gripped the little jar in her hand and stood to face the Io.  "Yes," she said, staring into the woman's hard eyes.  "I have fulfilled my teacher's final wish."

Liori shut her eyes and clenched her mouth.  She turned her head away for several moments, then said, "You may use the Priestess' tent for the night.  We leave at dawn."  With that, she strode away.

Zhava stood and watched the Ios and the soldiers as everyone went about their evening rituals.  Some of the soldiers set out for the perimeter guard to begin their shifts, but most of them retired to their tents or sat by the light of tiny camp stoves and drank hot ale.  The Ios all filed into a tent where Zhava could see several mats set in a circle upon the ground.  They sat, and the last one to enter shut the tent flap behind himself – no doubt to discuss Zhava's actions, and possibly muse on the blasphemous nature of "desecrated" Marmaran's body.  After a long while, she turned and stepped into her own tent, letting the flap close behind her.  She sat upon the ground and stared at the blankets laid out for Priestess Marmaran – for her friend. Her teacher. The last person in the world who truly loved her. She stared at that empty spot upon the ground, and drifted off to a teary sleep.

# CHAPTER 5

The dawn came with a miserable smattering of rain. A soldier helped Zhava carry blankets and secure them to the side of Liori's wet, stinky camel, then he returned to tear down the tent. Zhava stood in the rain and fingered the little clay jar around her neck, the jar that contained the last remains of Priestess Marmaran. She had found a bit of twine, tied it around the mouth of the jar, and looped it around her neck. It hung just beneath her collar, and she vowed to keep her Priestess with her forever.

She watched the soldiers and the Ios strike camp, their wet faces stern and stoic. There was no way for her to be sure which of them thought her a heretic for what she had done the night before and which of them thought her just a silly girl. Or if any of them thought of her at all. No one looked at her. No one bothered her. No one gave her so much as a morning greeting as they all tromped around her through the rain and the mud.

Zhava, wrapping the wet blanket more tightly about her shoulders, stood alone and shivering. She whispered a quick invitation, and two of her little flames danced joyously within her tight fists, warming her hands and quickly drying at least one tiny part of her soaked body. With the cold morning and a clear mind, Zhava began to wonder at the way she had acted last night. She loved Priestess Marmaran, certainly, but Liori was correct: What the Priestess had requested was not proper. A body simply was not tossed to the ground on bits of kindling; it was not wrapped in dirty, soldiers' blankets; and Priestess Marmaran's body most certainly should not have been burned up in a common bonfire, with only a few lines of poetic prayers spoken in her name. And placing any of her remains in a jar to be worn around someone's neck like common jewelry? Maybe blasphemy was exactly the correct word to describe her actions.

The last time Zhava had attended a burial, she had been only 7 seasons old. Her Onaa had passed suddenly and without notice sometime in the night. She had lived in the back room of their house, the same room that Priestess Marmaran had used as her own for the past couple seasons. Onaa had been perfectly fine the evening before, laughing and telling stories during the evening meal. She had even gone for a short walk to watch the sun set, something she rarely did because of her stiff bones, and then she had kissed Zhava on the cheek before retiring for the night. That was the last gift that Onaa had given Zhava, that kiss on the cheek, and Zhava had felt herself so special for receiving it. That burial had been proper, however. Mama had insisted on everything being just perfect, with the flowers and the singing and the prayers and the stories of Onaa's life – and all done with a proper respect for Onaa's body. They had rubbed oil upon her body, sprinkled the perfume around her neck, carried her body reverently to the tomb, knelt beside her body, cast flower petals upon the ground, arranged all the blankets and the wash basin and her two favorite pots for her to pick up and take with her as she left the tomb and entered into the next life, into the afterlife, and then they all offered hours upon hours of prayers to the Gods to care for Onaa forever and forever.

But Priestess Marmaran had insisted on none of that for herself, had made Zhava promise to treat her body exactly the way that she had instructed; made Zhava promise that those specific words, whatever their significance, would be spoken; insisted that Zhava offer not one single prayer to the Gods to care for her in the afterlife; and demanded that Zhava send those little flames to collect some of the bones for Zhava to carry with her. Zhava had promised…and she had fulfilled that promise. But in the dim morning glow and with the slow drizzle of rain running down her head and in front of her eyes and down her cold back, Zhava had to wonder if she really treated Priestess Marmaran's body with so little reverence.

A pair of boots stopped in the mud before her, and she looked up to see Liori standing there.

"You ride with me," Liori said.

"Yes, Sir."

Liori gripped the saddle and quickly swung up on the camel's back. She grabbed Zhava's hand and hoisted her up to sit in the front, then tapped the camel quickly on the neck, and the animal got to its feet, lifting them both high into the air. Zhava held on to the little pomel before her and hunched over against the rain.

"Eeya!" Liori yelled, and Zhava jerked at the noise though she knew it was coming.

"Eeya!" the others yelled back.

"Go forth!"

And with that, the procession began. The five Ios atop their camels set a slow pace, allowing the soldiers to file in behind as they marched along the muddy trail. Zhava glanced to the left and to the right, noting the muddy rings where the tents had stood throughout the night, and then her eyes met the long, skinny ditch – now filled with water – where Priestess Marmaran's burned remains still lay. She stared at that pool of water and tried to imagine what her teacher would say. Would she be pleased, or would she be cross? Zhava had done exactly what she had been told. She hadn't wanted to do any of it – she had never wanted Priestess Marmaran to leave her – but still she doubted. And now with the morning rains, the ashes and remaining bones of her lovely teacher's body lay buried in a pool of mud...along a dirty path...on the road to the Hibaro that Priestess Marmaran had called home. Zhava felt the tears begin down her cheeks, and she ducked her head and quickly wiped them away.

"You should look," Liori said. "You should remember what you have done."

The words burned within Zhava. What did this woman know? She had no idea of the love that Zhava felt for her teacher, or of the heartache she felt now. Zhava sat up straight in the saddle, turned her head again and stared at the retreating pool of Priestess Marmaran's grave. Yes, she would look.

"I have done," she said in a voice louder and more confident than she really felt, "exactly what my teacher instructed me to do. And I regret nothing. I made Priestess Marmaran proud with my devotion last night."

Liori gave one quick snort, but otherwise said nothing.

They followed the trail over a small hill, and within moments the gravesite was gone from sight. Zhava refused to hunch, however. She sat straight and proud in the saddle, refusing to let this Io woman see how truly heartbroken she was. Even when her mind drifted to those final moments with Priestess Marmaran, singing the little childhood song to her in the dim light of the tent, Zhava forced herself to reveal nothing of her sadness. She clenched her mouth, took a deep breath, and forced the memory away so that the emotions would not overwhelm.

They rode that way for much of the morning, the trudging broken only sporadically by one of the soldiers offering a report on their surroundings, or by one of the Io men confirming some bit of information with Liori and then riding away again. Otherwise, the soldiers spoke little, and the Ios kept their thoughts to themselves. Zhava felt herself drifting off in the plodding rhythms of the camel's steps.

"Priestess Marmaran was with you for how many seasons?" Liori suddenly asked.

Zhava forced her eyes open and sat up straight again. She had been almost asleep, and she did not like the interruption. "What?" she asked.

"How many seasons?" Liori repeated, an annoyed edge to her voice.

"Two."

Liori did not reply.

The camel continued walking.

Zhava yawned and shut her eyes again.

"And she taught you to call flames in only two seasons?"

"What?" Zhava asked, forcing her eyes back open again.

"Listen," Liori said, clapping her hand against the side of Zhava's head.

"Yes, Sir," Zhava replied, rubbing at the spot.

"Priestess Marmaran taught you in only two seasons to call forth flames?"

"She never taught me that."

"No?" She sounded as if she did not believe Zhava, and Zhava really did not care. "Then who taught you?"

"No one," she muttered. "He was simply there one day. And then one night–" She did not say it was just two nights before. "–more little flames came. They have been with me ever since. They are my friends."

"Then what did the Priestess teach you?"

Zhava took a deep breath. This woman was suddenly determined learn something of Zhava's life. It was raining, Zhava was cold and shivering, all she wanted to do was sleep, and it seemed as if none of that mattered to the Io Liori. So Zhava began to tell the story. She told of the night that Priestess Marmaran had arrived at their home – it was the night after her eldest brother had been married and moved far up the valley to begin his own home with his new wife. Of course, no one in the household had known that Marmaran was a Priestess. They knew nothing of the woman who suddenly appeared on their doorstep seeking shelter for the night. They welcomed her within, and then they saw that she could hardly see, that if they sent her away she was likely to wander someplace dangerous, possibly to be eaten by the wild animals or even preyed upon by some bandit along the path. Papa had insisted that if Marmaran wanted to stay at their home that she could do so.

Of course, Mama had insisted that if Marmaran remained in their home, she had to earn her keep. Mama had probably expected another helper in the kitchen, to assist her and the servant in the cooking and the cleaning. Marmaran offered to instruct their daughter in the ways of the Gods, to make her prepared for the life of a truly spiritual woman capable of not only directing the household staff but of directing the spiritual lives of her future husband and children and servants. Mama had not been pleased, but Papa had agreed to this arrangement, and so Zhava's education had begun the very next day.

That was not the extent of Marmaran's instruction, however. She instructed Zhava in the letters and words of the Kandor, demanded that Zhava read the texts on her own and become proficient in making her own letters and words – in two different languages. They practiced this every day without ceasing for nearly an entire moon before Mama discovered them crafting sentences in the dirt. She was furious, and she yelled at Marmaran, claiming that Marmaran had lied, that they were wasting time when there were so many chores on the farm that needed doing. She wanted the old woman gone. But when Papa returned that day from the fields, the three of them – Papa, Mama, and Marmaran – went in the courtyard and spoke in hushed, angry tones. Zhava was sent to her room, waiting for news that Marmaran would have to leave, but that was not what came. It was nearly sundown when Marmaran climbed the narrow stairs and told her simply that the lessons would resume in the morning – and that they would now include many more details on the proper operation of a wife's home. Nothing more was ever said again about that night.

After that, Zhava's lessons were split. She learned from Marmaran in the mornings about how to use the Kandor to best please those around her, her husband and her servants and her children, and she learned in the afternoon how to use the Kandor in service of the Gods and the King. That was not exactly what Mama had wanted, Zhava was certain of that, but Marmaran said that Mama and Papa could not know everything the Gods had planned for little Zhava's life, and so it was best to practice the Kandor in as many ways as possible. There were plenty of years for life to work itself out the way it should, but not so many years left for Marmaran to provide thorough instruction.

Zhava stopped speaking. She hadn't thought of that conversation in so long. Could Marmaran have known what was to come? Even then, could she have been preparing Zhava for a time when Marmaran's sickness would overwhelm her?

"That is all?" Liori asked.

"No," Zhava said, annoyed at the woman's insistence. There was something in that one comment from Marmaran that meant something. She wanted to think upon it some more, to wonder at how much Marmaran knew – how far her knowledge of the Kandor extended into every other area of life.

"Then continue," Liori said. "What else did she teach you?"

Zhava sighed. She just wanted to think, and she was tired of speaking. Her mouth was dry, her clothes were soaking wet and sticking to every part of her body, her backside hurt from the constant back-and-forth rocking of the camel's plodding procession, and she did not want to talk any longer. But she knew the Io Liori would continue asking. Better to tell more now than to get another cuff to the side of her head and have to tell more later.

So she told Liori about the Kandor lessons. Marmaran had been amazing, and simply so gifted in the arts of the Kandor. She taught Zhava to spread words across the sand, to move the pebbles and the rocks to blend with nature, to spread her arms and ride the waves of the wind through the morning light. She made Zhava memorize entire passages of the Kandor and to recite them for long afternoons until Zhava could speak them perfectly in two languages.

Liori interrupted the story there and recited a few lines of the Kandor, a passage near the beginning, about the earliest Initiates in the Time Before. Zhava picked up the line and continued it, reciting for several passages before Liori was satisfied and requested more about Priestess Marmaran's life and lessons.

Zhava remembered a funny story and decided to share that, something to break the monotony of the ride and maybe get some other reaction from Liori besides annoyance or grim determination.

"One time," Zhava said, "after Marmaran kept me out late at night in the fields reciting the names of the stars, I slept well past the sun's rising the next morning. I had been allowed a little morning time by Mama, so I was not ignoring any of my household chores, but Marmaran had made me promise to meet her in the woods to help search for wild herbs. I do not know why I did not awaken that morning, but I remember I was so very tired. To Marmaran, however, this was a terrible insult. I did not know it then, but she–"

"Hold," Liori said. She raised an arm into the air and yelled, "Ooya!"

"Ooya," the others called back.

"Mid-day food!"

"Mid-day food," they replied with far more cheer.

Liori brought her camel to a halt. Within moments, Kua was at their side and helping Zhava down. He hoisted her gently around and set her beside him in the mud.

"She is your responsibility for the remainder of the ride," Liori said.

"Yes, Sir," he said.

Liori guided her camel away, picking along the side of the trail as she barked orders at a small group of soldiers.

Kua turned to Zhava and smiled. "You impressed her," he said. He took her arm and began to lead her away.

Zhava was at a loss for words. She impressed the Io Liori? But...how? The woman barely spoke to her, and when she did it was only in the shortest of annoyed words. She had said several times that Zhava had blasphemed the Gods in her care of Priestess Marmaran's body. She had ordered Zhava to speak, cuffed her on the side of her head when she did not speak quickly enough, and interrupted Zhava several times. What about that impressed Liori?

Kua pointed to a fallen shrub with a long, narrow branch. "Sit there. I will find you some food."

Zhava sat. Kua returned moments later with a small tinn of dried meat with some kind of herb that Zhava did not recognize sprinkled across the top and a small handful of dayberries. She had not realized how hungry she was until she smelled the food in front of her, and then she ate so quickly that she barely tasted any of the flavors. She was licking her fingers when Kua returned with his own food and glanced at the empty tinn. His eyes went wide as he looked at her, and Zhava ducked her head in embarrassment. A moment later, he tossed another small strip of meat on her tinn and sat beside her. She chewed this one much more slowly as she sat in companionable silence with Kua.

After the mid-day break, Kua led her to his own camel and helped her on, then climbed on behind her, and they were back on the trail again within moments. Kua opened a sack beside him and pulled out a blanket. He tossed it around Zhava's shoulders and retied the bag.

"Thank you," Zhava said.

"Rest as best you can," Kua said.

"Will you tell me something of the Hibaro?" she asked.

"No. You will see it soon enough, and rest now will be the best thing for your arrival."

Zhava tucked herself into the new blanket, shivering in the cold rain even with the extra layer wrapped about her. She shut her eyes. She knew she should take the Io Kua's advice and get some rest, but she could not push his words from her mind. How could she have impressed the Io Liori? Was it something she said, something she did? Neither seemed likely. Then what? It wasn't because she had been Priestess Marmaran's student, or Liori would have been more pleased with Zhava at home. Perhaps it was simply the way she told her story? Or the things that Priestess Marmaran had taught her, the details of the Kandor?

It made little sense to her, and she quickly found her mind wandering to her Mama and her Papa, her brothers and her sisters-in-law, and the daily routine of her life. Just past the mid-day meal…back home she would have helped Mama wash the plates and utensils, and then she would have her time with Priestess Marmaran. They would have talked of the Kandor, and Priestess Marmaran would have made her recite passages from memory. They would have practiced their letters and words, and then Priestess would have made her study more, learn more of the techniques for control, for release and suspend, for exhale and dilate. They would have talked, and Priestess Marmaran would have listened. She would have smiled as Zhava began to sing…began to hum that little song from her childhood…sung the words of devotion to the Gods. Priestess Marmaran smiled at that, and she ran her fingers through Zhava's hair and told Zhava how very proud she was to have had such a dutiful student, how very proud she was that Zhava was on her way to the Hibaro, how very proud she was….

"…that you are growing into a spirit of fire," Marmaran said.

"Please, I do not know what you mean," Zhava said.

"Oh, dear child, I saw something within you. I saw something, but I never thought it could be this. Never thought you would blossom as you have."

"I have only done what you told me. I have done all that you told me."

"Not all." Marmaran looked down at Zhava's hands and pointed. Dozens of little flames clung to Zhava's hands, all staring at Marmaran and watching her, listening to every word she spoke.

Zhava looked back and saw that Marmaran's eyes were clear – that she was looking right at Zhava, that the blindness was gone.

"Marmaran, you can see!" Zhava said, jumping up and down. "How is this possible? You can see!"

"Oh, dear child," Marmaran said with a laugh and a huge grin. "Of course I can see. I can see all!"

Zhava slipped from the saddle and sat up straight.

Kua wrapped a hand around her so she did not fall off the camel.

Zhava shivered, blinked away the sleep and the remnants of the dream – that wonderful dream in which Priestess Marmaran was finally happy and well and could see again. Zhava smiled, and she reached up to grip the little clay jar hung around her neck. That had been a good dream. She was glad that Priestess Marmaran was so happy in her afterlife, and it felt so good to have been visited by her one last time.

The happiness quickly faded, however, as Zhava realized how cold and stiff she had grown on this journey. The clouds had only built throughout the day, and Zhava was thoroughly soaked through the layers of blankets draped across her. She tried to sit up, and her body complained, fighting against the sudden movements. The air was even colder now, and the clouds so obscured the sun and darkened their travel that Zhava could not tell if she had slept for only a short time, or if she had slept away most of the day.

Kua tapped her shoulder and pointed ahead. Zhava looked.

"The Hibaro," he said.

To Zhava, the sight was amazing. One tall building – the tallest building she had ever seen – sat in the center of a ring of smaller buildings. Lanterns flickered along each floor of that center building, and lanterns were lit in so many of the rooms all the way up that building, up all – she counted quickly – nine levels of just that one building! The smaller buildings encircling it were smaller only by comparison, though, for they were double and triple the size of Zhava's own home, several at least three floors tall. The lowest building stood closest to them, only one floor high, but it was also the longest building that Zhava saw. Lanterns were lit all along that one building, and she saw camels and...horses? She had never before seen horses, but she had heard them described to her in some of the greatest tales of adventure in the far-off lands. Squatter than camels, with shorter necks, but powerful animals that could pull far more than their weight. They could not traverse an entire desert, but they could run faster than the wind and carry their riders across great, gaping distances and over tall rocks and high fences.

As they approached, several children ran to meet them, taking the camels' reins and allowing the riders to dismount. Kua took Zhava's arm and eased her down while a boy ran over and helped her off. Kua slid down behind her while the boy walked the camel through the rain toward the long building with all the other animals.

"Take Zhava for processing," Liori yelled. Zhava turned to see the Io handing off her own camel to a young girl and pointing away from the animal stalls.

"Yes, Sir," Kua said. He gripped Zhava's shoulder and led her away.
They passed at least a dozen more boys and girls running to take charge of the camels and assist the soldiers with their gear.

"Candidates," Kua said.

"Sir?" She turned to look up at him through the rain.

"Candidates," he repeated, gesturing to the boys and girls running through the rain. "Like you. Well, not quite like you. But they all hope to remain at the Hibaro and train. I expect at least a couple will succeed."

They walked around the end of the building and ducked into a narrow tunnel lit with low lanterns. Zhava shivered at the sudden change. She loosened the blanket around her shoulders and wiped at the water running down her face. She slicked back her hair to get it away from her eyes and ears. The little lanterns against the walls puffed bits of smoke as they hurried past closed doors on their right and left all along the dim, musty tunnel.

Kua stopped at one door that looked like all the rest, and he knocked. Zhava looked back and forth down the tunnel. No one was here; the tunnel was empty. Kua knocked again.

A woman – a large woman in dirty and faded shirt and pants – opened the door.

"Sister Allenka," Kua said, bobbing his head in greeting.

"Io Kua," she replied. She stood a little taller and ran a finger through the hair by her ears. "Sir, welcome. How may I be of assistance?"

"Our newest Candidate," he said, pointing at Zhava.

"This?" Allenka said, glancing at Zhava. "She's...so old. A Candidate?"

"Living on a farm just this side of the Purneese Mountains – and training under Priestess Marmaran herself."

"That old jay?" Allenka said with a laugh. "What can she possibly be doing now? I thought she died ages ago."

"She died yesterday," Zhava interrupted.

Allenka's eyes narrowed on Zhava, and she seemed to really see the girl for the first time. She cocked her head to the side as her eyes flicked from Zhava's face to her hair, her soaked blankets, her bare legs, her muddy boots. She absorbed the details up and down Zhava's body, a small smile slowly forming at the corners of her lips. "Hm," she finally said. "What did the old bird see, I wonder?"

"Zhava is here for processing," Kua said.

"Of course she is," Allenka said, staring at Zhava's face some more.

"Deliver her to the Commons House when she is finished."

"Of course, Io." She turned back to Kua and bobbed her head. "Will that be all?"

"Ma'am."

"Sir."

Kua set his hand to Zhava's shoulder and gave it a quick squeeze, then he turned and went back down the tunnel toward the evening rains again.

"So you are Priestess Marmaran's little bird," Allenka whispered, studying Zhava more.

"Ma'am?"

Allenka reached up and slapped Zhava's cheek. The sudden sting surprised her, and she yelped at the pain, cupping a hand against her cheek.

"I did not ask you a question," Allenka said, "so you have no reason to speak. I did not give you an order, so you have no reason to speak."

Zhava shook her head and wiped at the spot where Allenka had hurt her, but she kept quiet and glared at the woman.

"Good." Allenka smiled, then shoved Zhava further down the tunnel. "Now walk."

There was a thud as Allenka slammed her door shut behind them. Zhava did not know where they were going, but Allenka continued shoving her in the back, urging her forward down the long tunnel. Allenka pounded on a couple more doors they passed, and a few young women rushed out to follow them, each hurriedly straightening their clothes and tying up their hair.

"A late-comer," Allenka called over her shoulder by way of explanation.

The women following along murmured their understanding.

Allenka yanked back on Zhava's dress and brought her to a halt before one door that looked the same as all the others. She fumbled at the lock, then led them all inside. The room was dark, but one of the young women rushed inside with a shunt and quickly lit a lantern. She turned up the flame, then went to the other six lanterns around the small room. Within moments, Zhava could see that it was a washroom, piles of clothes in the corners, buckets of powders, stacks of cut soap on the tables, and a tub and drain set in the center of the room.

Allenka pushed Zhava forward, kicked aside the wooden tub with a clatter, then set Zhava over the metal grate.

"Stand here," she said. "And remove your boots."

Zhava kicked off her boots as she looked down and saw through the metal grate a pool of water far beneath her, likely runoff from the washing that had been done throughout the day.

The other four women busied themselves around the room, each working at an individual station.

Allenka yanked away the blankets from Zhava's back. "Illy!" she called, tossing the blankets to the side. "Cleaned and mended, then back to the stables."

"Yes, Ma'am!" a woman said, catching the blankets in midair.

Allenka pointed at Zhava's dirty, blue dress. "Off," she said.

Zhava looked down, then back at Allenka. "But...it's all I have."

Another quick slap to Zhava's cheek. "Off," she repeated. "And the underclothes too."

Zhava rubbed at the spot as she glared at Allenka, but she quickly stripped off the dress and underclothes and handed them each over.

"Numwah," Allenka said, tossing the clothes to another woman. "Cleaned and taken to the Commons House."

"Yes, Ma'am."

Zhava crossed her arms and shivered as she stood naked in the center of the room. She looked at the floor, at the grate on which she stood and the sparkling water far beneath her, and tried to ignore Allenka. The woman did not seem to notice or care that Zhava held her in such contempt. Instead, she cocked her head to the side again and stared at the little rope around Zhava's neck and the clay jar dangling from it.

"Now what is this?" Allenka whispered, stepping forward.

Zhava wrapped her hand around it and glared at Allenka.

Allenka smiled. "A little trinket from home, is it?" She waved her hand and turned around. "Keep the toy, little bird. Trinkets from the Purneese Mountains are piled in the corners like so much rubbish." She waved an arm in the air and yelled, "Plishka!"

A woman at the side of the room yanked on a cord, a metal gear clanked in the ceiling, and Zhava glanced up in time to see a stream of water pour down on top of her. She ducked her head and coughed, the stinging cold water burning her throat and insides and causing the hairs all over her body to stand on end.

"Powder!" Allenka yelled.

The fourth woman stepped forward and flung a bucket of powder at Zhava.

"Wash!" Allenka yelled.

Two of the women stepped forward – Zhava could not see their faces through the water and the powder. They yanked her arms straight and began scrubbing while Zhava coughed and tried to stand steady in their grips. Another woman grabbed the back of Zhava's head, pushed it forward, and began cutting, snipping long strands of hair and letting them fall to their feet and get washed down the metal drain.

"Again!" Allenka yelled.

The women backed away. The metal hinge creaked. Zhava kept her head down as water dumped across her head, down her neck and back.

Another bucket of powder. The women returned, and there was more hair cutting and more scrubbing – this time of Zhava's chest and back. Her skin stung from the cold water and the cold air and the vigorous scrubbing, and she felt-

"Again!" Allenka yelled.

Women backed away.

Metal hinge – water.

Powder. Scrubbing.

Cutting – hair falling to the floor.

"Again!"

Water.

Powder.

Scrubbing.

Cutting.

"Again!"

Zhava stopped caring. It was a cycle that seemed without end. And then....

"Rinse!"

More cold water. No powder, but more scrubbing. Then drying. Then underwear was hiked up her legs, and a skirt was wrapped around her hips and tied tight. A shirt yanked down over her head, and her arms shoved through the narrow openings.

"Take her away," Allenka said with a dismissive wave of her hand as she turned away.

One of the women – Plishka? – pulled Zhava from the room and back into the narrow tunnel. Zhava stumbled along beside the woman, her entire body tingling. Her head felt lighter, and she ran her fingers through what remained of her hair, the little bits sticking up off her head. It had taken her two seasons to grow her hair that long, and these women had cut it all off in just moments.

"Here," Plishka said, shoving a slice of bread into Zhava's hand. "You missed the evening meal, but you can have this."

Zhava thanked her and ate as they walked.

"Sister Allenka isn't always like that," Plishka said. "Only with the new Candidates. And especially with the older ones. She's gentler with the little ones."

Zhava was unsure how that made her treatment any better. Was that supposed to make her happier, that Sister Allenka treated only some of the Candidates so badly?

They left the narrow tunnel and walked back outside, but this time along a covered walkway that kept the rain from pounding their heads. Wooden boards clacked as their shoes tapped along – though Zhava could not remember when someone had put shoes on her feet through all the washing and scrubbing and rinsing and drying.

She had little time to consider that before Plishka led them into another building, a taller building, up a narrow set of wooden stairs, and into a long room filled with beds and chatting girls, many of whom seemed far younger than Zhava. Plishka pointed to an empty bed in the corner.

"There," she said, and then she ducked back out and was gone. Zhava stood at the end of the room – the now-silent room – and stared at the faces of dozens of girls, some who had to be as young as only a handful of seasons. Their bright eyes and short-cropped hair and plain cloth outfits made them all appear as one. The nearest two girls were actually taller than Zhava by a good three or four fingers, but everyone else she saw was shorter. Most had dark hair, but a handful of girls in the back had the bright, golden hair of the farthest valleys.

Zhava shuffled over to the bed that Plishka had pointed out, and she sat down. It was far nicer than her little bed on the floor back home, and the wooden boards creaked beneath the wrapped straw. Some of the farthest girls began to turn away, to return to whatever conversation or game or activity they had been doing when Zhava arrived. The nearer girls continued studying her, however, staring at her with wide eyes and open mouths. They must have seen new Candidates arrive before, Zhava thought, so there was no reason to be so curious or rude. The polite thing would be for someone to greet her, but these girls did not seem to care about polite.

Then she began to wonder if there was something about herself that caused them to stare, something about her own clothes or her face or her body.  Had Allenka done something to her to cause the other girls to stare?  Had she dressed Zhava in something inappropriate?  She quickly swiped at her face, but she did not feel anything unusual; she glanced down at her clothes, her shirt and her skirt, but it seemed in all ways identical to the plain clothes worn by all the other girls in the room.  When she looked up again, several of the nearest girls were huddled together and whispering to one another, occasionally glancing at Zhava.

She did not like the attention, and so she swung her legs up and onto the bed, laid her head down on a lump of cloth, and shut her eyes.  Sleep, she decided, was what she needed far more than worrying about the concerns of a roomful of girls who had nothing better to do than stare and wonder.

But the room suddenly grew silent.  Zhava opened her eyes.

Someone's hard boots clipped against the wooden stairs, and Zhava turned her head to see.  The Io Liori stepped into the room with one of the Candidate girls leading the way.  The girl pointed at Zhava and stepped back.

"Good," Liori said to girl.  "You are dismissed."  She wound her way through the maze of beds to stand before Zhava.  She was dressed in black and red riding robes, just as she had been all day, but these were dry and clean – obviously Liori had taken the time to change and wash as well, though she had likely had a nicer time of it than Zhava.

Zhava stood and bowed.

"You are washed and fed?" Liori asked.

"Yes, Sir."  Though Zhava did not believe one slice of bread meant she was sufficiently "fed," she would not argue the point.  She had no idea how the people of the Hibaro ate.  If one slice of bread was a luxury, then she had eaten well.  She would not speak up until she knew the rules of this new household.

"Excellent," Liori said.  "Then follow me.  High Priest Viekoosh requests an audience immediately."

# CHAPTER 6

Zhava followed the Io back out of the Commons Room, down the wooden stairs, through a long hallway, and back outside by way of a different door than the one Plishka had used. Again, boots clapped against the wooden walkway and the rain was held at bay by a covering over their path. Zhava had trouble keeping up with the quick pace Liori set, but she was able to catch glimpses of people moving through the rain and the darkness. A group of soldiers walked and laughed as they entered a building on her left. A young boy on her right went running through the mud and rain, a leather satchel gripped in his hands. Two women in the black and red robes of the Ios talked quietly as they passed Zhava and Liori on the narrow walkway, casting quick glances at Zhava.

That made Zhava nervous, and she thought about what Liori had said. The High Priest Viekoosh had requested her. She had no idea how many high priests were at the Hibaro – only the one? – but it could not be a good thing to be summoned by one. Was she in trouble? Had she done something wrong? Perhaps Sister Allenka had already passed word that Zhava talked too much? That she had to be reprimanded more forcefully for speaking out of turn?

Lightning flashed above, startling Zhava. She looked up and saw the clouds and the last remnants of the bright light just as the thunder rumbled its way overhead. She also saw that she and Liori approached the centermost building, the one that was nine floors high – and then she noticed one more thing that made her stop. She stared straight up, where the path's roof should have been to block out the rain and the light. But there was no roof. She saw only the clouds and the dark all around.

Another dull glow as a second burst of lightning flitted above. The rain striking and then running off some ceiling she could not see…or…could see through…?

"You just noticed?" Liori called.

Zhava pointed up and tried to ask the question, but the words would not form. She was not even sure how to begin, how to even think it through. There was no roof? The rain just…didn't fall?

"You're not very observant," Liori said. "Now come along. We should not keep him waiting."

Zhava ran and caught up with Liori just as they entered that center building. The room was lit from above, from little sconces built into the ceiling that cast their flickering light straight down. Tables were arranged throughout the center of the large room, and many people sat around those tables with open books and papers spread out before them. A couple of those people were older – much older, with their long robes and gray hair – but most of the people were young like Zhava. A couple at a nearby table, a young man and young woman, were only pretending to read as they winked and grinned at each other from behind tall books they had set before them. At another table, a group of three – two women and a man – were tapping their fingers at a spot in a book and arguing with each other in hushed, heated voices. At another table, four boys sat playing cards, a discard pile scattered at the table's center. At a table near the back, a young woman was quietly reading aloud, and at least 10 boys and girls sat on the floor before her, engrossed in her story.

"Our study room," Liori said. She pointed to a set of wooden stairs along the far wall and gestured for Zhava to follow. "Nine flights to climb. I trust you do not tire easily."

They began up the steep steps to the second floor. That floor contained tall shelves with books and scrolls scattered upon them.

"Library," Liori said. "Quiet at all times."

They climbed another set of steps. The third floor contained rows of small desks and chairs, papers and writing quills scattered across the desks. One man sat on the far side of the room, slowly writing words on a roll of parchment.

"The copying room."

They climbed to the fourth floor. A long hallway ran down the length of this floor, narrow doorways opening to each side.

"Student clerical apartments."

The fifth floor, much the same as the fourth.

"Senior clerical apartments."

The sixth floor, a wide open space with benches and tables scattered around.

"Clerical dining hall."

The seventh floor, more books.

"Advanced studies. Open to anyone advanced enough to be responsible."

The eighth floor, another hallway with only four doors to the sides.

"The Hibaro Magistrates' apartments."

The ninth floor, the uppermost floor of the building, and Zhava found herself winded and struggling to climb the final few steps. A wooden bench was set along the wall at the top of the stairwell, and Zhava almost fell across it as she struggled to breathe.

Liori, not even sweating, stood at the top of the stairs and smiled as she watched Zhava. "You do not want to be summoned to this office very often," she said.

Zhava clutched her stomach and leaned forward across her legs, suddenly afraid that what little food she had eaten would come up and land on the polished, wooden floor before her. She shut her eyes.

Liori chuckled and said, "Tomorrow, we will set you up with regular exercise and endurance training."

Zhava took a deep breath and sat back again, more sure of herself. She at least felt she could keep down that slice of bread. She opened her eyes and saw that Liori was watching her, studying her, and smiling.

"What?" Zhava said between gasping breaths.

"I was like you once," Liori whispered. Her gaze seemed softer then, even caring – if that were possible. Surprisingly, Zhava realized, Liori's smile seemed genuinely warm. Perhaps...caring? Love? Then the woman noticed Zhava's gaze, stood up straight, her smile disappeared, and she put her hands at her back. "Are you ready?" she asked.

Zhava nodded and stood. They walked the short hallway to a large double-door of dark-stained wood and heavy, iron bands. Liori gripped the large, wooden knocker and tapped several times.

Within moments, a man said, "Come."

Liori pushed open the doors, and they entered the expansive room. Zhava gaped as she realized this one room was larger than the entire courtyard in her home. Shelves lined three of the walls, and books and scrolls were piled high on each. Three cushioned chairs – a luxury by any standard – were set near those shelves of books. Wall sconces flickered light throughout the entire room, and several more lights were inset in the ceiling, casting light straight down on a huge, wooden desk. The desk was larger than her dining table back home, and it had several small stacks of papers – real papers, not the rolled papyrus – set upon it. Lightning flickered outside, and Zhava noticed a set of double doors open behind the desk and a large balcony, now soaking wet, opened to the outside, night air.

Without thinking, she ran across the room and through those doors and stood on the threshold of that balcony, the evening breeze sending waves of rain to wash across her face and body.

"Zhava," Liori called.

"No," a man replied. "Let her be."

Zhava had never before seen such a sight, and she marveled. The darkness just beyond the brightly lit room. The wind and the rain. The clouds! It felt as if she was so high she floated in the clouds. She spread her arms and shut her eyes, and she imagined that from this perch high above the earth she could fly away into the darkness, fly away into the nighttime storm and visit the Gods themselves.

A hand gripped her shoulder.

She opened her eyes and looked back to see Liori. The woman was definitely upset, and Zhava ducked her head and allowed herself to be led back inside. She had not gotten very wet, but still water dripped off her clothes, and her boots left wet prints across the polished floor.

"I'm sorry," she whispered. "I didn't mean…."

"Sit," Liori said, pointing at one of the cushioned chairs, the one nearest the large desk. Zhava sat.

When she looked up, she saw the man sitting behind the desk, High Priest Viekoosh. He was younger than she expected, younger than her Papa and Mama. His dark hair was cut short, just like hers, and his brown beard was neatly trimmed. His eyes were also brown, the deep brown she'd heard described of those who lived near the heart of the land, nearest the King's own fortress city. He was leaning back in his own cushioned chair – how rich he must be! – and his black and purple robes hung loose about him.

"Zhava," he said, leaning his elbow on the chair's armrest and studying her.

"Yes, Sir."

"Io Liori tells me you grew up on a farm near the Purneese Mountains."

Zhava looked to her left and saw that Liori had also sat in a chair. Her legs were crossed, her hands were folded in her lap, and she simply watched. Zhava turned back to the Priest. "Yes, Sir."

"And so you have never seen a sight like that before." He gestured over his shoulder, at the balcony and the storm beyond.

"No, Sir."

He leaned back and stared at her. He casually ran a finger across his beard, smoothing down the hair. His eyes flicked to Liori, then back to Zhava again. He seemed to decide something, for he quickly sighed and continued, "Do you know what an Initiate is?"

"No, Sir."

"And yet you wish to become one?"

"Sir, I...." She glanced at Liori, but the woman sat still as stone in her chair. "Sir, I do not know. I was told those children outside are Candidates to become Initiates, and that the young people in the Commons Room are all Candidates. I do not know if I am a Candidate, though, or an Initiate. I'm sorry."

At this, Viekoosh seemed surprised. He sat forward in his chair, his eyes wide as he stared at her. "But you had engaged Priestess Marmaran as your teacher, yes?"

"Yes, Sir."

"And she was teaching you the ways of the Kandor?"

"Yes."

"Then why are you unsure if you wish to become an Initiate?"

"I'm sorry, Sir, but Priestess Marmaran's lessons did not include anything about becoming an Initiate."

High Priest Viekoosh simply sat and waited, so Zhava continued. "She taught me the letters and words, Sir, both Remmliite and Purneesite. She made me recite the Kandor, and she taught me how to be a good wife and mother, how to lead my family's spiritual journey. She wanted me to succeed."

Viekoosh let out a quick laugh at that, startling Zhava. The Priest looked long at Liori, his expression shifting slightly as his eyes and smile changed. He was talking to her without using words, but Zhava had no idea what they were saying with their small gestures. Finally, he looked back at Zhava and stood, walked around the large desk and knelt down at her eye level. He gripped her chin and looked her in the eyes. His eyes grew darker, and he studied her, his gaze flicking back and forth. Another quick sigh, and he clenched his jaw and stood.

"Io Liori, you waste my time," he said, walking back around to sit in that chair again. He reached for a book and a sheet of paper and set them to the center of his desk. "I must prepare for tomorrow's meeting. Take her back down to be with the other Candidates. She will fail, but let her have her chance at 'success.'"

"High Priest," Liori replied, "with your indulgence. Priestess Marmaran was many things, but she was never known to waste her time. I could not see it in Zhava either, but it is there. Allow her the opportunity to demonstrate."

He looked up from his book, his eyebrows lifted high as he waited. "Zhava," Liori said, turning to her. "Stand up and show the High Priest your little friends, the ones you used on Priestess Marmaran's body."

Zhava stood. She stepped away from the chair and stared at High Priest Viekoosh. He sat back, a look of annoyance on his face as he watched her. She didn't like that look on his face. Whatever he had been trying to find in her eyes was not there. Was he hoping that her eyes were a different color? Or a little bigger? A little smaller? Whatever he had been looking for, when he didn't find it, he had simply dismissed her as not even being worth his time, and she did not like that. Her Mama had done that, too. And her Papa had sold her for a few bags of coins to the first person willing to pay the bride price and take her away. She would not be cast aside again, and if the Io Liori believed that her little dancing, flaming man would change his mind, then she would gladly bring him forth.

But not just the one, she thought. She had become rather skilled at calling forth several of them at a time. How many could she call? She had not even thought to count when she cast them upon Priestess Marmaran's body, but she had to have called forth at least 20, perhaps even more. Could she do that again? Could she do even better?

High Priest Viekoosh sighed and tapped a finger on the desk. He was not a man who was accustomed to waiting.

Zhava decided that she would ask for as many as she could. She raised her arms before her, flicked her wrists, and invited the little flames once more.

The room flashed with light as dozens of the little flaming men burst to life. Her hands and arms seemed to writhe as the flaming men clambered to stay atop her, to hang on to her skin as they jostled each other for a place to remain. Zhava had never before heard them make a sound, but they now buzzed with excitement and anger and laughter. She saw a few of them dance, a few others push and shove, a few more roll across her fingers in joyous laughter. One of the little flames slipped from her wrist and fell to the floor in a flaming pile. He quickly jumped back up, ran to Zhava's boot, climbed back up her clothes – somehow without setting fire to any of them! – and raced back down her arm to rejoin the others.

Zhava looked back at High Priest Viekoosh, and she was pleased to see that he was now standing behind his desk, his eyes wide and his mouth open as he watched.

Zhava smiled. This man now thought better of her, and she liked that. He would not dismiss her so easily again. However, she felt the need to prove herself just a little more, to show off how much she could do. She knew these flaming men, and she knew they would listen to her and obey, and so she turned and faced the far wall. She rolled her hands together, balling up the flaming men until they were all contained in a tight sphere.

She knelt to the floor and tossed the ball of flame across the room. It landed in the corner – far from the books and parchments, Zhava had made certain of that – and it spread wide as the men split apart and began dancing their flaming jigs in the corner.

Zhava stood again. "Come," she said, snapping her fingers. The flaming men immediately raced back across the room, a bright fireball with a flaming tail skittering back over. The flames climbed back up Zhava's body and down her arms and to her hands again. She smiled, brought them all to her face, and gently whispered, "Good," to them. They all grinned back at her, then one by one they vanished in a quick flicker until her hands were once again empty.

Zhava turned to High Priest Viekoosh and smiled.

The High Priest stood staring at her, no longer in shock, however. He was studying her, as if truly seeing her for the first time.

Liori got up from her chair and gently tamped out the bits of flickering embers in their line across the floor and to the corner of the room, then she turned and stood with her hands behind her back and waited.

High Priest Viekoosh slid his chair far out from the desk and sat down again. He crossed his legs, steepled his fingers, and turned to Liori. He pursed his lips and sighed, then said, "Have her moved to Initiate quarters, somewhere near the Tower. Because of her age, I do not want her with the regular classes. Assign her a Mentor."

"I can Mentor her," Liori said.

"No. I need you maintaining the patrols to the north; you are my experienced eye on the Go'aab border. Where is Verece?"

"He left a week ago on a King's errand."

"Sandoval?"

"With a group of Candidate finalists on the High Plains. They are due back by the next moon."

Another sigh. Viekoosh frowned. "How about–"

"Io Kua," Zhava said.

High Priest Viekoosh turned to her and frowned.

"I'm sorry, Sir," Zhava said, ducking her head and awaiting the slap that was likely to come. Instead, however, the room remained silent.

Zhava waited for him to stand and walk around his desk, for him to tell her she had done wrong, just as Sister Allenka had done several times already. She should have taken that lesson to heart, remembered the order of things in the Hibaro and her place within – her lowest station within.

However, when neither High Priest Viekoosh nor Io Liori made any move toward her, Zhava flicked her gaze up, tentatively. They both watched her but made no move toward her.

"Zhava," Liori finally said. "You should not have interrupted, that is true, but now that you have, continue speaking. Why do you request Io Kua?"

"Um...," she said, standing up straight again. She did not know what they would think of her when she told them her reason, whether they would think her just a silly girl or whether they would be happy that she spoke her mind. Either way, she was expected to answer, and so she went with the simple truth and said, "He was nice to me, and...he seemed to care for Marmaran."

High Priest Viekoosh sighed and rubbed at his eyes.

Liori frowned. "Understand, Zhava, that the job of a Mentor is not to be nice to you. No matter how nice he may have been on the trail, he would be required to test you, to push you to your limits and then beyond. He would be required to make you do things you never before thought possible, with your body, with your mind, with your spirit. A Mentor is not your friend; he will be your greatest ally, but it is quite possible you end up despising him before you become promoted – assuming you do not die under his instruction."

Zhava's eyebrows went up at that.

"How long ago was Io Kua promoted?" Viekoosh asked.

Liori thought for a moment, then said, "About seven or eight moons ago. He just joined my patrol, and he is learning well."

"She would certainly be a challenge for him. Do you believe him capable?"

"Likely," she said with a slow nod of her head. "But I would want someone checking on her at regular intervals. I could do that."

High Priest Viekoosh slid his chair up to the desk with a sudden scrape of wood on wood, and he gestured toward the other end of the room.

"Zhava, you are dismissed. Wait on the bench at the head of the stairs, and Io Liori will see you to your quarters soon."

"Yes, Sir," she said with a quick bow. She turned to leave.

"And shut the door tightly behind you."

"Yes, Sir." She did as she was told, rushing from the room, and firmly shutting the door behind her. Then she smiled, yawned, and shuffled to the little bench at the end of the short hallway. As she walked, she casually flicked her wrist and called a flame. It sparked to life in her hand, and she giggled as it tickled her palm and played between her fingers. She turned and sat on the bench, called another flame in her other hand, and held her hands together to watch them play. They grabbed hold of each other's arms, swung around, fell down, leaped up again. She cupped her fingers down and blew on them, and they ducked down, putting their heads into the wind as their flames crackled behind them. She laughed at them, and they grinned at her.

Zhava sat back and watched them for a while, and then her eyes went back to the double doors into High Priest Viekoosh's office. She was very pleased with herself and how she had done in that office. She was not sure what an Initiate was supposed to do, but she had impressed the High Priest enough for him to decide she could be one. She probably should not have interrupted the High Priest and Io Liori as they discussed Mentors, but she had not been trying to do that. She had assumed a "Mentor" was a kind of teacher. Priestess Marmaran had been a wonderful teacher – she was so kind and loving, and she had always been working to make Zhava better. That was what she wanted from her next teacher, someone who would be nice to her just as Priestess Marmaran had been nice to her. That didn't mean her Mentor had to love her as Priestess Marmaran had loved her, but she wanted her next teacher to not be mean to her, to think of her as a real person and not just someone to push around – like that Sister Allenka pushed her around. That woman was awful, and Zhava hoped she never had to see her again.

The voices from High priest Viekoosh's office were suddenly raised, as if the High Priest and Io Liori shouted at each other, and then they were quiet again. That was interesting, Zhava thought. They had both been so calm when she had been in the room. They had looked at each other often enough, though, passing thoughts back and forth with the lifting of an eyebrow or the twitch of a smile. Zhava had seen that quite often when she was living at home. She had seen that with her oldest two brothers when they had chosen wives – she had known long before Papa or Mama had known which women had caught her brothers' attention simply by the way they spoke to each other without their words. With the lifting of the eyebrows, the little smiles, the playful gestures of their hands.

Zhava sat up straight. Had she missed something in that room? Had High Priest Viekoosh and Io Liori been looking at each other as her brothers and their wives looked at each other? That was an interesting thought. Neither of the two wore a bonding band on their arm, but...could she be sure? Io Liori had been in her riding clothes almost the entire time they had been together. And Zhava had not even thought to look at High Priest Viekoosh's arm. Did he wear a bonding band? She could not remember.

"I wish I knew what they were saying," she whispered.

The flames in her hands stopped dancing. They stared at her.

"What?" she asked.

One of the flames turned, sprinted from her hand, and jumped to the floor.

"Hey," she said, reaching to catch him – she missed. "Come back here."

The second flame jumped from her hand and bounded up her arm. She reached up to catch him, but he darted between her fingers.

"Stop that," she said. "Where are you going? Get back in my hand."

The first flame was halfway down the hall already. Zhava leaned forward and cupped her hands to her mouth.

"Get – back – here!" she hissed.

He didn't listen. He skidded to a halt at the double doors, braced his hands on the floor, and shoved his flaming head into the tiny crack between the door and the floor.

"What are you doing?" she said – and that's when she felt the second flame hop up onto the edge of her ear. It didn't hurt to have him there – if anything, it sort of tickled to have the heat of his flame perched in her ear – but she just wanted them both to behave themselves and get back into her hands. Why wouldn't they listen?

"My judgment is not clouded," the flame whispered into her ear.

"What?" she asked, turning to him.

"Io, your judgment was clouded fourteen seasons ago," the flame said.

Zhava sat still. Two thoughts went through her mind. First, she realized that she had never before heard her little flames speak – she did not even know they could speak. And second...whose words was he speaking?

"Yes," he said. "Yes. A dozen seasons ago. Not now."

He sighed. "I can accept the Io Kua. I can even accept that another Io should be held responsible for them both. You have not provided a compelling reason why it should be you – a reason based on logic."

Zhava turned to stare at the little flame at the other end of the hallway, the one with his head shoved beneath the door. This was amazing, she thought. How were they doing this? One listened beneath the door and heard the words...and the other repeated those words into her ear?

"I am commandant."

"Yes. A commandant who should not have gone riding out to the Purneese Mountains on this errand. And how much did the girl cost?"

"Sir – it was my own savings."

Zhava's eyes grew wide. The Io Liori had paid the bride price from her own savings? But...why?

"A waste."

"You see what she can do. The waste would have been to throw her away to some illiterate, Purneese, goat-milk sucker."

Zhava chuckled. Yes, that was a good description of little Ooleng. She gagged at even the thought of his name.

A sigh. High Priest Viekoosh seemed to do that quite often. She wondered if it was something he had done his whole life, or if he did it because of the demands of the priesthood and of now leading the Hibaro.

"If not me, then who? Who else would you trust to properly vet this girl?"

"There are many who could vet her. Your judgment could falter."

"I have never failed you. I will not fail you now."

"You were with her on the return ride. Does she realize her potential?"

"I do not believe so. Priestess Marmaran did not seem to reveal it to her, and she has only played with a couple Abilities. Had Priestess Marmaran been able to remain with her a few more seasons, I have no doubt Zhava would have grown quite formidable."

"How did Marmaran ever find the girl?"

"Zhava described it as a chance encounter. The Priestess simply showed up at their door one day, and she persuaded the family to let her stay."

"Do you believe she found them by accident?"

"I do not believe so, no. Priestess Marmaran did nothing by accident."

"And you? How did you happen upon her?"

"I will provide the details in my report, but an informant of mine along the Purneese happened upon her. I do not know how, but he said he saw the Gods within her."

That was interesting, Zhava thought. She couldn't remember the last time she had met someone new, so she had no idea who that "informant" would be. And if the Io and the High Priest could not see the Gods within her, then how did this random informant?

Another sigh, then, "Did I tell you that I saw Zhava once, many seasons back?"

"No. When? Why?"

"Purely by chance. I had business at the border, and I stopped to refresh myself. She was in the village center with her family, buying produce at the market."

"You never told me."

"I saw nothing in her eyes then either."

"I do not know how she masks it. Perhaps something Priestess Marmaran taught her?"

"From your report, Marmaran got to her only recently. Two seasons ago? She was but a child that one time I saw her."

"I do not know. Allow me the freedom to discover the truth."

"Fine. Do it. But your patrols continue. Allow Io Kua his chance at teaching, and then check on her progress when you return."

"Yes, High Priest."

"Go, Commandant."

"As you command, High Priest."

Zhava gasped. She turned to the doors just as they burst open. Her little flame with his head beneath the door disappeared in a flash, and Liori spun around to look.

Zhava reached up and scratched vigorously at her ear, willing that flame to disappear also.

Liori scuffed her boot across the floor, stamping out the little embers that still flickered at the end of the hallway. She shut the doors gently, then turned and stepped slowly, her eyes narrowed on Zhava as she approached.

"What were you doing?" Liori slowly asked.

"Nothing." Zhava shook her head, but she knew the lie sounded forced.

"Hmm...," Liori said, glancing at the doors again, then back to Zhava. "Why was one of your flames at the foot of that door?"

Zhava grinned – and she hoped it seemed like an honest grin. "I was playing," she said. "Want to see?"

She snapped her fingers, and a flame sprang to life in her hand. She leaned forward, cupped her hand, and tossed him away. He flew through the air, then landed on the ground, bounced a few times, and rolled over and over upon himself until he struck the doors and disappeared in a tiny flash.

"See?" Zhava said with a broad smile. "Fun."

Liori simply stared at her for several moments, as if willing her to admit the truth.

Zhava ducked her head, feigning remorse and hoping it looked real. "I'm sorry," she mumbled. "I didn't mean to do anything wrong by playing. High Priest Viekoosh told me to sit and wait, and that's what I was doing. But I was bored – and tired. I needed to do something to keep myself from falling over and sleeping. I wasn't trying to disturb you with my little game."

"Up," Liori said, snapping her fingers. "I will take you to your Initiate quarters. You will refrain from using any more of those flames until Io Kua has deemed you ready. I do not want you harming yourself or anyone else until you have learned better how to control these Abilities."

"Yes, Sir." She turned and walked down the stairs, Liori following behind.

# CHAPTER 7

The nine flights of stairs were only slightly less taxing going down. Zhava was winded but did not collapse when she reached the studying room, Liori led the way outside through a different door and along a different wooden path toward another building of the sprawling campus. Zhava felt hopelessly lost in the maze of pathways and muddy stretches of ground. She looked up to see if the invisible covering was still above her, but the storm had subsided. The rain had stopped, the clouds were breaking apart, and moonlight was beginning to shine down in small stretches. The air still felt damp, and a chilled wind had begun to blow in from...the north? Zhava looked all around, but she was not sure of her directions. That way felt like north, but as she had been asleep much of the afternoon, and the clouds and rain had obscured her view all evening, she had no way to be certain of her surroundings or her directions.

Liori led them to one of the lower buildings that had only two floors, but it was long with many small windows lining the way along each floor. Most of those windows were dark and shut tight, likely against the night's rain and cold. Liori stepped up to the door and knocked. Within moments, a young woman opened the door, her eyes large and bright as she stared at them from the brightly lit entryway.

"Io Liori," she whispered, her large smile beaming. "Welcome to our Initiate House on this fine evening. Please, step in from the darkness."

"Thank you, Sister Tegara," she said. She placed a hand at Zhava's back and ushered her inside.

Tegara shut the door gently and turned to Zhava. "You must be so excited to be chosen as an Initiate."

"Yes," Zhava said. She actually felt exhausted from the day's traveling and being led from one activity to another all evening, but this woman's quiet enthusiasm and constant smile felt infectious. Zhava smiled back, though she was not sure why.

"Oh, Zhava, you will blossom within these walls," Tegara said.

"You have a room ready?" Liori asked.

"Always. We shall place her in room 215."

"Um...of course," Liori said, blinking. "Whatever's available, of course."

"I know you will like it there," Tegara said to Zhava. "The morning sun is especially beautiful through the open window, and you will get a wonderful view of the Tower. It is a room meant to inspire. Is that not true?"

That last was directed to Io Liori, who gave only a noncommittal grunt.

Zhava was unsure how to respond to Sister Tegara's praise of a room and its view. A bedroom was simply a place to rest and store clothing, possibly even a few personal items, such as her little carvings back home, but Tegara seemed to value the beauty of the morning sun and the view of a building. How could those possibly be of any value? Her room back home showed her the farm yard and many of the night's stars. Was that not enough?

"I leave with the dawn," Liori said. "Initiate Zhava is now in your care."

"Of course." Sister Tegara gave a smooth, graceful bow at the waist. "All blessings be upon you this lovely evening, Io Liori."

"And upon you," Liori responded with a quick, curt bow of her own and then turned to Zhava. "High Priest Viekoosh approved your request for Io Kua as a Mentor. I must resume my patrols along the border, but I will return by the next moon. I will be approving your progress – or not – when next I see you."

"Yes, Sir."

Liori stood there a moment, simply staring at Zhava. She reached a hand toward Zhava's face, brushing back a loose strand of hair – and smiling.

"You will not disappoint," she whispered.

"No, Sir," Zhava whispered back. It was an odd exchange. Liori was so cold, so professional, but then she would show just a little tenderness to Zhava in moments like this. It left Zhava so unsure how to respond. The woman had berated her on the trek to the Hibaro for blaspheming the gods in her treatment of Priestess Marmaran's body, but then she had insisted on knowing about Zhava's life. Did she like Zhava, did she barely tolerate Zhava, or did she want to know Zhava better?

And just as quickly as the moment had begun, it was over. Io Liori straightened up, tugged at her cloak, and bowed crisply to them both. "Good night," she said, turning and stepping back into the cold dark.

"Oh, she is a beauty, is she not?" Sister Tegara said, watching Io Liori walk away. She gently closed the door, then turned back to Zhava. She was still smiling, and that somehow made Zhava feel more comfortable, more relaxed. "And you," she whispered, stepping closer. "You are even more beautiful than I imagined. You are going to grow into the most wonderful Initiate."

"Thank you."

"Oh!" She clasped her hands before her. "And so polite. You truly are a gem. Come with me."

Sister Tegara led the way. They turned a quick corner to the right and walked down the dimly lit hallway, doors lining each side. Tegara talked quietly the entire way. "This is the oldest of the Initiate Houses, built over 200 years ago, and we have seen many of our people go on to do great and glorious things – such incredible adventures! Why did you wish to become an Initiate?"

"Um …I didn't. I mean…I don't know."

Sister Tegara quizzically glanced back at Zhava as they walked. "'I didn't.' My, that is telling. You must keep that answer to yourself from now on, Zhava. You give away too much of yourself with that answer."

Zhava opened her mouth to apologize, but Sister Tegara stopped suddenly before an open door. Inside was a small, dark room, and a young woman sat on the end of a bed, looking out to the hallway.

"Initiate Barae," Tegara said. "You have an early morning. Why do you not use this time to rest?"

"I wanted to see her." Barae looked Zhava in the eyes and smiled as she gave a quick wave.

Zhava tentatively waved back.

"Now you have seen her," Tegara said. "Rest well." She pulled the door shut with a dull thud and secured the bolt.

"Why would she want to see me?" Zhava asked.

Sister Tegara turned to her and stared, her eyes narrowed. "You really know nothing of the Hibaro?"

Zhava shook her head.

"My, this is the most glorious place." She turned and continued down the hall. "The center of all knowledge. The seat of the Kandor. The advisors to the King himself." They reached a narrow stairwell at the end of the hall, and they climbed the dark steps slowly, a small glow from above them the only light to guide. "Many children arrive at all stages of life. Some are young, others old – but they all want to learn and to grow. Sometimes children are willed to us for one reason or another. Sometimes the parents are too poor, and they know that we will care for and feed their children – at least as long as they remain viable Candidates. We get children here who have been training in the ways of the Kandor their entire lives, and some children who have only heard the name Kandor upon arrival."

They reached the top of the stairs and stopped at a door on their left. Sister Tegara pulled a ring of keys from her belt, checked the numbers, and pulled two off the ring. She held them up before Zhava. "One key is yours. One key is mine. Do not lose yours."

"Yes, Ma'am." Zhava took one of the offered keys, and she stared at it. She had never before been given a key to anything. At home, Mama and Papa had all the keys to everything. Not even the servants held the keys when they had to go for supplies – that was still Mama or Papa. She slid the key into the metal lock, turned it and felt the bolts sliding out of place, then she pushed the door open.

"But you," Sister Tegara whispered. "The Ios went to retrieve you. My, but that is rare." She reached forward and kissed Zhava on the cheek.

Startled, Zhava stepped back and stared at Sister Tegara, rubbing at the damp spot on her cheek.

"Welcome to our Initiate House," Tegara said with a smile. Then she spun on her toes and quietly retreated back down the stairs.

Zhava slipped into the room and quickly shut the door behind her. She slid the lock back into place and leaned against the heavy wood, listening. Sister Tegara's footsteps quietly echoed from the stairs, and Zhava counted the steps. Nine down to the first landing, then another six down to the main floor of the Initiate house. Sister Tegara was gone.

Zhava rubbed at her cheek again, wiping away the last bit of that strange kiss. Why would Sister Tegara do that? A kiss was something special, something delivered from one who loved to another who was loved. Zhava herself had received only a handful of kisses her entire life, most of them when she was a little girl and her Papa used to tell her stories in the evening. He would tell her about his day, about his time in the fields with the sheep and the cattle, or about his time tending to the hired men doing the planting or the harvesting. He would tell her his tale, spin it out into a grand adventure, and then he would kiss her and tell her it was time for bed. But Papa had not done that in many seasons, not since Zhava was so young. So again, what would make Sister Tegara share something so intimate with her?

She pushed away from the door and turned to face the darkened room. A sliver of moonlight cut from the closed shutters, and she slowly stepped forward. She felt a bed at her left and a small table at her right and – she cracked her knee into something that banged across the floor. She rubbed at her knee and felt with her hand until she reached the small chair she had accidentally kicked. She pushed it back toward the little table as she continued toward the fading light at the shutters. She slid her hands along the seam, found the latch, and flicked it open. Pushing open the shutters, allowing the chilled night air to drift into the room, and she saw the moon casting its light from behind the fast-moving clouds overhead.

She shut her eyes and listened. Unlike back home, the Hibaro was noisy. The pack animals shuffled and snorted. Men and women – probably patrols of some kind – walked in pairs throughout the yard and away in the distance. A couple people, two women by the high pitch of their voices, laughed from within one of the rooms beneath her. All around, she felt the strangeness of this place to which she had been brought, felt the wrongness from deep within her. She wondered how she would find her place here, how she would survive in a place so foreign to everything she had ever known.

She knelt before the open window and pulled the twine from around her neck. She pulled the loop over her head and fingered the little jar the Ios had found for her, the one Priestess Marmaran had insisted upon, the one that now held bits of the Priestess' bones. She set it on the narrow ledge before the open window and wondered why Priestess Marmaran had insisted on this treatment of her body. As Io Liori – and probably every other man and woman on that trip – had said, this was not proper. The dead simply were not treated this way, carried around like a piece of jewelry. But Priestess Marmaran had made it clear that Zhava was to do this. Even when Zhava had cried that she could not do it, Marmaran quietly insisted that it was her final wish.

Zhava gripped the jar in her hand, wound the twine about her wrist, and turned back to the room. The bed was a city type, with the four legs lifting it a little above the floor. She had slept on one once when she was little, and she knew it would be comfortable, but the idea of it always seemed like a waste of wood. A straw or feather mattress on the floor was all anyone really needed. The little table along the wall held a small lamp – again, a city style, with the handle on the side, the bulging oil tank just below the wick, and a frosted, glass chimney to disperse the light and heat. On a second shelf were stacked three piles of clothes: a couple shirts, pants, skirts, and underclothes. They looked large, and Zhava assumed she would have to alter them to fit.

She went to the bed and pulled back the thin quilt. Gripping Priestess Marmaran's jar in her hand, she curled up in a tight ball, wrapped herself against the cool breeze, and stared at the bare wall before her, lit occasionally by the moon drifting out from behind the clouds. She thought about saying a prayer...or casting a blessing upon her family back home...or even asking the Gods to keep her safe in this new world...but before any of those things could happen, she drifted to sleep.

It was a fitful sleep, though, and her dreams were misshapen. She was riding a horse down a mountain of snow –

– but the river before her would not allow her to cross. She asked the river what it wanted, but it only said the same thing each time, that it wanted –

– and then Sister Tegara was cutting Zhava's hair and placing it in a small jar to keep for later, but Priestess Marmaran walked over, took the jar from Sister Tegara's hand, looked at Zhava, and said,

"Dear child, you are in danger."

Zhava sat on a stool made of doe skin and smiled at Priestess Marmaran. "I have missed you."

"Dear child, you are in danger." Priestess Marmaran emptied the jar full of hair upon the ground.

"But I am at the Hibaro," Zhava said. "I am at my new home – your home."

"Dear child," Priestess Marmaran said, stepping close and gripping Zhava's head in her hands. "You are in danger. Pay heed to the midnight bird."

Something pounded through the darkened night of her dream, and Zhava sat up in her bed to the blinding rays of sunrise streaming through the open window. She wiped away the sleep from her eyes and squinted into the bright light. There was another pounding, and Zhava realized it was someone knocking on her door. She shook her head, rubbed at her eyes, and quickly looped the twine with the little jar around her neck and tucked it beneath her dress. She must keep Priestess Marmaran close, because…of danger? The dream was fading quickly, but there had been something about a bird, that she had to watch for the midnight bird. That made no sense; most birds slept at midnight.

Again, someone pounded, and Zhava slipped out of bed, unlatched the metal bolt, and opened the door. Before her stood the girl from the night before, the one who had left her door open so she could see Zhava.

"Hello, cutie," the girl said with a wide smile. She raised her hand in greeting.

"Hello." She wondered what this girl could want. Other girls chatted quietly from farther down the hallway, and a couple more walked slowly past, linens draped across their arms as they stole quick looks at Zhava and into her room.

"I'm Barae," the girl said.

"Yes, I remember," Zhava said, though she had forgotten the name sometime in the night. This girl had made two attempts at a meeting, so Zhava should at least appear to remember the name. That seemed the polite thing to do. "I'm Zhava."

The girl, Barae, smiled. "'Zhava,'" she repeated. "That's a beautiful name."

That startled her. A beautiful name? Zhava had never before heard anyone say that to her – and she had certainly never thought of her own name as beautiful. Her brothers had made a point of mispronouncing it on purpose whenever they were outside the home; her Mama usually said her name to order her to do something or to chastise her when she did something wrong; and her Papa, though he had said it lovingly, spoke her name so seldom that it hardly mattered. Zhava was so surprised by Barae's statement that she could think of no way to reply, and instead she stood at the door with her mouth open, thinking she should say something but unable to say anything.

Finally, Barae leaned forward and said, "You needed a sponsor. I volunteered."

"Thank you. What's a sponsor?"

Barae's smiled widened, and she grabbed Zhava's hand. "Come. I'll show you."

Zhava had just enough time to shut the door behind her before Barae pulled her down the hallway and toward the center of the long building. The girl chattered as they walked, pointing to the left and right, front and back the entire way. "This is the second floor of the North Wing – the girls' wing – of our Initiate House. And you have a beautiful room, by the way, with a great view of the Tower in the morning light. Your room is directly above mine."

"Yes, I remember."

"The South Wing is the boys' wing, and in the center – directly over there – is the House Commons where we can get together in the evenings to study and talk and play games – quietly, of course – if we want to do so before lights out." She gave a quick wave above her head to a boy walking through the empty Commons. "Good morning, Posef!" she called.

"Barae, hello," the boy – Posef – called back, returning the wave. He was dressed only in a pair of pants – no shirt – and Zhava looked away. "Who is that with you?" he said, walking over.

Zhava stared intently at the floor.

"New girl," Barae said. "Her name is Zhava."

"Greetings," Posef said, extending a hand.

Zhava took his hand as she tried not to stare at his bare chest. She looked at his face instead and saw the deepest, greenest eyes she had ever seen in her life. She had heard of the green-eyed people of the western Highlands, but she had never thought to see any of them – and certainly not to meet one in her lifetime. His people were said to be nomads who drove their herds across the mountains with the changing of the seasons. From the few stories Zhava had heard, it was a hard life, and it built hard men and women with little humor or time for games – but this young man before her grinned as if he was about to tell the greatest joke ever.

Instead, Posef laughed at her. "You're staring," he said. "You like what you see, don't you?" He pulled his hand free and backed away. He turned around, his arms spread wide as he gestured up and down his shirtless body. "Take a good look – especially at the back. Go on."
Zhava ducked her head, but not before seeing the cut lines of the muscles down his back and shoulders. She stifled a grin.

"Stop it," Barae said.

"Yes, I knew it," he said, turning back around again. "Zhava likes men. Not like you, eh, Barae?"

"We shall be on our way now," Barae said, taking Zhava's hand and turning them around. She called over her shoulder, "You better get dressed before Tegara sees you."

"Meet you for breakfast?" he yelled after them.

"If you're lucky." Barae leaned in to Zhava as they briskly walked away and talked quieter. "He's really nice once you get to know him – a little wild, but he will do anything for his friends, and he and I have been the best of friends since he was promoted to Initiate last season. Still very untrained, but he has a talent – and that's his problem. He doesn't think he has to work for anything, and it gets him into trouble with several of the teachers."

"Okay," Zhava said, "but...why wasn't he wearing a shirt? Or shoes?"

Barae burst out laughing. "Do not even think about that," she said. "He is always doing things like that, and Sister Tegara is always telling him to stop. He gets into serious trouble at least once a moon, and he often ends up having to do perimeter patrol. I think he secretly enjoys perimeter patrol." She stopped and tugged Zhava to a halt beside her. "Unless...did you actually like his body?"

Zhava had no idea what to say. Everything with this morning was happening so quickly, and she was still trying to take it all in. Being at the Hibaro, being a Candidate, and then being an Initiate, meeting all these new people, and then her dream last night...and there had been something there. Something she should hold on to. Something about...Priestess Marmaran....? And a midnight bird...flying through the winter trees? She shut her eyes and tried to remember.

"You did like him!" Barae said with a grin.

"What?" Zhava asked, returning to the moment. Her mind flashed on Posef turning around and flexing the muscles in his back, and she felt her face flush. "No. I mean, I'm just not – my brothers and my Papa did not do things like that at home."

"Hmm," Barae said. "Okay, well, to each her own, I guess."

"And you...do not like men?"

She waved a hand through the air and scoffed. "No," she said with a chuckle. "More trouble than they're worth." She gripped Zhava's hand again and started back down the North Wing. "As I was saying, sleeping quarters are all inside, the Commons room is wonderful if you have any time to yourself – which, depending on your area of focus, you might. I don't know your focus – and you might not even know it yet – but everyone is given a little time throughout the day. I hope your study time is with me, but we'll find out today."

A bell rang from somewhere outside.

"Don't worry," Barae said. "That's first warning. That's to let us know we should be awake by now, and we obviously are. This way." They headed back down the hallway, Barae greeting several others as they walked. She seemed to know almost everyone in the Initiate house. They passed Zhava's room, went down the narrow stairs at the end of the building, passed Barae's room – where she stopped briefly to bolt her door tight – and went back to the main entrance at the center of the building. Sister Tegara was just coming in from outside as they reached the front door.

"Oh, Zhava, how lovely to greet you this beautiful morning," Tegara said. "And it is good that Barae has already found you. How are you doing?"

"Very well, thank you," Zhava said, giving a quick bow of her head.

"Oh, so formal," Tegara said with a laugh. She returned the quick bow. "Thank you. Barae volunteered to be your sponsor."

Barae squeezed Zhava's hand.

"That means," Tegara continued, "that she will take you around the Hibaro today. She will show you where to find anything you might need, and she will help you to find a set of instructors who will better prepare you as a new Candidate."

"Thank you," Zhava said.

"She will also help you to find a task appropriate to your skills. Everyone here performs a task. That is how we keep the Hibaro running smoothly."

Another bell rang outside.

"Oh, second bell already," Sister Tegara said, stepping aside. "Go, quickly. I will meet you both back here after your breakfast."

"Yes, Sister Tegara," Barae said. "Thank you."

"Thank you," Zhava repeated.

They went outside, careful to stay on the wooden paths built between the buildings. They passed dozens of other people, boys and girls, men and women. Zhava was trying not to stare, but the variety and number of people was amazing to her. She recognized a few people speaking languages near the Purneese Mountains, as she did, but she heard several other languages she did not recognize. Most people were dressed in simple tunics or dresses or pants and shirts, but some others were dressed in fancier clothes with buttons down the sides or wide belts or vibrant colors – such as purple or red or green. She saw several priests in their black robes, Ios on horseback with their flowing red and black uniforms, soldiers training in the distance. She was so enraptured by the bustle of the open yard that she realized she hadn't heard anything Barae had said until they entered a small building and Barae turned, grinned, and said, "Here we are."

Zhava looked around the dimly lit room with its rows of doors down each side. The smell was horrible, and she covered her face.

"The toilette's bad, I know," Barae said, wrinkling her own nose. "Posef has been on toilette cleaning duty several times too, and you really want to avoid him after that."

They found two open stalls next to each other, Barae continuing to chatter the entire time. She explained the standard schedule of courses for the days, the different types of meals that were served to the Candidates versus those served to the Initiates – and even some of the fancy meals the Priests and Ios ate in the Tower.

As they left the toilette building, Barae told Zhava about some of her favorite teachers, a few of her favorite books, which Initiates were likely to be sent out of the Hibaro because they simply could not learn, which of the Initiates were likely to be promoted early because they excelled in their studies, and which mentors were the best for training. Zhava noticed that Barae did not mention Io Kua's name among the best mentors, and she wondered if she might have made a mistake requesting him.

Before she had time to finish that thought, however, she saw Plishka walking along the path, and she waved. Plishka did not return the wave, however. Instead, she frowned, turned away, and continued talking with the woman beside her.

"Don't bother being nice to her," Barae said. "Plishka is one of Sister Allenka's little toads, and she trains them to be mean."

"But she was nice to me last night," Zhava said.

"Plishka? What did she do, hit you or just say nasty things to you?"

"No, she gave me some bread."

Barae stopped, turned to Zhava, and stared. "She...but why?"

"I don't know. Because I was hungry?"

Barae shook her head and continued leading. "Well, if you ate bread that Plishka gave you, I'm surprised you lived to see the morning light."

They entered a large hall with tables and benches set in long aisles. People were filing into the building and being given bowls of some of the most delicious soup that Zhava had smelled in a long time. Her stomach growled, and that was the first time she realized how hungry she had grown during the whirlwind tour Barae had been leading.

They stood in the fast-moving line, were given full bowls and wooden spoons, and found where Posef was already sitting and eating. He waved them over and pointed to the two empty spots on the bench across from him.

"Welcome, ladies," he said with a quick bow.

"Greetings," Zhava said, returning the bow and trying not to blush. He was dressed now – thank the Gods – but those green eyes were still so vibrant.

"What's the word?" Barae asked as they all sat and dug into their morning soup.

"Emsterold is missing," he said.

Barae gasped and nearly dropped her spoon.

Zhava had no idea what an "emsterold" was, so she was unsure whether she should be concerned by the fact that it had gone missing. She took a mouthful of soup instead, and savored the creamy broth and bits of chicken and highlights of dill. She shut her eyes. This was a very good soup, and her body shivered as the warmth ran down her throat and into her stomach. She had given no thought to the food she would eat, but she was thrilled it was so good.

"She was on patrol," Posef said. "Wasn't supposed to be by herself, but she wandered into the woods during the third watch. Never came back."

"Who was she?" Zhava asked between spoonfuls.

"Emsterold," Barae said. "Came here nearly ten seasons back, off the Storm Coasts. She had recently become an Apprentice – she was incredibly tuned in to the spirits. She could summon the recently departed and actually get them to answer questions – I snuck in to the Apprentice house this past winter and watched her. I have never been so scared in my life as I was watching that dead man's spirit drift around the room."

"So she...communed with the dead?" Zhava asked, staring at the two.

"That was her Ability," Posef said. "And she was damn good at it, too."

"This is a blow to the Hibaro," Barae said.

"It's more than that. If someone as talented as Emsterold could be killed, where could this all end?"

"But," Zhava said. "Wait. People here can commune with the dead? How? Why?"

"Where are you from?" Posef asked.

"Just this side of the Purneese," she replied.

"Does no one this side of the Purneese have any Gods-granted Abilities?" Posef said, tapping the table as he asked his question. "How did you get to be an Initiate? You must have some Ability. Or are you a pretender?"

"Posef," Barae said. "Remember, she's new here. And I'm her sponsor – I will not have you speaking like that to her."

"Well go on then," Posef said to Zhava. "You must have some ability, or the Ios wouldn't have gone all the way out to the Purneese to drag you back here. What can you do? What is your Ability? If you have one."

Zhava glanced around and saw that Posef's voice had attracted the attention of several people nearby. They were turning to stare, their conversations quietening down or simply stopping altogether. She looked back down at her soup and wished that she hadn't asked the question.

"It's okay," Barae said to her. "Posef is just mad because of Emsterold. He didn't mean it."

"You want to know what I can do?" Zhava asked, her anger suddenly flaring. She did not need her new friend defending her, and if Posef really wanted a demonstration, she could certainly give him one. She would call forth her little flames and scatter them across the wooden table. Maybe set a few of these soup bowls aflame – maybe burn up the one Posef was using and let the soup spill into his lap. That would stop him questioning her.

"It must be something good," Posef said, wagging his head as he spoke.

But then Zhava remembered her promise to Io Liori, that she would not call forth the flames again until she had learned better how to control them, until she had met with Io Kua and begun her training. She wanted so badly to use them now, but she also wanted to honor her promise to Liori. She looked around. If her flames danced atop this table and burned up soup bowls, that would certainly be learned throughout the Hibaro. Even if Liori had left for her duties at the border patrol, she would hear about this when she returned, and she would be even angrier then.

"Well?" Posef said. He sat back on the bench and clapped his hands against his chest. "Show me what you can do. I'm ready."

Zhava took a quick breath, focused her will, flicked her fingers – and sent a sudden gust of wind across the table that struck Posef in the chest. He was sent sprawling off the bench, across the aisle, and into the back of a boy sitting behind him. The boy was knocked from his spot, and Posef fell to the floor with a thud and a yelp of pain.

The room grew silent. Zhava looked around and saw everyone staring from Posef to her and back again. She had no idea what to do – she would certainly get into trouble now. And what if she had hurt Posef?

"Hah!" Barae said with a huge grin, slapping Zhava's shoulder. "That was wonderful."

The people around them burst into applause, several of those nearest Zhava reaching out to touch her, to clap her on the back or to tap her shoulder or squeeze her arm. She was jostled about on the little bench so much she almost toppled off, but Barae reached out a hand to steady her.

Posef stumbled up from the floor, dusted himself off, and gave an extravagant bow to those around him, grinning and flashing those green eyes toward Zhava.

When the noise began to settle and people returned to their breakfasts, Posef sat down again and extended a hand toward Zhava. She tentatively reached out and shook it.

"Zhava," he said, "I am ever so thrilled to be your friend."

"Thank you," she said.

"Are you satisfied?" Barae said to him. "She truly has a Gods'-given Ability."

Posef was about to respond, when a hush suddenly settled on the room. The three of them turned to look. A figure stood in the doorway of the building, hands on his hips, and his black and red robes fluttering around him. His face was flushed, and his mouth was clenched in a tight line. He scanned the now-silent room until he caught sight of Zhava – and began striding over.

"That's Io Kua," Barae whispered.

"What's he doing here?" Posef whispered back.

Kua stepped up to the table, anger in his eyes, and pointed at Zhava. "You," he said. "Come with me. Now."

# CHAPTER 8

Zhava hung her head as she hurried after Io Kua. They left the dining hall and set off at a brisk pace across the yard. He did not care about mud or paths or people, cutting a straight line through the campus where people ducked aside as he passed. Zhava knew she was in trouble. Even though she had not set loose her flames, she had used one of her Abilities – impressively used one of her Abilities, she thought with pride – and nearly hurt another student. Her new friend. She smiled at that thought. She had actually made friends, she realized. Two friends in only her first day.

She looked up at the flowing black and red robes of Io Kua's back. Now she might lose those two friends because of what she had done, losing her control in a fit of anger. Priestess Marmaran had taught her better than that. Io Liori had made her promise to be better than that. She had done something wrong on her very first morning at the Hibaro, and now...what?

She looked around and realized they were walking along the edge of the Hibaro, past the outer patrols. Oh no. They were leaving. Io Kua was walking her out of the Hibaro. He was going to send her on her way – kick her out and send her back home again. She would have to go home and explain to Mama and Papa that Priestess Marmaran was dead, that the Ios had kicked her out, and that she now had nowhere to go and no one to teach her and no real skills that she could use around the home or around the farm...and she would probably now be sent off to spend the rest of her life with that pig Ooleng.

It was simply too much for her, and she stopped walking. "No!" she yelled.

Io Kua stopped, turned, and stared, his eyes still flaring with anger.

"I'm sorry for what I did, but I do not want to leave," she said. She stared at the ground and clenched her fists. "I know Io Liori told me not to use my flames, but I did not. I should not have let that boy make me angry, and I know Priestess Marmaran would reprimand me, but that is no reason to kick me out. I want to learn. I want to be an Initiate."

"Oh stop," Kua stepped forward and yelled into her face. "I don't care what you do with that boy. Knock him into the side of a building if you want."

Zhava looked up. This was not about Posef?

"You...." He clenched his fists and beat at the air as he shook with rage. "You! Had no right to keep me here."

She blinked. Keep him here? Keep him where?

He took one more step closer and pointed a finger into her face. "I had just been promoted." A second finger. "I had successfully completed my first field assignment." A third finger. "I was supposed to be riding with Io Liori's patrol for the next six moons."

Zhava took a step back. Kua followed with a step closer of his own.

"I was not supposed to have a student of my own for another full season."

This was not about her at all, Zhava realized. This was about Kua. Yes, he was mad at her, but this wasn't about anything she had done. At least not directly. She was being reprimanded, certainly, but she had been reprimanded so many times in her life by Mama or Papa or one of her brothers that she could survive the experience again. Relief washed over her as she realized she was not being kicked out, and that relief escaped in a soft giggle.

Kua stepped back and stared at her, his mouth open. "You laugh?"

"Oh." She covered her mouth. "No, Sir. I'm sorry, Sir."

"My problems – they're funny?"

"No, Sir. Really–"

He held up a hand to cut off any further comments. "Fine. You want a Mentor? You want me to pick up where Priestess Marmaran left off? You want me to mentor you properly in the ways of the Kandor?"

Zhava wasn't sure how to respond. He was asking her questions so quickly, but he was still holding up his hand as if he wanted her silent. Her Mama had sometimes done that when she was particularly angry, and whichever response Zhava chose was always wrong. As silence was often the safest option in those moments, she choose not to speak.

"Io Liori says you lack endurance," Kua said, looking her up and down. He turned around and scanned the trees and hills, then pointed. "You see those fallen stones on the edge of the clearing?"

Zhava looked. In the far distance was a small clearing with a mound of stones piled near the edge. It sat at the base of a tall hill that looked unnatural, as if many people had piled buckets of dirt until they could no longer pile it any higher. She nodded.

"We're going there. Keep up." He took off at a run.

Zhava, stunned at his sudden departure, stood and watched him for a moment. Then she bolted to try and catch up. They quickly left the hard-pack of the Hibaro grounds and entered the surrounding forest. There weren't many trees, but Kua darted left and right as he ran, making it hard for her to keep an eye on him the entire time. Within only a few minutes, he was so far ahead of her and moving back and forth so quickly that she lost track of him. She stopped and bent over to catch her breath. He was fast, and he and Io Liori were correct: she did not have the endurance she needed. At home she was always working, but she was allowed to work at her own pace. As long as she got where she was going with whatever she had been given to carry or to fetch within whatever general time she had been told – early morning, late morning, high sun – no one complained. This, however, this was different. These were the King's Ios, and she was not prepared to work with them the way they expected.

She stood straight and looked around. She knew the general direction she had last seen Kua run, but she had completely lost track of the direction she was supposed to travel. The tree next to her was thick and tall, so she jumped up and gripped the nearest branch. She loved climbing trees. Whenever she could get free of Mama and Papa, she would always climb the trees around their fields and look out on the world around her. Not that she had ever expected to travel much farther than she could see, but she enjoyed the feeling of freedom she got from watching the world from so high.

She hoisted herself up, got her footing, and started climbing. The bark was just a little sticky, and within moments her white shirt and pants were covered in sap and dirt and a few leaves. The branches easily supported her all the way to the top, and she braced herself in a split of new growth where she could see the surrounding area. She found the Hibaro grounds quickly enough and realized she had not traveled as far as she expected. She turned in her perch until she could see the groupings of rocks in the distance. That was not the direction in which Io Kua had been traveling, and Zhava frowned. Either he had changed his mind, or he had gotten himself lost...or he had been leading her by an indirect path.

Zhava clenched her jaw tight at that realization. She had thought him nice when they were riding to the Hibaro and he let her sleep, but to lead her astray like this.... Angry that he would treat her so unfairly, she took a quick sighting of several landmarks in her path, then hurried back down. She flung herself from one branch to the next, caring little about the snaps she heard the tree make or the small tears that peppered her clothes. Within moments she was back on the ground and running again, this time heading in the correct direction.

She darted around trees, leaped over branches, ducked beneath a tangled webbing of vines, jumped across a shallow creek, and climbed up a tall ravine. She struggled to pull herself up on the exposed roots that snaked through the sandy soil. When she felt the top, she groped about until her hands wrapped around a stone set in the ground, and she struggled up, her feet kicking wildly to get good purchase on the steep wall. Someone grabbed her hands, and she shrieked.

"Get up here," Io Kua barked, yanking her the final way to the top.

Zhava rolled over on the ground, breathing hard and looking into Kua's stern face as he stood above her. She pulled in gasping breaths, and she wiped away the sweat and dirt from her face.

"What were you doing?" he asked.

"You...left me," she said between breaths.

His eyes narrowed.

"And you...led me...in the wrong...direction," she finished.

"Get up."

She rolled over and struggled to her feet. She was unsteady, and she felt her body swaying between breaths.

"I lied to you, did I?" he said, crossing his arms. "You are out of shape, you're barely trained in the Kandor, you're irresponsible in your skills, you requested me as your Mentor even though I'm not supposed to be Mentoring anyone for at least another season, you find my troubles laughable – and now I lied to you?" He was yelling by the time he finished, and Zhava took a hesitant step back. He pointed behind him. "What is that?"

Zhava looked. The pile of rocks – more like large building stones – was behind Kua, and beside those was a path that led straight into the small clearing in which they now stood.

"The trail," he said when she did not reply. "The trail that leads from the Hibaro to this sparring ground – so you don't have to climb out of a steep ravine."

Again, Zhava did not know what to say. She remained silent.

"Add to your list of problems that you do not obey, and you do not trust," Kua said. He reached behind his back and yanked out two small sticks. "Here." He tossed one to her. It struck her in the chest, and she fumbled to grip it before it fell to the ground. He flicked his stick down, and several extensions snapped out from within it, making it nearly four times as long as it had been when he started. "Defend yourself."

Kua swiped through the air, and Zhava felt the snap of the rod on her arm. She cried out in pain and gripped the spot. Her hand came away, a long, red mark spread across her arm. She backed out of his reach, nearly tripping on the sandy ground, and tried to flick her own rod down to open it. It did not open. She had heard of training rods such as these, but she had never before seen one – and she had certainly never been taught how to open or fight with one.

"Again," Kua yelled, leaping forward and swinging from the other direction.

Zhava stumbled backward and tripped. She fell to the ground hard, but at least Kua had missed striking her other arm.

"Again." Another swing.

Zhava kicked away, scraped across the ground, and rolled out of his reach. She stumbled up, ran for several lengths into the forest, then turned to face him, her small stick held before her. He had not followed her, however. He was still standing in the clearing and watching her, gently swinging the rod through the air around him.

"Get back here," he said. "The clearing is the sparring ground. Our score is now two to nothing – one point for the arm strike and one point for you leaving the clearing."

Zhava took a deep breath, wiped more sweat from her eyes, and glanced down at her arm. A trickle of blood ran down through the dirty and torn sleeve.

"Or am I lying to you again?" he called. "Maybe I've led you out here to torture you until you run back home to your Mama and your Papa. Do you prefer a life with Ooleng? Maybe we can still find him out along some of the Purneese trails, on his way home with his illiterate family. Maybe that is where you belong?"

Zhava clenched her jaw. She was now certain: Io Kua hated her.

He pressed his palm to the tip of the rod and pushed, the extensions sliding back into place with little snicks. Then he raised his hand into the air and sliced in a short arc away from his body. The extensions snapped back out again.

Zhava imitated the rapid movement, and the rod in her own hand extended until it was just as long as the one Kua held. She stepped slowly forward, trying to get her breathing back under control.

Kua turned, walked to the other side of the clearing, then turned back to face her. He held his training rod down and at his side.

She stepped forward, back into the clearing, and held her own training rod down and at her side, imitating his stance. He narrowed his gaze at her.

"You're capable of learning," he said. "Or perhaps only copying?"

He moved so quickly she could barely respond. His swing circled high, and she tried to block it. The snap of the sparring rod against her other arm confirmed the hit.

"Three to nothing," he said, stepping away.

"What in the Gods' names are you doing?" she yelled, squeezing the spot he'd just struck. Her hand came away slick with more blood.

"Some passion," he said, casually slicing the air around him as he circled her. "I'd wondered if you were capable. So cold on the trail. Even burning up your beloved Priestess Marmaran's body you barely shed a tear. More animal than person, I thought."

She leaped and struck out at him. She missed, and he brought his rod down across her legs.

"Four – five – six!" he yelled.

Zhava staggered at the cuts along the back of her leg. She bit her lip to keep from crying out as she turned and held her own rod up before her.

Kua sliced forward, and she clumsily blocked the hit. He smiled.

"I've never done this!" she yelled, staggering backwards.

He flicked his rod around and snapped her in the wrist. She dropped her sparring rod and stumbled, nearly falling in the dirt. She stood up straight and gripped her throbbing wrist. She was defenseless. If he was going to do something harsh to her, now was the time.

"This is my point," Kua said, flicking a hand at her. He reached down, retrieved her sparring rod from the ground, folded them both back together, and reattached them at his back. "You've never done this. You've never done any of this. And yet I'm supposed to be your Mentor?"

"I didn't ask for one."

"You asked for me! You requested me. You're not ready for a Mentor – for any Mentor – and yet you requested the one person on this entire campus the least ready to train you." He shook his head and sighed, then looked to the sky and screamed. He clenched his fists and beat at the air above him.

Zhava took a step back, ready to run away. She was unsure what he might do next, but her arms and leg throbbed painfully from the lessons she had endured so far.

Kua took a deep breath, shut his eyes, and seemed to be muttering quietly to himself. She made out a couple numbers, as if he was counting to himself. When he finished, he opened his eyes and stared at Zhava, apparently thinking. He turned to look up the pile of stones at the edge of the sparring ground. "There's a path back there," he said, flicking his hand at the rocks. "Follow it to the top, then go inside."

Zhava turned to look at the pile of stones. She hadn't thought much about them the entire time they'd been sparring. They were large, each the size of a yearling calf, and they were piled high against the side of a cut in the hillside. They looked to be hiding something. A cave perhaps?

"What's inside?" she asked.

Kua sighed, plopped to the ground in a small cloud of dust, and crossed his legs before him. "The future," he said. "The past. The present – just go. Let's see what happens." He shut his eyes and rubbed at his head. Within moments he had begun a muttering chant in some language Zhava did not know.

Zhava limped forward. She wiped her blood-stained hands on her torn pants. The cuts throbbed, and her body ached, not only from the sparring but also from the running and the climbing she had done. She couldn't remember a day ever that had begun with this much pain. Even back home, though her daily chores were hard, the work was steady and slow. She could walk, she could carry loads at her own pace, she could fetch and tote and haul sacks of grain or clothes or weeds as slowly as she wanted. And she never had to fight – except with her brothers, but they had outgrown fighting with her several seasons back. Perhaps Kua was correct; she was not ready for this. But if not for this, then what?

She stepped to the back side of the pile of stones and found the steps just as he had said. They were made by flat rocks piled atop each other. They were steep, far steeper than any normal person could easily climb, and they seemed to stop about halfway up the hillside. She glanced back at Kua, but he still sat in the middle of the sparring grounds, his eyes closed, muttering his foreign chants. She stretched one leg high, grabbed hold of the rocky hillside, and pulled herself up. Her knee scraped against the rock, and she gasped. She looked down; blood was soaking through the leg of her pants, mixing with the dirt and tears. She had no idea how she would get these clothes clean.

She limped forward and hoisted herself up the next step. Another scrape. Her fingers slipped on the stones, and she winced as sharp pebbles bit into her palm. She cursed, flicked her wrist, and sent a force of wind to scatter the pebbles and sand away from her. At the next step, she used her Ability to clean away all the dirt and rocks before she climbed, and though she cracked her shin into the edge of the step, she didn't lose her grip on the rocky hillside. After several more steps, clearing her way before each one, she finally reached the top. She looked back down, but Kua was completely hidden by the rocks piled along the side of the steps.

Zhava turned back to the entrance. It was small, with strings of moss draping down before it. She parted the moss and peered inside. Within only a short distance, the darkness seemed to swallow the light. She called forth one of her little flames, and he flared to life in her palm. She held him out before her, and he actually shrank back from the darkness, peering out from between her fingers. She didn't like that. She had never known her flames to show anything but excitement – and certainly never fear. She called forth a couple more to her hand, and they immediately wrapped themselves about the first, forming a cowering little ball of flame. Whatever Kua sent her to face, she wondered if she was truly ready.

Should she go back? She turned and looked down the steep steps. She certainly could – it would be difficult to navigate back down those large stones, and she would probably get several more cuts and bruises, but she could do it. But what would Io Kua say then? He already believed she wasn't ready for a Mentor, wasn't ready to be trained. He had already said she disobeyed and didn't listen to authority. If she climbed back down and refused to enter this small cave...would he really kick her out of the Hibaro?

She turned back to the cave. She had disappointed him enough; she would see this through.

She stepped forward, the ropes of moss leaving damp streaks along her shoulders and back. The flames in the palm of her hand seemed to shiver, but their glow cut through the extreme dark, casting finger-shaped shadows on the slick walls around her. The dampness quickly seeped into her thin shoes, and she felt something sticky oozing between her toes. She looked down. The floor was covered in a shallow layer of mud. She wrinkled her nose. What a waste; there would be no saving these clothes.

The narrow cave angled down, and she kept one hand against the slick wall to stop herself from slipping. Her fingers scraped against some spindly plants growing in the seams of the rock, little pinpricks of blood quickly seeping from her fingertips. She winced, shook her hand to dull the pain, then continued walking. The flames nervously rode in her other hand, their gazes flicking up and down and all around. The air began to stink, a pungent smell that made her not want to breathe. She knew the smell; something had died in here, and recently.

"Yuck," she muttered. She turned away. She had no intention of leaving, but she just needed a few moments to compose herself, to get her mind accustomed to the smell of death so she could go on. She looked back up the tunnel to the little moss-covered entrance – and saw that it was closing behind her, shutting as if someone pushed the walls together until the light outside simply vanished.

She stood there several moments, just staring at the darkness where the cave entrance had been only moments before. Her heart started thumping in her chest, and she had to work to calm her breathing, to keep herself from panicking. She had never seen anything like that before, had never seen a wall of rock close in on itself like that, but there had to be an explanation.

"Kua," she whispered. She could move little rocks, but Kua was an Io, trained for years in the Kandor – of course it made sense that he could move much larger rocks than she. That he could shut the entrance to a cave. This was simply the next part of the test, she was sure of it. He was forcing her to find her own path through the cave, to find her way out. She could do this. She would do this. She had her flames to light her way, and she had her control of the wind and the stones to keep herself safe.

Something gurgled from deep within the cave.

Zhava spun around and held the flames up high.

The gurgling continued, slower...and slower...until finally it stopped. She saw nothing. It had sounded like the big toads that came up from the river, especially after a spring rain, but it had sounded so much larger than any toad. Or like the kind of loud noise the cows made bellowing into the evening, but harsher than that, less melancholy. She realized Kua had never truly answered her question about what was inside this cave. Instead he had said something cryptic about the future and the past. That was not helpful.

Another gurgle, from behind. She turned, and something moved in the darkness where the cave entrance had been only moments before. A deeper shadow, shuffling low just outside the light from her flames. It was big, too. She could tell even in the darkness that the shadow animal was large as it lumbered across the path. More gurgling, and the shadow stopped. Gurgle...gurgle.

It spun around, its eyes glowing red from the light of the flames, and it stared at Zhava. Its bulky shape shifted in the darkness, four massive legs moving slowly, deliberately as the creature turned. All the time it kept watching Zhava, gurgling at her in the darkness.

She took a step back. She had lived with wildlife her entire life, but she had never seen anything like this before. Its shape seemed to shift in the darkness, to blur at the edges, so that Zhava could never quite see it. The gurgling seemed to come from deep within its throat, as if with each breath it also took in a mouth full of water.

Suddenly, it lunged. Where it had been sitting motionless one moment, it leapt straight at Zhava's head the next, its glowing eyes fierce.

Zhava screamed and scuttled backward. She slipped in the muck at her feet and fell – and fell and fell. She continued screaming, watching the roof of the cave recede into the distance, the glowing-eyed creature watching her from the lip of a cliff. She fell so far that the creature became a spot in the distance. The cavern wall rushed past her, and she struggled to grab hold, to stop herself from falling.

She struck the ground hard. Her breath was knocked out of her, and her head slammed into the floor so hard the world turned black. Within moments, spots bounced before her eyes. Her vision began to clear, and she could see a pinprick of light.

She struggled to make herself breathe again, to pull in even a tiny breath of air. The back of her head ached. She tried to move her hands up, to feel her head, but she couldn't make them work.

The light began to grow in her eyes, and she realized it was her three little flames standing on her chest and imploring her to get up.

Her breathing started again. She coughed and gasped, and a blessed burst of air filled her. With it, however, came a rush of pain from every corner of her body. Her head throbbed. Her back felt as if she had been kicked by a camel. Her arms and hands tingled from the hundreds of cuts and bruises she had gotten in the fall...

...the fall that should have killed her.

She tried to focus on the ceiling high above, but she couldn't even see it. She had fallen into a cavern so deep she couldn't even see the top of it...but she had survived?

The creature's gurgling echoed down to her.

Zhava panicked. It was still up there. It had attacked her, and it was still up there. She struggled to roll over on the floor of the cavern. Her little flames slipped off her shirt and landed in a pile beside her. She scrabbled across the slick surface, her entire body screaming at her to stop moving. She finally rolled onto all fours and looked around – and the room began to spin. The pain in the back of her head nearly crushed her to the floor, but she refused to give in. She refused to give up.

The creature gurgled again, closer this time.

As Zhava struggled to stand, her little flames clambered up her arms and rushed to her shoulders. They snuggled against her neck, and she could feel their warmth like a comforting shawl. She now understood their fear. They had sensed this creature in the cave long before she had, and they'd understood how scared they should be.

She used the wall to right herself, leaning against it to keep from falling over. She looked up and saw the shadowy creature leaping its way down the steep cliff face. She still couldn't see it well, and if she was going to survive, she had to know what she was fighting. She called several more of her flames, and they sprang to life along her shoulders and arms.

The darkness drifted away with the light of so many fires. The shadow creature landed with a thud several paces away. It no longer lay squat on all fours. It now stood hunched over, its massive arms dangling nearly to the floor, and its hind legs crouched beneath it. Somehow, though, it remained in shadow, its black fur waving along its body as if in a wind that Zhava could not feel. Its small eyes glowed brighter red in the light from her flames.

Suddenly, it leaped again – but this time Zhava was ready. She raised her hand and willed the wind to beat it back. Just as she had knocked Posef from his seat, this shadow creature was shoved backward and slammed into the far wall. It fell to the floor and shook its head.

Zhava didn't wait for it to recover. She sent another blast of wind at the thing and sent it flying farther into the darkness. It growled and screamed as it was pushed far away, then went silent.

Zhava collapsed to the floor. She sat in a heap, leaning against the wall and just trying to breathe and not fall over. She couldn't believe she had actually done that. She couldn't believe she had actually used her powers to fight off some creature in the darkness. She felt giddy at what she had done – like laughing – but she hurt too much to even try. She looked down and examined the muddy, torn clothes. She had streaks of blood across her arms and legs, along her chest and belly, and – she reached up – running down her face. Her head was throbbing so hard it felt like one of her brothers was using it as a drum. She looked around to see if there was a way out.

The creature gurgled in the darkness.

"No," Zhava muttered, tensing.

Another gurgle, followed by a low growl.

"No, no, no, no." She struggled to push herself up.

The creature shuffled back into the light. It now stood straight and tall, and Zhava could see it was shaped like a person – a very tall, very powerful person. Its black fur rippled along its body, and its glowing, red eyes narrowed on her.

The area seemed to grow dimmer, and Zhava looked down to see her little flames tucking themselves behind her arms and peering out at the creature.

She found her footing beneath her, pushed against the slick wall, and stood up straight.

The creature leaned forward and growled at her, its black mouth open wide.

Zhava raised her hand and willed the wind again – but nothing happened.

The creature bobbed its head and watched her, gurgling and growling on the edge of the darkness.

Zhava focused her will again – pushed out with all her strength to make the wind do her bidding, but again, nothing happened.

The creature stood tall and waved its arm at her.

The force of the blast caught Zhava by surprise. The wind knocked her aside, and she fell to the ground, skidding across the slick muck and gravel. She coughed and sputtered and struggled to push herself up.

The creature stood tall, raised its head into the air, and gurgled a high-pitched, steady rhythm into the cavern. Then it brought one arm down through the air.

The wind slammed against Zhava's back, shoving her into the ground.

Again, the creature raised its arm and brought it down, and again the wind drove Zhava into the floor.

She cried at the pain. Cried at the beating force of the wind. Cried at the injustice of it all, that she should be beaten by her own stolen Ability.

The wind struck her back a third time, and she nearly blacked out from the pain. But then the little flames tumbled down before her eyes, pleading with her, begging her to let them loose. They wanted to attack this creature. They wanted to be set upon this creature and burn it to ashes as they had done with Priestess Marmaran's dead body. They wanted to be used as her weapon, to defend her, to attack her enemy.

"Go," she whispered.

Dozens of the little flames poured forth from Zhava's body. The cavern lit like daylight as hundreds of them leaped to the ground around Zhava, all aiming at the creature in the darkness. They roared to action, their screams like a tidal wave of sound, as they burned so hot they flickered blue. The army of little flames rushed across the cavern floor, burning up the damp ground and leaving a flaming trail in their wake. They swarmed atop the creature, biting into it and burrowing into its thick hide. The creature thrashed and moaned and bellowed and tore at the little flames. It tried to brush them off, but they climbed right back on. It tried to slap them dead, but they popped back to life. It tried to squeeze them tight, but they wriggled loose and continued burning bright. Within moments, they had subdued the creature, and it fell to the floor. They roiled across its body, tumbling and flickering and playing.

Zhava coughed, and that sent a spasm of pain through her head and body. She just wanted to lie there and rest...forever. She couldn't think what more she could do. Every part of her body was in pain, she had no energy left to move, and she had no idea how she would ever climb back out of this cavern...or even find another way out, a side passage or a back exit or anything. And now with her command of the rocks and the wind gone, her Gods-given Abilities seemingly taken away from her by that creature, she didn't know how she could even begin to move aside the rocks from the cave's entrance. Her little flames could do many things, but she didn't think they could burn their way through rocks.

A faint gurgle echoed through the cavern.

Zhava shifted. Her little flames had gone back to their pretty orange/red color, but they had stopped moving.

The creature's body twitched. It gurgled again, more forcefully this time.

Zhava lay paralyzed in fear as she watched. What did it take to kill this thing?

It shifted on the ground, getting its legs beneath it and pushing up.

Zhava called on her little flames.

The creature's body rippled, and the flames flared brighter for a moment. They shifted across the thing's body, each one taking a step to the right, and then they turned to look at Zhava. Their eyes burned black within their little flaming heads.

Zhava struggled to move. The bruises and cuts all screamed at her to remain still as she desperately tried to sit up. She called to the flames again, but they only stared at her across the distance.

The creature let loose a series of sharp, rattling breaths, almost a laughing, barking sound, as it got up on all fours. It turned to face Zhava, its red eyes gleaming in the darkness.

Zhava shoved herself up and tried to stand. Her legs were weak, and she couldn't force them to work. Again she called to the flames, and again they would not come.

The creature stood tall, the black-eyed flames clinging to its fur and humming with excitement.

"No!" Zhava screamed.

The thing ran at her, gripped her by the shoulders, and knocked her back to the ground. It stood over her, pressing her down and leaning in close to her face. The flames grinned their hollow smiles at her, and the creature's mouth opened and closed as it gurgled joyously at her. She could smell the thing's breath, like some animal had died deep within it. Its body had pinned her to the ground so hard she could not move, she could not even squirm. She could barely breathe.

It bent its head down low, and the black fur brushed against her. It peered into her face, and she could see her own reflection staring back from within its dead, red eyes.

Zhava realized this thing was going to kill her, and there was nothing she could do to stop it. It had taken away her Abilities, her control of the rocks and the wind and her little flames. It had beaten her until she could not move. It had sat on her to keep her from running away. This would be her end, at the bottom of a cavern inside a cave on the edge of the Hibaro. She wondered if Io Kua would even venture this deep to retrieve her body.

A scraping sound came from...somewhere.

The creature heard it too, and it tensed its body and turned toward the sound.

Zhava looked and saw that a light was coming from far away.
The creature crouched down atop Zhava and began growling low in its throat. The little flames dimmed, as if trying to hide from this new noise.

The pinprick of light grew wider, and Zhava could see movement from within. A person...two people were standing in the light.

The creature began to snarl, and she could feel its muscles tensing as it prepared to strike.

The people in the light raced forward, rushing down the long tunnel as if propelled by magic. They had scarves wrapped around their faces and bandages bound over their hands, but even so, Zhava recognized them immediately. It was her friend Barae and Sister Tegara. They were coming to get her, to rescue her.

Zhava panicked. They didn't know about the creature.

"No," she tried to yell, but her voice wouldn't come.

The creature reached down and snapped its jaws in her face, then turned back and growled at her rescuers.

Zhava would not let this creature hurt her friends – she could not let it hurt them. She lifted her pounding head and slammed her forehead into the creature's snout. It let out a surprised bark, then jumped down the tunnel – straight for Barae and Tegara.

Zhava rolled over and gripped the thing's tail. The little flames bit into her hands and ran down her arms, burning her and trying to get her to let go, but she would not. This creature might eat her, but she would not let it harm her friends. She was dragged across the floor of the cavern, through the mud and across the sharp stones, but still the creature bore down on her friends.

"Get away," she yelled at them. "It's coming for you. I can't stop it. Just get away!"

The creature leaped into the air, its jaw open wide and its razor claws flashing in the light of a thousand flaming men as it pounced upon –

– Zhava sat up with a gasp. She blinked to find herself lying in her own bed, back home, in her own room.

She looked around. The early morning glow poured in through the open window. The rooster crowed somewhere across the yard, and the birds were singing their morning songs. A small breeze ruffled the curtains. Her little table along the wall was all set with two of her wood carvings – a chicken and a camel. Her clothes were laid out neatly folded on the shelf beneath. Her straw bed was lumpy, and the covers were scattered about her, but it was all perfectly normal...and home.

The door cracked open, and Mama poked her head in and smiled at her.

"I heard you cry out, Beloved. Are you all right?"

Zhava looked down at herself. She sat in the bed in her night gown with no cuts or bruises, no blood – and no creature attacking her.

"Um...yes," she said.

"That's good," Mama said, her smile beaming. "You don't want to start off this day with any bad dreams."

"This day?"

"Your wedding day, of course. Ooleng and his family arrived late last night, and you will love him. He is the most handsome and charming young man I've seen...well since I met your Papa."

Zhava just stared. She couldn't remember ever hearing her Mama speak like that about anyone.

"Get dressed and come downstairs, Beloved," she said with a wink. "A good breakfast of eggs will get you ready for the day."

# CHAPTER 9

Zhava changed quickly into her favorite dress, the blue one with the little rooster embroidered along the hem. She fluffed her straw mattress and straightened the coverings, then folded her nightgown and set it on the bottom shelf of her table. She was ready to go downstairs. She was ready for the day when everything would begin to change. When she would meet her future husband.

She ran down the short hall, took the narrow steps two at a time, and burst into the kitchen. Mama was at the little cooktop with a skillet and had just cracked two eggs. At the table, sat...no one. That didn't feel right. The table in the corner of the kitchen always had someone sitting at it the first thing every morning. It was...

"Priestess Marmaran," she said.

"What's that, Beloved?" Mama asked.

"Where is Priestess Marmaran this morning?"

"Oh, don't you remember?" Mama turned from her cooking and knelt down before Zhava. "Priestess Marmaran got sick last year. She died."

"Last year?"

"Yes, Beloved. I'm so sorry. It was hard on all of us, and I know how special she was to you. But she taught you all those wonderful skills you will use now that you are to be married, and that is all that matters."

"Yes." She nodded. That was all that mattered. She sat at the table while her Mama went back to frying the eggs. She casually flicked a rock into the center of the table and stared at it. She could make that rock move if she wanted to. She could make that rock skip and dance and roll across the table...if she wanted to. She waved her hand at it, but it did nothing. She sighed. She didn't want that rock to do anything but sit there. It was fine where it was.

She turned and stared out the window. The morning sun was beginning to brighten the yard, and she could see the yellow flowers growing around the base of the fig tree near the road. They were so bright in the early morning, with the sun glinting off the petals. She loved the look of the yard first thing in the morning, when everything came alive and greeted the new dawn.

"Where is Papa?" she asked.

"Tending a newborn calf. He'll be back by noonday meal, don't worry."

"Hmm." She casually played with the sand in the window ledge and watched the chickens peck their way across the yard. She looked off into the distance, to the end of the main path, and she saw the dark outline of a person out there. The person seemed to be just standing there, doing nothing but...waiting. Or watching. "Mama, who is that?" Zhava asked, pointing.

"What are you seeing, Beloved?" Mama asked, leaning down to peer out the window.

"Right there. That person at the end of the path."

"Oh, that trouble-maker is back." Mama flicked her towel to the floor and stomped off. "Zhava, you stay away from that one, that sister of yours. She has always been trouble, and now she wants to ruin this wonderful day for you." She went outside and around the side of the house. Within moments, one of the servants was running down the path and brandishing a club. The person at the end of the path – her sister? – ran away, and Mama came back inside. She quickly finished the eggs and piled them high on a plate, but she did not set the plate on the table as Zhava expected. Instead she went outside and gestured for Zhava to follow.

They went around the side of the house to where the sun was bright and a low table had been set with three small stools. A young man, a handsome young man dressed in fine robes of purple and blue, sat at the table with a plate of food before him. He sat with his hands in his lap and waiting as Zhava and Mama approached.

The man stood and bowed. "Greetings this fine morning," he said, with just a hint of a mountain accent. Zhava liked the way he sounded, the way he spoke the words with just a slight hint of a foreign pronunciation. She had met several people from the Purneese Mountains, especially with Papa making annual trips into the mountains to buy and sell, but she had never before heard someone speak with such a unique accent. If she didn't know that Ooleng came from the Purneese, she never would have been able to guess it. Maybe from...the coast.

She and Mama sat at the little table, and Ooleng sat down last. Mama set the plate of eggs before Zhava and smiled at her and Ooleng.

"A prayer of thanks?" Mama asked. "Ooleng, would you do the honors?"

"Of course," Ooleng said with a quick wink at Zhava. She gasped as she noticed his bright green eyes – just a moment before he shut them and bowed his head. "Great Goddess Preizhavan, you are most honored. We thank you for the bounty of this harvest." He lifted his head.

"Short and simple," Mama said, nodding her head.

"The Goddess Preizhavan does not honor lengthy prayers full of ornate words and empty sayings." He turned to Zhava and looked her in the eyes. "She already knows her value."

"I approve," Mama said. She gripped Zhava's hand, and Zhava reluctantly broke her gaze with Ooleng. "And you should also approve. How many others have we met who revere your namesake, the Goddess Preizhavan?"

"Very few," Zhava said. She began picking at the eggs on her plate. "We have been so blessed with our little Beloved," Mama continued, this time to Ooleng. "Until just last year, she was being trained in the ways of a proper household – under a Priestess of the household."

"Really?" Ooleng said, his beautiful green eyes growing bigger at the news. "And what kinds of things did you learn?"

"I learned," Zhava began. But she realized she could not quite remember what she had learned. She knew that the Priestess had taught her how to...move away the dust and the rocks from the floor and the tables and the little window ledges...to sweep. And she had taught Zhava to...do something with her hands...to properly hold a candle. She spread her hand wide and gently closed her fingers. She had held a friend within that hand. No, she had held many friends. But they were all gone now.

She looked up. Someone stood at the edge of the yard, someone that Zhava should recognize but could not quite place in her mind. It was a young woman like her, a young woman dressed in simple clothes, a tan skirt and old shirt. She was gesturing to Zhava, beckoning her to come forward.

Mama turned to look. "Oh, not her too," she muttered. "Zhava, pay her no mind. That is the little orphan beggar who came to our door just yesterday. I gave her some food, and now she will not be on her way. Beloved – and Ooleng – please excuse me. I will see to it that the little orphan beggar does not disturb us again." She stood up and began walking across the yard. The girl quickly ran away, and Mama began to chase her. Within moments they were gone.

"I was hoping we would have some time to ourselves," Ooleng said quietly.

Zhava turned back. This was improper. They were pledged to be married, but they should not have been left alone without at least one of their parents as chaperone. Still...Zhava did not really mind the impropriety of the moment. And if it meant that Ooleng could speak honestly with her, then she quite preferred the solitude.

"I know that we have been pledged for many seasons," he began.
"We have?" Zhava asked. That did not seem right. She thought they had been pledged only recently. Why would she think that?

"For many seasons, yes," Ooleng continued. "But we have never truly had the chance to speak with each other as one, to speak in our own voices."

"I do not speak in anyone's voice but my own," Zhava insisted.

"And yet I do not know if this marriage is truly your heart's desire."

Zhava opened her mouth to protest, to assure Ooleng that of course her greatest heart's desire was to be married to him. She wanted nothing more than to travel with him into the Purneese Mountains, to set up a home with him in the wilderness so that they could call it their own. He would take care of her, provide for her needs and her protection, and she would bear him a son – a dozen sons, and a half-dozen daughters. But she couldn't say that. Something else was pulling at her. She had to do something else...she had done something else when...those people...arrived.

"Zhava," Ooleng whispered, taking her hand in his. "I love you with all that is within me. I love you from the top of the highest mountain to the bottom of the deepest ocean. I love you to the ends of the highest Heavens and to the firmament beyond. Zhava, you are my one and only true love."

Zhava yanked her hand away and jumped up, her stool falling back and banging against the side of the home.

"I...," she began. "I...um...I have to...go back." She rushed off before Ooleng could even reply. She ran around the side of the house and then walked on. She flicked her hands at her sides, trying to bring something forth, trying to provide light for her path, trying to remember where she had left her friends. This was all so wonderful, this was all so perfect. Mama loved her, and Ooleng loved her, and Papa...well, Papa was off with a newborn calf, but she was certain that he loved her, too. But there was something more than what she was seeing here. There was something more than what her Mama and Ooleng were discussing. This had all happened before, but it had happened differently. It had happened much worse, she realized. It had happened with...raised voices...and with a troop of soldiers and Ios...and with the death of Priestess Marmaran. Except Priestess Marmaran had died last year...that's what Mama said.

"Ah, my little Beloved," Papa said, and Zhava's head jerked up. She had not been paying attention, but she had walked into the fields. She had found her Papa, quite by accident, but he was here with her now. "Come to me, Zhava," he said, his arms open wide.

Zhava ran to him and hugged him tight. She squeezed her eyes shut and just embraced him, took in all the love that he would give to her. His strong arms held her, and she felt safe. She felt as if nothing in the world could harm her as long as she was wrapped in these arms. He was sweaty, of course, and kind of stinky from dealing with the newborn calf, but he was her Papa, and he loved her, and that made everything perfect.

"Ah, my little Beloved," Papa said, gently lowering them to the ground in the middle of the open field. "You have been crying. Tell me what happened. Tell me how we can make it right."

So Zhava told him. She told her tale of coming downstairs and eating a wonderful breakfast at the little table around back and meeting her wonderful, loving betrothed and how he had expressed his undying love for her...and how it was all so wrong. This was not the way it had happened. It was not the way it could happen. Things were too perfect. Things were too loving. Things were too....

She opened her eyes. He was smiling at her, stroking her long hair and soothing her. Milling about them in the open field, however, were five newborn chicks that circled them, pecking at the dirt. They were plump little fuzzballs, filled with the wild seeds they had found among the hedgerows and the slop buckets. They were filled with the bride price, waddling around like plump little sacks upon the ground, and Zhava knew that this was wrong too.

"Ah, my little Beloved," Papa said. "Everything will be all right. It is all over now. You have come home, and nothing more can ever harm you again."

Zhava turned her head away. Plenty had already harmed her. She did not like what had become of her life, of the things that had been done to her, but she knew this love, as wonderful as it was, was not a part of it. She knew that this was the lie, that the harm that had come to her had made her the person she was. She was not this person who lived at the edge of the Purneese Mountains. She was someone else now – had maybe always been someone else.

"Good bye," she whispered, and she stood.

"But, my little Beloved," Papa said. She did not look. "We need you here."

She shut her eyes and walked.

"Little Beloved, you must remain where you are loved."

The sun beat down on her head and warmed her body. Her head began to ache, but she knew that would happen when she cast aside the love. Her feet and hands began to tingle, and she felt her body slowing, stumbling in the plow ruts of the harvest field. She tried to open her eyes once, just to be sure she could find the path, but her eyes no longer opened.

That did not even bother her. She would end up where she was meant to end up.

Someone began walking beside her, shuffling through the dirt, and she reached a hand to grab hold. A companion was needed for this journey to anywhere. The hand that held hers was old and frail, and she knew in an instant that she could trace every line of that palm and every callous upon those roughened fingers. She smiled.

"Marmaran."

"Child," Marmaran whispered back. "I am so very proud."

Zhava gasped – and came up out of the water with a splash and a scream. Hands held her down, and wet cloths wrapped quickly about her arms and legs. She tried to see, but something blocked her vision, and she fumbled at the wrappings, fumbled at the cloth stretched across her eyes.

"Zhava, please," a voice whispered in her ear. "Calm down. Calm down."

Zhava stopped struggling, and she noticed that every part of her body was in some kind of pain. Her head, chest, arms, back, stomach, hips, legs, feet – even her toes were tingling. What had happened? Where was her Papa? Her Mama? Where was Priestess–?

"Marmaran," she muttered.

"No, Zhava," the woman's soothing voice said. "Not Marmaran. Calm down – relax. You are safe."

"I can't see."

"Shh," the woman whispered, and Zhava finally recognized the voice.

"Sister Tegara?"

"Yes."

"I can't see."

Another pair of hands touched Zhava's head, and she felt the cloth being pulled away. Dim light began to show through, and she could just make out two shapes standing above her. The cloth was unwound again, and the shapes resolved into two people, the one leaning in close and whispering soothing sounds into her ear, and the other unwinding the cloth from around her head and eyes. Finally the cloth came free, and

Zhava blinked at the dim light of torches set high into the rough ceiling above.

Sister Allenka tossed the cloth aside and grunted. "Hm," she said. "So the little bird lives."

Zhava turned to the other woman, to Sister Tegara.

"You decided to come back to us," Tegara said with a smile. "I'm glad."

# CHAPTER 10

The wash basin in which she had been placed was narrow and shallow, but it was deep enough for the water to cover her. She blinked in the dim light of the small room, but it was not the light that hurt her eyes. Something stung them, as if bees were jabbing at her every time she tried to look around. She recognized the room as the same one in which Sister Allenka and her girls had washed her and cut her hair when she first arrived. The basin had been placed over the draining grate at the room's center, and she could hear water dripping down to the cistern below. The room and the water smelled far better than the first time she had been here. She recognized lavender, and she smiled at that, though there was also an undercurrent of blood lily to the water's scent.

While Sister Tegara and Sister Allenka tended to her injuries, several other people came and went from the wash room. She recognized Plishka, who smiled at her this time, and Barae gave her a big grin and a wave, but the other young women were strangers to her. They brought in fresh towels and carried away the bloodied ones, they refilled the bottles of ointment and buckets of hot water, and they mopped the floors. This was all done because Zhava's body was covered in bloody cuts and bruises. She had trouble focusing, and her head wanted to flop to the side, but she could see the extent of her injuries. The smallest cuts were easily as long as her fingers, and those were spread across her entire body. She had a long, deep slice along her right arm that Sister Allenka continued to rub with ointment and another high up on her inner thigh that seemed to have stopped bleeding but was still dark red with a deep purple bruise all along. Her left arm was covered in a webbing of slashes and looked as if she had fallen through a thorn bush. The bruises across her body were deep, and several had already blossomed to brilliant purples. The back of her leg throbbed where Io Kua had struck her with his sparring rod. Her knees ached where she had slipped and fallen when the creature first attacked, and her back felt as if someone had punched it repeatedly – which, as she remembered, the creature had done.

"The creature?" she mumbled.

"It's gone," Tegara whispered soothingly.

Allenka snorted and wrung out another towel.

"But how?" Zhava asked.

"Shh," Tegara said. She slipped her hand into the water at Zhava's shoulder. That water began to warm, and Zhava turned to see ripples of heat pulsing from Tegara's palm. Where the ripples touched her body, Zhava felt soothed, calmed. The throbbing eased, and the stinging lacerations did not hurt as badly.

Zhava wanted to shut her eyes and let the women continue to minister to her, but she felt she had to know. That monster in the cavern could get loose and hurt people in the Hibaro.

"But it's down there," she said. "And it was so strong."

"It usually is," Tegara said. "But it will not leave the cave. You are safe."

"You don't understand," she insisted. "It took away my Abilities – my wind and my flames."

At this, Allenka began chuckling.

"Shh!" Tegara said.

Allenka shut up.

"Zhava," Tegara said, "you have your Abilities. Try one now – a little one, though, not what you did with Posef."

Zhava lifted her hand from the water and held out her palm. She called to her little flame, and he appeared in a flash of light, spinning and dancing and leaping across her fingertips, but cautiously avoiding the rivers of water running off her hand.

Allenka gasped, sat back and stared.

"Now calm yourself," Tegara said. "Let me heal you."

Zhava let the flame flicker away, then lowered herself deeper into the water and shut her eyes. She had so many questions yet to ask, but Sister Tegara seemed unconcerned by any of them – and she had been right about Zhava's Abilities. The little flames still came when she called to them. She could play with stones and wind another time, but for now she would trust that those Abilities remained.

The healings continued for a long time after that. Sister Allenka soaked cloths in ointments – some that smelled of pretty wildflowers and others that stank like dead animals – and wrapped the worst of Zhava's injuries while Sister Tegara ran her pulsing-warm hand through the water and over Zhava's many injuries. With each pressing of Tegara's palm the throbbing and the stings of pain subsided, and she felt more like her old self again.

When she asked Sister Tegara to explain how they had rescued her from that monstrous creature in the cavern, Tegara instead launched into a tirade about Io Kua's irresponsibility as a Mentor and how High Priest Viekoosh himself would be dealing with this situation. Tegara's anger was so great that Sister Allenka told her to quiet down – it was late, and they did not want to disturb anyone else.

Then Tegara began a story of how Barae had come running. Io Kua had been angry, and he had taken Zhava out of the Hibaro, and they were worried that Kua would send her away. A quick check of the stables confirmed he had not, and then Tegara remembered the sparring grounds. By the time they arrived, Zhava had already entered the cavern – the "Proving Cove," Tegara called it – and they went in to retrieve her. Io Kua had helped them carry her back to the Hibaro, then Tegara and Allenka sent him away. They'd brought Zhava into the wash room, set up the basin with hot water and ointments, and she had been awake for much of the rest.

"Thank you," Zhava said when Tegara finished the telling.

"This is what I do for my Initiates."

After what seemed like days, Tegara and Allenka finally said Zhava could leave. Allenka bandaged the deep wounds on Zhava's arm and thigh – both of which looked so much better already – and then pulled out a fresh set of clothes for Zhava to wear. Tegara and Barae helped her dress because even though some of the cuts had healed completely and the others were well on their way, Zhava's body still did not want to move. Tegara assured her the stiffness was due as much to the healing as it was to the injuries, and Zhava would be moving much better within a couple days.

She hobbled from the washing room and down the long hallway of the processing building, Tegara supporting her on one side and Barae on the other. They emerged to a starlit night, a sliver of a moon low along the trees. The air was chilled and damp, and Zhava stood there for a moment, soaking it all in. She was glad to be alive.

"How many days?" she asked.

Barae laughed and hugged her gently across the shoulders. "Only one, sister."

It took what seemed an eternity for them to walk all the way back to Sister Tegara's Initiate House, and Zhava had to stop several times to catch her breath. Her body was weak, both from the sparring and the creature's attack as well as from Tegara and Allenka's healings of her. They passed only a few random people so late into the night, but a line of soldiers grinned at them and gave Zhava little salutes as they headed out for patrol.

"They think this is funny?" Zhava asked after the soldiers walked off.

"No, that is not mockery. It is respect. They have all been through the Proving Cove," Tegara said. "As have I, and as will Barae when she is ready. Most people must endure it several times – but none go into the Cove when they are as inexperienced as you." That last had the bitter edge of anger, and Zhava thought that anger was probably aimed at Io Kua.

They finally reached the door to the Initiate House, and Sister Tegara opened it and led them inside. Several people were standing or sitting in the front hall, and when Barae helped Zhava inside, those people stood and applauded her, some whistling and others yelling their congratulations. Within moments, doors up and down the hallways swung open, and more young people poured out, their cheers and smiles overwhelming.

Zhava was amazed at the outpouring of support, and she bowed her head to avoid their eyes. She didn't feel like she had done anything but survive – and even then she had only managed that because of Barae and Tegara rescuing her. These young people, though, were shouting their praise at her, congratulating her and commending her for doing so well. Tears welled up in Zhava's eyes, and she wiped them away on the sleeve of her shirt.

"All right, young ones," Sister Tegara called. "You are all wonderful for cheering her on, but it is time for bed."

The noise hardly diminished as they made their way slowly down the hallway. Almost every door was open, and the young women all stood and applauded Zhava as she walked past.

"Bedtime," Tegara continued calling out. "You all have busy schedules tomorrow, so back in bed."

The men shambled back to their wing of the house, and the women soon quieted down. Doors began shutting, and the noise died away almost completely by the time they reached the narrow stairs at the end of the building.

"You were great, sister," Barae said, supporting her from behind as they climbed the steps.

"I just want to sleep," Zhava said. "Forever."

They reached Zhava's room at the top of the steps, and Barae helped her inside through the dark. Zhava kicked off the new shoes Sister Allenka had given her, eased back onto the bed, and shut her eyes.

"You really were great," Barae whispered before shutting the door. Zhava didn't even have the strength to thank her, and within moments she was sound asleep.

***

The next day arrived too soon for Zhava. The morning sun streamed through her open windows, lighting up the room and ending any more thought of sleep. She didn't remember her windows being open last night, but she didn't remember much about last night once she collapsed on her bed. She thought she might even be in the same position she was in when she fell asleep. She shifted beneath the blankets and regretted it immediately. Her stiff, aching body did not want to move. At all. She groaned, forced herself to roll over, then sucked in a wincing breath and waited for each part of her body to stop complaining. It took several moments.

She heard people moving in the hallway, so she knew she was not one of the first to wake. More likely, she was one of the last. She knew she should get up and begin her morning routine, but even the thought of shifting again made her slightly nauseated. There wasn't a spot on her body that didn't hurt. Her head no longer throbbed, but there was a lump at the back of it that would likely be there for several more days. The bandage on her arm felt a little looser than it had after Sister Allenka tied it, and the gash tingled. She didn't know if that was good or bad. The bandage on her thigh was still tight, and she couldn't feel that cut at all. Zhava had watched Sister Allenka clean the wounds and apply so many ointments she was surprised more of them weren't numb. That creature in the cavern had hurt her so badly, she felt lucky to be alive.

A knock at the door.

Zhava grunted. She wasn't even sure if it had been a "Come in" or a "Go away" grunt.

Another knock.

"What?" Zhava mumbled.

"Zhava, it's me," a voice said. "Barae. I don't know if you're awake, but I'm coming in. You don't mind if I come in, do you?"

Zhava didn't even care enough to respond.

"I didn't hear you say 'no,' so I'm coming in."

The bolt in the door clicked, and Barae gently eased the door wide. Her face lit when she saw Zhava's open eyes.

"Hello, sister," she said, quietly closing the door behind her.
Zhava grunted again. Barae grinned.

"It's so wonderful to see you awake," Barae said, shutting the door and kneeling down to eye level with Zhava. "You look good. Well, you don't really look good. I mean you look better than you did last night, what with all the screaming and all the blood and everything. I thought you were going to die, and I'm so glad you didn't."

Zhava just stared at her. Was that supposed to make her feel better?

"Anyway, this is yours," Barae said, setting something on the blanket beside Zhava's face. "It looked important, and I thought you would want it back."

Zhava fished along the blanket until her hand wrapped around the little jar with the string tied to it. "Oh, thank you," she said, relief flooding her. In all the confusion of her day and night, she hadn't even realized she'd lost it. She loosed the tie and slipped it over her head, glad to have Priestess Marmaran's remains so close to her again.

"After we got you to the processing room, I saw Sister Allenka pull that off you and set it aside. I knew you'd want it back. Allenka was messing with it, trying to untie the string and pull the little stopper out of the top. She didn't seem to know what she was doing, but when Sister Tegara came over to see it, I asked to keep it and return it to you. Sister Allenka was mad at me for that, but she gets mad at someone every day. "

Zhava gripped the jar in her hands and shut her eyes, thanking the Gods it had come back to her safely.

"So, it's...uh...something from home?"

"The last remains of my teacher," Zhava said. She quickly wiped a tear from her eye.

"Bones?"

"And ashes." She looked up and smiled at Barae. "Thank you again. I would have been lost without this."

"Sounds morbid."

"It was her final wish, that I would keep her with me while I trained at the Hibaro."

"Hm," Barae said as she walked to the window. "Okay, so, now that you have that back...we've been given a light schedule today."
As if on cue, a bell resounded across the campus, and the people in the hallway began rushing.

"Sister Tegara made special arrangements for us – well, mostly for you, but I'm your sponsor, so they apply to me, too. We're going to do today all the things we should have done yesterday. Get you into some of the more basic Initiate classes and then find you a job."

"Ugh," Zhava said, flipping the blanket across her face. Neither of those sounded like something she was even capable of doing at the moment.

Barae laughed. "You can't do that all day," she said. "We have a light schedule, but it's still a schedule. Come. Let's start the day."

She pulled back the blankets and helped Zhava ease out of bed. Surprisingly, once she was upright, Zhava actually felt a little better. She was stiff, her legs were weak, and her back felt like someone was constantly cracking it with a wooden hammer, but she could move more quickly than she expected – which merely meant she could shuffle along at something faster than a crawl. Many of the smaller cuts on her hands and arms had already smoothed over, no doubt from Sister Tegara's healing Ability – which was something Zhava would have to ask her about when she had the chance.

Their first stop was the toilette, and then to see Sister Allenka about the bandages on her arm and leg. Allenka applied more ointment, rewrapped the bandages, and sent them on their way with barely a half-dozen words to either of them. By the time they arrived at the dining hall, almost everyone else had eaten and left. The cook staff had set aside a bowl of breakfast soup for Zhava, though it was likely more of Sister Tegara's special instructions. Posef waved them over to join him.

"Don't you have lessons?" Barae asked him.

"I can't go to my lessons without seeing Zhava," he said, with a quick wink of those green eyes.

Zhava ducked her head and started in on the soup. Her stomach grumbled. Really, the food could have been almost anything and she would have enjoyed it. She didn't remember eating anything since yesterday's breakfast. She looked up long enough to notice that Barae wasn't eating.

"Did they not set aside anything for you?"

"Already ate," she said. Then, to Posef, "What news from last night?"

"Io Kua got called before High Priest Viekoosh at dawn," he said with a grin.

Zhava kept her eyes down, but listened intently. Sister Tegara had said last night that the High Priest would hear about what happened at the Proving Cove.

"He was up there for a long time," Posef continued. "No one else allowed into the meeting, and when Io Kua left the Tower, he went to the stables and took out a horse. Last anyone saw of him, he was riding south."

"South?" Barae said. "But Io Liori and her people went north. He's not rejoining them?"

"No one knows where he went."

Zhava wasn't sure how she felt about that. She had thought Io Kua was nice to her, and that was the only reason she had requested him. He took out his anger on her, though, when he learned he had to stay and be her Mentor – and she could understand that anger. She had seldom been given free choices when she was home, always doing what Mama or Papa said to do, but on those few occasions when she could do what she wanted, she expected to be able to complete her task. If someone came and interrupted her, she got angry also. If she acted out that anger, she got punished. Io Kua was probably being punished for his anger. She wondered how often he had ever had her same experience, of expecting to be able to do one thing and being told he could not. She didn't think it had happened to him very often, though, especially if he chose to indulge his anger.

"Posef," Sister Tegara called as she entered the room.

He shut his eyes and dropped his head into his hands. "Yes, Ma'am," he said.

"Zhava and Barae have special dispensation for the day," she said, striding toward them. "You do not."

"No, Ma'am."

"Riding lessons this morning?"

"Yes, Ma'am."

She reached their table and stood behind him, her hands on her hips. "Then get to it."

"Yes, Ma'am." He collected his empty bowl and utensils.

"And the south stairs will need a good scrubbing before lights-out tonight."

"Of course, Ma'am." He grinned as he stood up, then winked again at Zhava and strode away.

Tegara watched him dump his bowl and utensils in the wash room and leave, then she turned and sat at the table. "I think he enjoys being punished," she quipped.

Barae laughed. Zhava scraped the bottom of her soup bowl.

"I am pleased to see you doing so well this morning," Tegara said to Zhava. "Sister Allenka told me the leg was still swollen, but your arm was healing quite well. You will have a couple nice scars from those, though I am sure they will not be your last."

"Thank you for coming for me," Zhava said.

"Of course. You are my charge, and I always protect my own."

"But that creature in the cave," Zhava began.

"Shall not be spoken of again," Tegara finished. "You will return to that cave some day, but not for a long while. You are an Initiate, yes, but you have less training than most of the Candidates who get sent away."

"Then why am I an Initiate?" She looked Tegara in the eye. This was important. Io Kua did not believe she was ready, Io Liori and High Priest Viekoosh had argued about where to place her, and even the other women in the Initiate House had looked askance at her, as if she was an oddity who did not belong.

Tegara reached forward and cupped Zhava's hands. "What do you know of Priestess Marmaran?"

"She was my teacher." She wasn't sure she liked her hands being held so tightly, but she sat still and let Sister Tegara continue.

"Priestess Marmaran is responsible for training some of the most powerful people to ever graduate the Hibaro. High Priest Viekoosh studied under her for a season when he was an Apprentice, and his abilities expanded to amazing proportions in just that short time. But she left the Hibaro nearly a dozen seasons ago, and no one ever saw her or heard of her again – until Io Liori found you studying with her at a little farm along the border."

Zhava didn't realize her teacher had been so famous. Around the farm she had simply been "Marmaran," the old woman who taught her nice lessons in exchange for room and board.

"Zhava, what you can do with controlling the wind – that is impressive. Many of our Priests and Ios can do that too. It makes them very popular when crews set out to sea. But what you can do with fire?" She glanced at Barae, then back to Zhava. "Hear me clearly: no one else can do that."

Zhava's eyes grew wide.

"You were Priestess Marmaran's student for only a few short seasons, and she taught you something that not even the High Priest is capable of doing."

Zhava wanted to say that Marmaran had not taught her that. The little flames had simply appeared one day, and she had actually kept them hidden from Marmaran. Instead, she stayed quiet.

"You lack training and discipline," Tegara said. "We will give you that. But the lessons Priestess Marmaran taught you make you truly unique – and right now we could use more people with the power to protect us all."

# CHAPTER 11

"What did Sister Tegara mean about needing people to protect us all?" Zhava asked as she and Barae walked from the dining hall.

Sister Tegara had given them their instructions for the day and then left for a meeting. Barae was slowly leading them across the yard to their first destination, the fitness trainer. Zhava wasn't sure what she could do with a fitness trainer the way she was limping now, but she didn't question Sister Tegara's instructions.

"Do you remember when Posef said that Emsterold had gone missing?"

Zhava nodded. She had forgotten the name, but she remembered that someone had disappeared.

"We've been losing several people a moon since last season. We're up to 27 gone, and it's been quite scary."

"Lost?"

"Taken," Barae said, shaking her head. "A few were definitely killed, and the others just vanished. At first the Ios thought we were being raided because the people all vanished at night, but there was never any sign of intruders. Then over the winter, a First Salient – a good friend of High Priest Viekoosh – came to the Hibaro and questioned everyone. He was...even scarier, actually."

"What did he do?"

"You saw Io Liori," Barae said with a shiver. "She's First of the King's Third Salient – and she is amazing in a fight. She can kill a wild boar with a single arrow; when she would compete in the tournaments, before she graduated, she would usually take 1$^{st}$ or 2$^{nd}$ place in hand-to-hand combat; and one time I got to sit in on a self-defense class she taught. That was right after the killings began, late last season, and she was incredible."

"I've never seen her fight."

"Watch her some time – just don't cross her."

Zhava nodded. She had thought Liori was scary enough when she chastised Zhava during their trip to the Hibaro.

"As good as Io Liori is at fighting with a sword and with her hands, that First Salient was just as good at fighting in the mind. We were all lined up outside the Tower, and he met with each of us, one by one. I remember him digging through my memories like they were nothing but stories around a fire. He pulled things from my childhood that even I had forgotten. By the time he was done with us, some people were in tears and others didn't speak for days. All of that to learn that no one on the Hibaro campus was responsible for the deaths and disappearances."

"It sounds horrible." She stopped and leaned against Barae, catching her breath and massaging her aching leg.

"It was," Barae said with a nod. "But we also learned we could trust each other. Whatever is happening here, it's an outside enemy, not an inside one."

When Zhava was ready again, she limped onward. Barae knew the way to the fitness field and directed them through the maze of buildings and past dozens of people. After the scary story of the First Salient, Barae changed moods to stories about her childhood. She'd been raised along the coast, and she had gone out on fishing trips with her father and his crew when she was very little. Her mother had died giving birth to her younger brother, and Barae had very few memories of her, but that meant she and her five siblings had to leave their small home. They worked and lived on the fishing boats with their father from then on. He hired a shipboard tutor of the Kandor for several seasons for his children, hoping at least a couple of them would show promise and catch the King's attention. Her two older brothers never took the time to study, though, always so busy at the nets, and her older sister simply could not make sense of the Kandor philosophies. Her younger brother enjoyed the lessons, but spent most of his time on ship below decks and lying in a cot, sick with the fever or with the runs or with the spotted skin. He had finally been sent to live inland with one of her father's childhood friends, and the last Barae heard of him he was enjoying life on a valley farm raising horses.

Barae, however, excelled at the Kandor lessons, and she seemed to have a talent for manipulating cloth, which she was perfectly happy to demonstrate with the sails on the open ocean. Since she was attracted to girls, her father couldn't find any of the fishermen's sons to take her in marriage, so the tutor took her to the Hibaro. She had been a Candidate for only one season before her talent with cloth got her promoted to Initiate. The lessons were harder, and she was struggling – her second full season as an Initiate, she said – but her teachers believed she was finally making progress. If she continued to work hard and grow, she might even be promoted to Novice by the first snowfall.

Barae wrapped up her story just as they reached the fitness fields. The fields stretched along the southern edge of the Hibaro, almost as far away from the Initiate House as they could walk and still remain on the campus. To the west was a series of looping tracks surrounding an open, grassy plain. Several groups of children were running along the innermost track, and a few men and women were running along the outer tracks, yelling encouragement to the children each time they passed. All throughout the grassy field stood equipment stations, a few with people at them. Zhava saw people lifting weighted harvest baskets, and a couple people throwing spears as far as they could. There was also an open tent in the center of the field, and Zhava could see piles of equipment stacked within it.

To the east, however, was a far more interesting sight. That field contained groups of people practicing with sparring rods, shooting arrows into straw targets, and throwing axes and knives into wooden stumps. In the center of that field was a roped off square where a woman stood with a large group of children teaching them how to set their feet in the dirt and swing their arms. Zhava hadn't liked being beaten by Io Kua with the sparring rods – and she was terrified of having to fight off that creature in the cave again – but if someone could teach her how to defend herself and fight, that would make all the difference.

"Are we going there?" she asked, pointing to the sparring fields and smiling.

"Later." Barae pointed the other way. "Right now we have to meet Priest Qi at the track."

"Oh." Running and jumping...yay....

They slowly trekked to the edge of the track, and Zhava watched the children as they shuffled by. They were sweating, but their faces were scowling and determined as they made slow progress. Three women easily caught up to the children, cheered them on, then continued running. Next down the track was a tall, lean man with short-cropped blonde hair. He wore only shorts and leather shoes, and sweat was running down his toned body. He saw them, turned from the marked path, and ran to meet them. Zhava had trouble not staring. Even on the farm, she had never seen a man whose muscles seemed to pop out so much from his body. He looked more like he'd been cut from stone than simply a man of flesh and blood. As he ran toward them, Zhava realized the man's hair wasn't actually blonde; it was light brown with flecks of gray scattered at the top and prominent along the sides. She also noticed the lines at the corners of his eyes and his bigger ears. This man had to be older than her Papa, but his body was in better shape than most of the young men she'd ever met.

"Close your mouth, little girl," the man said with a grin as he stopped before them. He wiped his arm across his sweaty face.

"Priest Qi," Barae said, "Sister Tegara told us to meet you. This is Zhava. She needs to be in an endurance class."

"Does she?" He looked her up and down, his gaze stopping at the bandages on her arm and leg. "No, she belongs in a healer's bed." He turned to leave.

"But Priest Qi," Zhava yelled. She raised her bandaged arm. "This isn't my fault."

"Hah!" He turned to her again, pointing at the various injuries up and down her body. "I heard all about you, Zhava. Second day at the Hibaro, and you walk yourself into the Proving Cove? Were you trying to get yourself killed, or are you just that stupid?"

Anger flared within her. "I didn't walk myself into it – Io Kua told me to go in there."

"Oh, so you do everything people tell you. Now I understand. Well, you'll make yourself a good little soldier."

"Priest-" Barae started.

"No, Barae" Qi said. "You are on my field at the start of the next moon. Until then, you can go take a walk. I'm speaking with Initiate Zhava, and if she is incapable of defending herself from a few harsh words, then she might not have any place at all on my field."

"Yes, Sir." Barae turned and walked away.

"Now you," Qi said, turning back to Zhava. "Sister Tegara says you're quite impressive, but you look more like a child playing dress-up at your father's work. Why should I allow you onto my field?"

Zhava just stared at the ground. She had no good answer to that question. Everything she'd done since leaving home had been because someone else willed it. Mama wanted her gone? She was sent away. Papa wanted the bride's price for her? He received it. Io Liori wanted her to have a Mentor? She got Io Kua. He told her to walk into a cave and fight a monster? She did it – without argument. The only time she'd truly done something because she wanted to had been inside her dream. Inside that dream, she had received everything she thought she wanted – Mama's heartfelt love, a husband who put her before himself, and a Papa who sat in a field and held her while she cried. But she had turned her back on that. She had returned to this world, the real world. Not some dream world that wasn't true. But why? This man was asking her, and she wasn't sure what she really wanted.

She noticed she was looking at Priest Qi's legs – and she realized again how truly impressive they were. For a man of his age, she couldn't see any fat on him. He looked as if he spent every moment honing his body – and Zhava realized something she wanted.

"I want to look like you," she said, looking him in the eyes as she said it.

He burst out laughing. His laugh was quite loud, and he leaned over and held his stomach. She noticed people on the fields turning to look at them, and Zhava turned away. Barae was nearby, and even she was watching, a frown on her face. Priest Qi put a hand on Zhava's shoulder as he continued laughing, and now she was getting upset at him. If he didn't like that answer, all he had to do was tell her. He didn't need to laugh at her.

She wrenched herself from his grip and turned to stride away.

He stopped laughing. "Where are you going?"

"You don't want me here."

"When you say you want to look like me, I absolutely want you on my field."

Zhava stood there, confused. He laughed at her...because he liked her?

"But first," he said, a smile on his face. "Who told you to say that? Sister Tegara? Your friend Barae?"

"No one. It's simply what I want."

"Fine," he said with a wave. He turned and pointed to the field. "Let's see what you can do – which probably isn't much in your condition. Go to the inner lane. 'Turtle Lane' we call it because that's where all the turtles go, and that would certainly be you. Let's see how fast you can get yourself around a half-lap – walk it or run it, I don't care. I'll know which class to put you in after I see your form."

"Yes, Sir," she said, limping forward. "Thank you, Sir."

"Don't thank me yet," he said with a chuckle. "You want a body like mine, you'll get it, but you will work for it."

Zhava walked across the paths on the field. There were no markings separating one lane from the next, but the ground was packed hard along sharply defined grooves in the ground where people ran or walked. At the innermost groove sat a little, stone-carved turtle. She grinned. Someone had a sense of humor.

She looked up and around, wondering if people would watch her. She wasn't a great runner, even when she wasn't injured. It wasn't that she couldn't run, but she rarely saw the purpose of it – unless Mama was yelling at her. Then she'd better run, either to her or away from her. No one on the field seemed to be looking at her, though, except Priest Qi – and Barae from farther away. Barae gave a quick wave, and Zhava smiled. She'd never had a friend like her before, and she liked it.

Zhava started running. It wasn't exactly a run, though. More of a fast walk, which she stopped doing almost as soon as she started. The cut in her leg felt as if someone had stabbed her. She almost tripped from the sudden pain, and that jostling made the back of her head feel like someone knocked her with a club. She stood there a moment, one hand to her head, her eyes shut, trying to block out the stinging pain in her leg and regain her balance. She took several deep breaths, then turned to look at Priest Qi. He still stood there, watching her with his hands on his hips. Barae waved again and grinned. Zhava waved back, then limped forward. This would be a long, painful half-lap.

A group of older students ran past her and offered her a cheer. That felt good. Soon after that, however, a group of children at least half her age ran past and offered her their own cheer. That didn't feel good.

Priest Qi said he would choose a class for her based on her "form," whatever that meant. She wondered if he expected her to walk a certain way or move her arms a certain way. She didn't have many options with as much pain as she was in, but she tried to make her limping look as good as she could. As if the pain didn't bother her. As if she wasn't injured. She stumbled, regained her footing, and limped on. She wiped a sheen of sweat from her face.

The older students ran by and cheered her again. She smiled at them but didn't say anything. This was getting embarrassing.

"Hello."

Zhava jerked at the sudden greeting, and she almost stumbled again, but the young woman walking beside her put her arm around Zhava's shoulders and steadied her.

"Careful," the woman said. "I wasn't trying to scare you."

Zhava glanced over. Plishka.

"I'm Plishka."

"Yeah," Zhava said between breaths. "I remember."

"You're Zhava?"

She nodded.

"You were really hurt yesterday in the Proving Cove. Why are you on the track today? You should be resting."

"Trying to...get into a class." It was starting to hurt to breathe, and she still hadn't gone more than a fast limp.

"Well that's stupid," Plishka said with a laugh. "We spent half the night patching you up, and Qi is going to make you pop some bandages. That will get Allenka mad at you."

"Then I'm glad...you're here...to fix me."

Plishka laughed even harder. "And risk Allenka's wrath on me, too? Sorry, but you're on your own. So what was in the Proving Cove? What did this to you?"

"You've...never been?"

"If I finish my philosophy research before the end of this moon, I'm being sent in right away. If I don't finish the research, I get another half-season in Brother Micah's boring class. I'm not sure which is worse."

"The Cove...is horrible," Zhava said with a shiver.

"I heard there's a giant snake in there."

"No snake. A shadow monster."

"Initiate Plishka," Priest Qi said as he stepped onto the path beside them. "You are dismissed."

They stopped. Zhava leaned over to catch her breath and let the sweat drip onto the ground instead of into her eyes.

"Goodbye," Plishka said with a wave as she ran off. "Thanks for the talk. Heal quickly – and say 'Hello' next time you see me."

"Initiate Zhava," Qi said, turning to her. "That was the slowest half-lap I have ever seen anyone do."

"Sorry," she gasped.

"But I've also never sent anyone onto my field as beat up as yourself. I expected you to quit, but you didn't. Might have been because of your friend there. Might have been something deep within you. Or it might have been that you really do want to push yourself as hard as I push myself. Looking this good isn't easy, you know."

Zhava just stood there and breathed. She hoped he wasn't expecting an answer.

"Whatever it is, I like it," he finally said. "I'm putting you in Candidate Group 3. I think you've got more potential than any of those worthless kids, but not with that bum leg and arm. I'll keep you with them for the first moon, though, and then we'll transfer you up to a proper Initiate class. Take off tomorrow and rest. Get yourself moving a little faster than you did today, and we'll see about putting some real muscles on that scrawny little body of yours."

"Yes, Sir," Zhava said. She stood straight. "Thank you, Sir."

"And there you go thanking me again," he said with a laugh. "You don't know what you've got yourself into."

She met Barae on the edge of the field and told her everything that had happened as they walked to the weapons field, including her short conversation with Plishka.

"I don't understand her," Zhava said. "She was nice to me both times I saw her with Sister Allenka – she even gave me that bit of bread. But when I saw her yesterday morning she wouldn't even say hello to me. But then she was nice and walked with me on the field."

"Don't even try to understand her," Barae said. "I gave up trying to be friends with Plishka a long time ago because that is exactly what happens with her. Nice in the morning; mean in the evening. Or mean in the morning, and then nice in the evening. She asked for my help with a reading she was doing from the Kandor, and I spent an entire afternoon helping her study and practice and answer questions. The next day, did she even thank me? Did she acknowledge all that work? No, not a single word of thanks."

"She seemed nice just now," Zhava said.

But that didn't stop Barae as she continued telling stories about Plishka all the way to the weapons field. One day Plishka had lunch with Barae, and the next day she wouldn't look her in the eye. She agreed to help Barae with a research project, but then never showed up when they were supposed to meet. They were paired as sparring partners for a while, and sometimes Plishka would laugh and joke and go easy on Barae; the next time they sparred, she was like a goddess on the court, beating Barae 12 to 0. Zhava was glad when they finally arrived at the second field and Barae had to stop talking about Plishka long enough to make introductions.

"Io Suleenuo," Barae said with a quick bow of her head. "This is Initiate Zhava. Sister Tegara made arrangements with you to admit her into a class."

"Thank you," Suleenuo said. She stood before them with a helmet under one arm, brown leather armor wrapped snugly around her chest and waist, leather boots almost to her knees, and bands of leather wrapped around her arms and hands. Where she wasn't covered in protective gear, her muscles shown through, even more defined across her body than Priest Qi's muscles had been. Zhava just stared. She had never seen a woman with such a sharply defined body in her life. She didn't even know a woman's body could look like that.

Barae nudged her.

"Oh," Zhava said. She also bowed. "Thank you, Io Suleenuo."

"Why were you taking a lap over there?" Suleenuo asked, gesturing to the other field. She had a sharp accent, far more northern than any of the people Zhava had met at the Hibaro.

"Priest Qi wanted to see my form."

Suleenuo snorted and rolled her eyes. "I will speak with him. You are obviously injured."

"Sir, it was fine," Zhava blurted. "I do not wish to get him in trouble."

"Trouble?" she said, raising her eyebrows. "He is my husband. He is in trouble much of the time." She grinned.

Zhava smiled, but she wasn't sure that was the best response. What would Qi say if he learned she was laughing at him?

"As for you," Suleenuo said as she walked around Zhava. "It is also obvious you do not know how to use a sword if you cannot even defend yourself from a sparring rod. Have you ever held a bow?"

"No, Sir."

"Whip?"

"No, Sir."

"Knives?"

"Kitchen knives."

Suleenuo stopped circling Zhava. She ran her gaze over Zhava's arms and shoulders. "It is a place to start," she muttered. "Follow me."

Zhava was almost able to keep pace with Io Suleenuo who walked slowly toward a weapons rack at the edge of the field. The woman said nothing the entire way, and Barae trailed behind them – also not saying anything. Barae's silence was probably so that Suleenuo didn't send her away as Qi had done.

They passed dozens of people practicing with more weapons than Zhava had ever before seen. Several students were sparring, some of them even using real weapons, but most of them using practice weapons like she and Io Kua had done. But these students were so much better than she was. The teachers were giving instructions on how to stand, how to move, how to swing, how to throw, how to balance – it was all so exciting, and Zhava felt she might burst at the chance to do some of the things she saw these students doing.

When they reached the table, Suleenuo chose two pieces of wood cut very thin and very short. Each had a round, wooden handle at one end and a dull tip at the other. She gave one to Zhava and held the other.

"Show me how you kitchen knife," she said.

Zhava set the blade of the wooden knife against the table and mimicked chopping an onion or a garlic clove.

"Hmm, yes." Suleenuo gripped Zhava's fingers, reset them on the handle, positioned her hand in the air, and twisted the wooden blade perpendicular. "Now it is a fighting knife."

Zhava grinned.

Suleenuo repositioned Zhava's hand and arm so the blade was held down near her side. "Defend," she said. She pulled Zhava's arm forward with the blade pointing out. "Attack."

Zhava nodded.

"The knife is both your sword and your shield. Now, show me defend."

Blade at the side.

"Attack."

Blade out.

"Again."

She did it again.

"Again."

She did it a third time, and she really liked how it felt to learn something so simple. It felt like the first step of a child, but it was such a wonderful first step for her.

"Hmm." Suleenuo took the wooden blade. She picked up two smaller, real, knives from the table and gave one to Zhava. "Watch." She gripped her own knife by the handle, raised her arm, and flicked the little knife away. It stuck into the side of a nearby post. "Grasp it," she said.

Zhava held the knife the way she had seen Suleenuo do it.

"Raise your arm like this." She bent Zhava's arm up and back, then positioned her wrist. "When you are ready, throw the knife and release it."

Zhava took a breath. No one was near the post, so she wasn't worried about hitting anyone, but she had never before thrown a knife.

"Like a small stone," Suleenuo whispered. "You throw those on the farm, yes?"

Zhava tensed, then threw the knife. It spun through the air several times and stuck into the side of the post very near to Suleenuo's own knife.

Suleenuo took another knife from the table and handed it over.

Zhava wiped her sweaty hands, took the second knife, and threw it. This one bounced off the post and skittered into the dust.

"Hm." Suleenuo turned and glanced up and down Zhava's body. "Good form. Middling talent. Excellent enthusiasm. I will place you in Initiate Weapons Class 1. Return tomorrow at third bell."

"Thank you," Zhava said with a quick bow.

"Yes," she said with a wave of her hand. "You are dismissed. You may go."

Zhava grabbed Barae's hand, and they smiled at each other as they turned to leave. She couldn't believe what a great morning they'd had – far better than yesterday with Io Kua. She wished Priestess Marmaran could have been here for this, but she was glad to share it with a friend. The teachers said she could join their classes, which was far more than Zhava had expected. Back home, she would have been told she couldn't, that she wasn't allowed, that it wasn't the proper place for a girl or a future wife. Throwing knives! She had never thought to be throwing knives at targets, to be learning how to do "defend" and "attack." Those were things her brothers did when they were protecting the flocks, not things she had to do when she was cleaning the house or preparing the evening meal.

"You were great," Barae whispered when they were far enough from Io Suleenuo that she wouldn't hear. "I knew you would be, of course – but you hit that post on your first throw!"

"And missed it on my second."

"But hit it on the first."

Zhava couldn't help it. She just laughed. Barae was right. She could focus on that second miss, or she could focus on that first hit. It might have been nothing more than luck on that first throw, but it had still been a hit.

Barae stopped laughing, squeezed Zhava's hand, and slowed them to a stop. "Oh no," she said.

Zhava looked up. Io Kua was striding across the field...and straight toward them.

# CHAPTER 12

Io Kua was still dressed for riding, with his black and red robes flowing behind him and his black leather boots up to his knees. His hood was flopped down behind his head, and he held a small pouch across his shoulder by a leather cord. Zhava held on tightly to Barae's hand and slid behind her friend, putting at least that small barrier between her and the Io. He had been angry with her yesterday, furious enough with her to take out his anger with the sparring rods and then send her into that creature's den – into the Proving Cove when she so obviously was not prepared to defend herself. She had asked for him to be her Mentor on a whim, simply because he had been nice to her on the trail to the Hibaro. That had obviously been a lie. Or a trick. Or something like that. Why else would he change so drastically from one day to the next?

"Greetings," he said as he stopped before them. "Initiate Barae, I would speak with Initiate Zhava alone. Leave us."

"Sir," Barae said, averting her eyes and giving a quick bow of her head. "I do not wish to offend, but Sister Tegara gave me instructions to remain with Initiate Zhava at all times as we go about our duties today."

He sighed and shook his head. "Very good. Then you may remain with Initiate Zhava as you walk with us – from ten paces behind. Now go."

She gave him a much deeper bow, squeezed Zhava's hand reassuringly, then stepped away. Zhava watched her count ten paces away, stop, and turn.

"Walk with me," Kua said as he gestured forward.

"I can't walk fast yet," she said, taking a hesitant limp forward. "Sister Allenka said my leg will take another couple days to heal."

"Indeed." He kept pace beside her and walked in silence for a bit. "I spoke with her this morning before I left. She said you took to the healing quite well."

She wouldn't have needed any healing at all if he had been nice to her. "It hurt," she quietly replied.

"Healings often do. As does truth."

She glanced at him but did not say anything. What truth? Would he admit when had he not been truthful to her?

"Sister Tegara also spoke with me this morning," he continued. "She said you will be requesting a different Mentor."

Zhava did not know how to respond. She hadn't said that, and Tegara had said nothing about that to her.

"She also said I am incapable of being a good Mentor to you."

"I did not tell her that," Zhava blurted. She had thought it, certainly, but it was not something she had said to anyone – not even to Barae.

"I wondered," he said with a nod of his head. "It had the ring of Tegara far more than of you."

"I'm sorry. I didn't say that. She never should have told you that."

"And I never should have taken out my anger on you. That was my mistake. I was packed and on my mount to leave for the patrol when Io Liori told me I had to stay at the Hibaro – apparently a late-night message she sent was never delivered to my room. That Candidate boy has now been sent home."

Zhava bit her lip. His anger was far more relatable now, even if it had been scary. She would have been angry too if she had been ready to leave and then told she had to stay and Mentor someone, especially an Initiate who was just new to the Hibaro, who didn't know how to do anything or where she should go…or even what it meant to be a Mentor.

"But, that is not your problem," Kua continued. "Your problem, apparently, is to find a new Mentor. I felt you deserved to know everything, however. I already told you – quite angrily – what you did wrong. Now you know what I did wrong. If there is anything more to say, you may ask. Until then, good day to you."

With that, he strode off. Zhava stood there and watched him walk away, his black robes flowing behind him and the small bag bouncing heavily against his back. She wasn't sure how she felt about this. What he did was awful – she wasn't trained in sparring, and she could have been killed in the Proving Cove. It was her first day at the Hibaro, she didn't know how to do anything yet, she hadn't been to any of the classes she was supposed to attend, she had never used a sword even once in her life – and he sent her off to be killed by a monster in a cave. She should be mad at him, and she should be relieved that he was leaving…but still it felt wrong.

"Zhava?" Barae whispered, taking her hand. Zhava hadn't heard her friend approach. "What happened?"

"Stay here," she said. Then she yelled to Io Kua, "Wait!"

He stopped and turned.

Zhava released Barae's hand and limped forward. She hadn't planned to stop him, but she had to know. She had been so certain on the trail that he was nice – he had been angry about the situation, as he said, and at her for requesting him – but she had to know what else he had been thinking. She had to know…if there was anything more to it all. Was he simply being mean to her? Had he hoped to drive her from the Hibaro? Had he hoped she would die?

"Why did you send me into that cave?" she asked when she finally stood before him. "That thing almost killed me."

"Hmm," he said, rubbing at the stubble on his chin. He set his bag in the dirt beside him and crossed his arms. "Tell me what happened – in your words, not Tegara's words – when you went inside the Proving Cove."

So she did. She first told him how mad she was for him shutting the cave behind her. Then the creature had attacked her and knocked into a deep cavern. It stole her wind and her flames, and it used them against her. Then when Tegara and Barae broke into the cave to rescue her, she tried desperately to stop the monster from attacking them. She had no idea how they'd actually fought off the beast because then she had a strange dream about being home – except her Mama was nice to her, Ooleng actually listened to her, and Papa…well, he really loved her. By the time she finished the telling to Io Kua, she used the back of her sleeve to wipe a tear from her eye. That had been the hardest part, to walk away from a loving Papa. But she had known it wasn't true, because though he might protect her and care for her and provide for her, she had never really felt loved by him. When she left, she had seen him standing in the yard with the bags around his feet, the five little bags filled with the bride price that Io Liori had paid from her own money.

"What you experienced sounds awful," Kua whispered.

"I was terrified. I thought I was going to die. If they hadn't found me when they did, that thing would have eaten me."

"Do you know what I saw when I watched you on the trail from your home?"

She shook her head.

"A scared little girl clinging to her Priestess, too afraid of the world around her and the people within it to even survive."

She had been scared. Her whole world had changed in a single day, and not at all the way she expected. She was supposed to be crossing the Purneese Mountains right now, wife to Ooleng. Instead she was at the Hibaro, making friends and learning…something. This was better, certainly, but it was still so different. It felt like walking the dunes on shifting sand.

"Do you know what I saw, though, when I watched you at the morning table?"

She shook her head. "I didn't know you were watching me."

"For several moments. And I saw a scared little girl clinging to her Abilities, using a power she doesn't understand and cannot control simply to intimidate someone else – another Initiate such as herself."

She stared at the ground. She had no idea what to say. She hadn't thought of what she did in quite that way, and it didn't seem completely fair. Posef had made her angry, and Kua must have witnessed that too. The boy had been mocking her. She knew it had been wrong to use her powers as she did, but she wasn't scared of him. And now he knew that.

"Initiate Posef is a braggart," Kua said. "He is talented, certainly, but he breaks the rules and flaunts his Ability – which, actually, is impressive. No one takes him seriously anymore though, and that is his biggest stumbling block. He will have to confront that one day."

"I should not have knocked him off the bench," Zhava whispered. "I'm sorry."

"You are correct, but that is the wrong lesson to learn. The lesson you need to remember is the lesson from the cave: when the creature down there stole your wind and stole your flames...what was left? A scared little girl who rushed forward to save her friends, certainly, but someone who lacked any real talent to do it – because the only power you rely upon is your mystical one. You must grow. As I said – so badly – in the sparring ring, you do not know how to wield a weapon, and you have no endurance. Then that dream you had, of living at home with a loving family? That is a good dream, but that is, sadly, not the truth. You know that, and you accept it, which is good."

"I walked away from my Papa," she said, a hiccup in her voice as another tear ran down her cheek, "and Priestess Marmaran said...that was a good thing."

Io Kua reached forward and wrapped his hand across Zhava's shoulder. "Priestess Marmaran," he said, "was commending you for choosing truth. Had you chosen the dream, had you wished so fiercely for that false reality, you would have remained within it, and then you would have been lost from us forever. I know because it has happened to others." He leaned down, very near to her ear, and whispered, "And I would have very much regretted losing you."

"So you like me?" she blurted out – then clamped her hand over her mouth. She hadn't meant to ask that question, no matter how honest it had been. She had meant to ask if he thought she could do the work, if he thought she could learn the skills he wanted her to learn, if he thought she could be a good Initiate – not whether he liked her. That was a question that children asked, and yet it had been the first thing she said when he seemed kind to her again.

He smiled. He squeezed her shoulder a couple times, then asked, "Do you want me to remain as your Mentor?"

She nodded, too embarrassed to do more than simply glance up at him and back down to the ground.

"Then I have something for you," he said. He picked up the bag from the ground and began untying the leather cords. "I was older than you when I was assigned a Mentor – most students are – and he said this was a tradition he was handing down to me. Now I hand it down to you. I was away this morning because High Priest Viekoosh asked me to run an errand for him."

"I heard," Zhava said.

"I'm sure you did. The Hibaro gossip vine is always ripe for the picking. But while I was gone, I happened upon a caravan of traders and found this." He dropped the bag to the ground and held a bundle of leather in his hand.

At first, Zhava could not make sense of it. A wide band of leather was wrapped around itself several times, and it was all tied about a short sheath in the center. Then she realized what she was seeing, and she took a step back and stared at Io Kua.

He grinned. "So you like it?" he asked. He unwrapped the leather belt and pulled a gleaming blade from a sheath. The blade was almost as long as two hands, and the handle was wrapped in darkly oiled, black leather. "My Mentor told me that any student of his would learn the art of using a fine blade. He gave me a short sword when I began training under him. I found this one at the caravan market this morning, so I now tell you the same: You must learn the art of using a fine blade."

"But I have no skill with a blade – you said so."

"We all begin our journey from the point of ignorance," he said with a smile. "You shall learn by doing."

She gently brushed a finger along the cold metal. It was beautiful. It gleamed in the sunlight, and lightly smelled of cloves.

Kua took her hand and wrapped it around the handle. "It is a Felton sword," he said. He let go, and she held the sword tightly in her grip, afraid it would fall from her hand. "One of the shorter swords available, but they have excellent balance and a fine grip."

Zhava nodded. She balanced the sword in the air before her.

Kua leaned forward and pointed to the little ball of gleaming metal at the end of the handle. "Pomel," he said. He pointed to the handle. "Grip." Then the metal bar above it. "Cross-guard." The sharp edge. "The edge – I had them sharpen it when I purchased it, so be careful." Finally he pointed to the end of the blade. "The point."

Zhava nodded again.

"Now your turn."

"Pomel," she said, pointing. "Grip. Um...cross-guard. Edge. Point."

"Very good." He held her hand and gently lowered the point into the end of the sheath and slid it forward until the Felton sword was tucked back inside. Then he reached forward, looped the belt around her waist and buckled it securely above her hips. The sheath dangled at her right thigh – and she really liked how it looked and felt.

She turned to Kua and studied him, though. He'd had this with him when he met her. Why?

"Did you know I would ask you to remain my Mentor?" she asked.

"I hoped to remain your Mentor. High Priest Viekoosh said the decision was mine, not yours, but I wanted to know your feelings first. As your Mentor, I will be overseeing all of your training, and I will conduct your final trials in all disciplines. You will also meet with me every couple days to review your studies of Hibaro philosophies, mantras, and copas."

"Like I did with Priestess Marmaran?"

"Very likely. Not today, however. I have two more errands to run for the High Priest, and I expect to return to the Hibaro within two days, possibly three at the most. We will meet then, following your weapons training that day." He pointed at the sheath. "Until then, you wear that at all times so you get accustomed to the weight. Show it to Io Suleenuo, and she will begin giving you proper instructions with it."

"Yes, Sir," she said, smiling and with her hand wrapped around the sword's grip.

He sternly pointed a finger at her and said, "No flames until I return. No wind either. You are to build your endurance on the field and your skill with weapons." He glanced behind her. "And remind your shadow back there that she has her own classes to attend."

# CHAPTER 13

*Five nights later....*

"Hmm, why aren't you working?" Brother Tymare said.

Zhava stood up straight. She had been leaning against a shelf of papers, lost in thought, and she hadn't even heard the Tower's Book Master approach. He was a quiet, studious man who spent more time perusing books and scrolls on the shelves than he did conversing with people, but he was also brilliant. He had devised the Tower's system of organizing its documents by letters and numbers that allowed him to look up anything and find it within moments, and – most astonishing of all – Brother Tymare could recite almost any sentence from almost any document, and he could cite the title and author instantly.

For all of his brilliance, however, he was one of the shyest people Zhava had ever met. He seemed to prefer solitude, and he had arranged one corner of the Tower reading room with shelves piled high with books so that no one could see him when he was seated at his desk. When he discovered Zhava could read and write two different languages, however, he had agreed immediately to bring her on as his assistant. Apparently she was the first assistant he had allowed to work with him in almost a dozen seasons.

And now he had caught her daydreaming instead of working.

She ducked her head. Brother Tymare didn't like looking people in the eyes, and he preferred it when they looked away from him too.

"I'm sorry, Brother Tymare," she said. "I was distracted."

"Hmm, well, get back to work." He pointed to a pile of parchment on a table near the door. "File those."

"Yes, Sir," she said. She bowed and hurried on her way.

Even considering Brother Tymare's personality quirks, Zhava could not remember a time in her life when she had ever been this happy. Her weapons training with Io Suleenuo was hard, but she was having fun. Suleenuo said the Felton sword was a good, all-purpose weapon, and she had begun giving Zhava basic instructions with it after class. They had practiced how to hold it for offense and defense, how to swing it through the air, and, the most important of all, how to properly care for it. Zhava's primary task, however, was learning with the throwing knives. Every day, Suleenuo led a class with the throwing knives, teaching Zhava and the other students how to properly hold them, how to store them in small sheaths at the hip, under the arm, behind the back, or even against the leg. Then there was the throwing practice, which Zhava discovered she could do very well. That first throw had not been a fluke – with very little instruction and correction, she could easily hit targets within 10 or 12 steps of her. Unfortunately, though Io Suleenuo taught many students how to throw knives, it was not a skill she valued highly in a fight.

"If you throw away your knife," she had said to them on the first day of class. "Then, you no longer have a knife. Worse yet, you may have just given your opponent a weapon to use against you."

That was why she spent far more time teaching the students basic fighting techniques they could use in any situation. For every lesson she conducted on throwing knives, she spent at least twice as long teaching the students how to fight with their hands and with the sparring rods. Zhava didn't like those lessons – the sparring rods still made her flinch when she heard them snick open – but she appreciated the opportunities to learn, especially because the skills were so easily used with her Felton sword.

She finished organizing the pile of parchments and climbed the stairs to the second floor where she could put them in their proper locations. Reflexively, she dropped her right hand to the hilt of her sword and smiled.

As much as she was enjoying the weapons training, though, she was having a miserable time with her endurance training. She had returned to the field two days later, as Priest Qi had requested, to join a group of Candidates who were all younger than she by at least a couple seasons – and one boy who could not have been older than 7 or 8 seasons. With her injured leg, she couldn't do more than walk the field that first day. When the children shouted encouragement, it only reminded her how slowly she was walking. By her third day on the field, she could finally run, though not for long, and today she had actually completed two laps without stopping to rest. Priest Qi, who seemed to never wear anything more than shorts and shoes, commended her effort and told her to try harder tomorrow.

As slowly as her weapons and endurance training were progressing, her lessons with Io Kua had gone almost nowhere – though not through any fault of hers. He had said he would return within two or three days, but he had been gone on his errand until late last night. They had met briefly this morning, but he was exhausted and distracted and a little angry. High Priest Viekoosh had sent him to retrieve Salient Kretsch, but that man had been sent on a mission for the King and would not return for at least another two moons. After much searching, Kua had found another Salient willing to travel to the Hibaro, a woman named Noomira – but the High Priest and Salient Noomira did not like each other. Kua hadn't known about the animosity until he returned to deliver his report to Viekoosh, who became quite angry – and directed his anger at Kua. The High Priest had actually left the Tower and was said to be meditating – alone – somewhere in the woods outside the Hibaro. Kua was miserable for delivering such an unsatisfactory report to the High Priest. He had tried to do the right thing, and he had managed to create a situation that was apparently quite distressing – and his telling of that story took up more of their morning meeting than Zhava had ever cared to hear.

She found where the parchment was stored in the second floor holdings, piled them neatly in a row, dusted her hands, and headed back down the stairs. She saw a couple Novices reading their philosophies at a table near the center of the room and a lone Initiate against the far wall with her head bent down and writing something. She had actually become quite good at recognizing the divisions of people at the Hibaro, all of them dressed in outfits of varying colors. Those in white, as she herself was dressed, were Initiates; light blue for Candidates; red for Novices; and dark green for Apprentices.  The Ios wore robes of red and black; the priests wore solid black or purple; the support staff of Sisters and Brothers seemed to have the most variety in their clothes, with many of them in different colors that seemed more often to reflect the levels of people with whom they worked the most; and the soldiers wore their tanned leather and polished metal armor.  Though Zhava had noticed all of those varieties of colors, it had been Barae who told her over the noon meal yesterday what they all meant.

"Sir," she said with a bow as she approached Brother Tymare's desk.  She could just see the top of his head above the stacks of books and scrolls precariously balanced around him.  "I've finished the filing you gave me. If that is all, I would like to return to my room to study. Io Kua gave me some philosophies to read."

He stood up and looked around the dim room.  "Hmm, no.  Light the sconces before you go."

"Um...with you?"

"No."  He reached behind him and grabbed a sconce rod, then held it out to her.

Zhava just stared at him.  There were at least 40 ceiling sconces scattered around the main floor and another 25 on the second floor between all the stacks of books and scrolls.  He had shown her just last night how to do the job, but it was slow and tedious.  It would probably take her at least until dark if she did them by herself.

"And then I can go read my philosophies?" she asked, taking the sconce rod.

"Hmm, yes.  Good night."  He sat down again and returned to his reading.

She slowly turned and trudged across the room.  Io Kua had given her a basic philosophies scroll and said she had two days to read it and be prepared to explain it to him.  Priestess Marmaran had never given her an assignment like that, and she was excited to begin.  Now it looked as if she would be reading by lamp light.

She walked outside and around the corner to the Tower's everlight, the lamp with the large tub of oil that kept the flame alive both day and night so that all had quick and easy access to fire. She held the sconce rod to the little flame and gently spun the rod until the fire caught hold. Of course, she could do this task far more easily by simply calling forth her own little flames, but Io Kua had again made her promise to keep her Abilities in check. "For now, hone your physical," he had said, and she promised to do just that. But she still missed their company.

She returned to the Tower with a sigh as she stared at the rows of sconce lights set into the ceiling. This was a tedious job, and she couldn't believe Brother Tymare was making her do it by herself. Again, her fingers itched to call forth her flames. She could set them loose to run wild through the room and have every sconce lit before the sun set. She would have plenty of time to study her philosophies. *Promises*, she reminded herself. *I've made promises.* She sighed again and started forward.

She did the task just as Brother Tymare had shown her. Politely ask any people seated at a table to step away for a moment. Climb atop the table – careful not to disturb anyone's reading or writing materials. Set the lit sconce rod against the wick in the ceiling and slowly rotate the rod until the flame caught. Count to three. If the wick went out, try lighting it again, but that rarely happened. Climb down from the table. Thank the people at the table for their patience. Move on to the next table...and repeat another 30 or 40 times.

She started with the empty tables. There were several near the center of the room. People watched her, so they weren't surprised when she approached. Several of them smiled at her, chatted about the weather – it had been a beautiful, sunny day, and it looked to be a chilly, moonlit night – or simply stepped back and patiently let her go about her duty. A couple Novices studying the history of their Abilities grumbled at her for interrupting them, but after the ceiling sconce lit up their scrolls scattered across the table, they smiled and thanked her – then settled intently back into their studies.

It was well past sunset when Zhava finished the first floor and trudged up the steep, corner steps to the second floor. Far fewer people were at work up here, and she went from table to table right down the center of the room without interrupting anyone's work. This was actually a much prettier room at night than the first floor study room. This one had far more dark little corners where the light wouldn't reach, casting those spaces in dramatic shadows where someone would need a handheld lantern to peruse the scrolls and books. The early night's quarter-moon shone brightly through the row of windows on the far side, gently lighting the tables pressed against that wall. As Zhava turned to climb down from the center table, she noticed Plishka sitting nearby and reading a scroll by moonlight. She had scattered several scrolls around her, and she had a couple small books propped open. Zhava smiled and walked over.

"Hello," she whispered, sitting in the chair across from her.

"Um...hello," Plishka said with a frown.

"I haven't seen you since that day at the field. You were so nice to walk with me. Thank you."

"You're welcome." She flicked the scroll in her hands, shifted in her chair, and continued reading.

Zhava just stared. Barae was right – Plishka could be smiling and friendly one day and then cold and mean the next. What made her do that? Why would she change so much?

"What are you working on?" she asked, gesturing at the scrolls and books scattered across the table.

"A project," she said without looking up. "Not your concern. You may leave now – you're dismissed."

Zhava chuckled. She was "dismissed"? What did that mean? Plishka was an Initiate the same as Zhava – and Zhava certainly wasn't a servant...though, she thought with a quick glance at the ceiling, she did have to light that sconce above Plishka's table.

"Maybe I can help," Zhava continued, picking up one of the scrolls. "I can read two languages."

Plishka yanked the scroll from her hand and slammed it on the table with a thud. "You can't help. This is too important. Go away."

*Wow*, Zhava thought, backing her chair away. She had never met someone like Plishka, someone who would change so dramatically from one conversation to the next. And it wasn't as if Plishka was putting on some act for her friends – no one had been around when they'd been on the field the other day, and no one was sitting anywhere near their conversation now.

"Well," Zhava whispered, slowly standing up. "I'll light this sconce and...leave you alone."

"Don't light the sconce," she muttered. "Just leave."

Zhava chuckled. That would be a problem. Brother Tymare wasn't going to let her leave until she finished her task, and she knew he would check both floors to be sure she did it correctly – that would mean lighting every sconce on these two floors. Better to do it now than to be chastised by him later and then told to do it while he stood behind her and watched. Besides, she had her own philosophies to read, and she was already going to be awake far too late getting that done.

"It's all right," Zhava said, gently sliding aside one of the books on the table. "This will just take a moment, and then I'll leave you alone."

Plishka slammed her hand on the table and glared. "No! Leave it!" Now the others in the room turned to stare.

"Plishka, this is my job." Zhava waved the sconce rod in the air before her. "I'll be quick, and then you can get back to your work." She climbed on the chair and started to brace herself on the table.

Plishka jumped up and yanked the sconce rod from Zhava's hand. Zhava lost her balance, slipped from the chair, and tumbled to the floor. She landed on her elbow and yelped at the pain. Tiny prickles shot up and down her arm as it went numb, and she cradled it against her chest. She rolled over to see Plishka standing above her and waving the rod in the air between them.

"I don't need the sconce lit! I want to be left alone! Now get out of here!" Her hands lit with blue sparks that crackled and flashed through the air like lightning. She set one hand to the end of the rod and pushed. The crackling light burst against the sconce rod, and splinters of wood flew around them. She kept pushing, sparking her hand to the rod's end and sending shards flying until finally she reached the other end – and the final bits of cindered wood fluttered through the air between them.

Plishka looked around, her breathing heavy and the sparks slowly dimming from her hands. The room was silent, and even from the floor, Zhava could see that the few others in the room were standing and staring at them. Plishka turned back at Zhava and screamed, her fists shaking at her sides.

"Now look what you made me do!" She spun around to the table, hurriedly scooped up her scrolls and books, and stomped from the room. Her footsteps echoed down the stairs as she descended.

Zhava sat where she'd fallen, stunned. Other than from her own Mama (and that several times throughout her life), Zhava had never been yelled at so loudly. She had rarely seen anyone so mad. She thought back over the conversation, and she couldn't even think what had so offended Plishka – aside from Zhava being friendly. But who would reject friendliness?

"Are you hurt?" an older man asked, leaning down and offering her a hand up.

"No, I'm not hurt," Zhava said. Her numb arm had become tingly and throbbing, and she expected a large bruise to develop on her elbow, but other than that she was fine. She accepted his offered hand and slowly stood up again.

"Do not take her words to heart," the man whispered. "That is Plishka. She always says something like that to someone, whether it is here or in a room with other students or even on a field and practicing her Abilities."

"Thank you." Zhava sighed and walked away. Everyone seemed to expect Plishka to misbehave, but that didn't excuse it. It also didn't explain why she would be so nice to people once and then so mean to them the next time.

She went back downstairs and retrieved another sconce rod from the supplies behind Tymare's desk. He watched her but didn't say anything. She had known him such a short time, but it seemed impossible for anyone to know what the man was thinking. He could just as easily be critiquing the hem of her skirt, as he did the first day they met ("Hmm, your skirt's hem is very tight. The stitching is only 1/8-bits wide."), or noticing the pace of her walking, as he did the second day she worked for him ("Hmm, you're walking almost 10 percent faster today than you were yesterday"). He chose not to talk to her this time, though, so she didn't talk to him either. Let him wonder why she needed a second sconce rod.

She went outside, lit the new rod, climbed back up to the second floor, which was now deserted, and went back to the table where Plishka had been studying. She lit the sconce in the ceiling and climbed down from the table – and noticed one of Plishka's scrolls had fallen near the table's leg. She retrieved it. It was small and rolled into a tight bind. She loosened it and read the heading: "Coredor and the Women of Saed." Of all the Gods, Coredor was her least favorite. He was mean, he bullied those around him, and he enjoyed hurting people. Why would Plishka be reading about him? She shuddered and rolled up the scroll again.

She leaned out the open window by the table and looked outside, but she did not see Plishka. She slipped the scroll into her belt, gently tapping the Felton sword at her side and smiling at its familiar, comfortable weight, then continued on her way to lighting the remaining sconces. No matter how much she hurried, the sun was well past set before she finished the task. Her neck ached from staring up for so long, and it cracked several times as she stretched and went back downstairs. She set the used rod in an alcove behind Brother Tymare's desk.

"Hmm, you'll be faster next time if you take two rods with you."

"What?"

"For when you've finished the first rod. Then you'll have the second with you already."

"Thanks." She turned to leave.

"Hmm, this message came for you."

She plucked the message from his fingers and smiled. "Thanks. Good night."

He grinned, his eyebrows high and his eyes bright. "Good night."

She unfolded the small piece of paper. It seemed an extravagant waste to write something on a piece of actual paper. Even the scrolls were expensive, but this little piece of paper must have cost someone a small fortune.

*I want that book*, the note read. *Bring it to the Sparring Grounds.*

Zhava clenched her eyes and rubbed at the bridge of her nose. Plishka. Plishka! She got mad and stormed off, dropped her book on the floor, and now Zhava was supposed to fix everything for her.

She felt in the waistband of her skirt and found the little scroll. She could pretend she didn't have it and quickly return it to its place on the shelf, but that would be somewhere upstairs, and she had already been up and down those stairs too many times today. It was already dark, and Zhava would not get to her studies until much later no matter what she did. Plishka obviously needed the scroll, and whatever her "project," it seemed to consume her thoughts – and her manners. Barae would say not to bother, but she wasn't Zhava. Zhava would be a friend, no matter what Plishka did.

She set off from the Tower, found the path to the Sparring Grounds – now that she knew where to find the trail, she could see how easy a trek it would have been if she had just followed Io Kua that first day – and began hiking through the dark.

She had noticed that neither Barae nor Posef liked the dark. They would walk the Hibaro grounds at night with no trouble, but torches were stuck in the ground near different wooden paths, and lanterns were lit near most doors. The Hibaro itself could hardly be described as "dark" even on the cloudiest nights. However, neither of them was interested in venturing far beyond the Hibaro once the sun set. They stayed nearer to the buildings or within the buildings themselves. Their evening and nighttime paths through the grounds seemed to veer from one spot of light to the next, though she doubted either was purposefully following such a wildly crooked path. She thought it to be an effect of where they were raised. Posef, though he said he travelled with his family through the highland countryside, had frequently mentioned a small village that seemed to be the center of his journeys. Many of his stories began, "It was a day's ride away," and they frequently ended with, "When we got back to the village...." As for Barae, she was in and out of her portside village every few days, and her nights were spent on the open seas with the gentle lapping of the water against the hull of her father's fishing boat. Just last night, Zhava had actually noticed her shiver as she stared at the darkened tree line just beyond the Hibaro grounds. Barae was obviously nervous about the forest at night.

Zhava, however, loved the dark. Even without her little flames, she could see the dusty trail at her feet and the wide path through the trees just by the twinkling stars and the gently rising quarter-moon. The forest was alive, but she had spent enough time walking her farm and fields at night to know that the only things out there were the animals beginning their hunt for food. She swished her feet along the trail every so often to make noise and scare away anything that might take an interest in her. Her father had taught her that. Most of the animals, he said, did not want to fight with a person. Most animals preferred moving far away from people. Just in case, however, she slid her Felton sword from its sheath and held it down by her side. She wasn't very skilled with it yet, but its presence in her hand made her feel a bit more secure.

She turned the final bend in the trail and entered the cleared area of the Sparring Grounds. She eyed the pile of rocks on the far side that hid the stone stairs to the Proving Cove. She shivered at the thought of that dark creature resting within, but everyone she had spoken to assured her the monster never ventured from the Cove. Sister Tegara had gone so far as to say that Zhava could stand at the mouth of that cave and scream taunts at the thing all day and all night, and the monster would never emerge. It was only when someone ventured into the Cove itself that the creature attacked. Zhava had never heard of any animal that acted that way, but everyone assured her it was true.

She looked around the darkened ring, a bit exasperated at the emptiness. Plishka had said to meet her here for the book, but she was nowhere to be seen. Zhava slid the sword back into its sheath and cupped her hands to her face.

"Plishka," she yelled. "I brought your book."

The nighttime insects stopped their chirping. Zhava looked around, but still did not see Plishka. The insects started up again.

Zhava thought back to the note she had received. *I want the book*, it had read. *Bring it to the Sparring Grounds.* However, there had been no signature. Nothing on the note indicated Plishka had sent it. Zhava had assumed it was Plishka because Plishka had dropped the book. And now Zhava was out in the woods...late at night...by herself...when everyone said that someone was out here and killing people from the Hibaro.

She gasped. *No, no, no*, she thought, glancing around the Sparring Grounds. She hadn't thought this through – she hadn't been cautious. She had been tired from a day's work, and she had been irritated at Plishka for yelling at her and dropping the book, and she had been thinking of getting her own work done back in her room. She wasn't afraid of the dark, and it was nothing to her to go out into the dark and meet her friend. But what if it wasn't her friend who sent the note?

She gently slid the sword back out again, this time holding it before her in the dark. She turned to walk back down the trail and return to the Hibaro, to return to the safety of the buildings and the light and all the other people. She stepped lightly along the edge of the trail, trying to keep to the shadows. Where she had been enjoying the moon's gentle light only moments ago, she now feared it would expose her to whatever – whomever – might be waiting in the dark to attack. Her white Initiate clothes did not help, catching the light like a flare.

A shadow stepped from the trees and into the center of the path several lengths before her, and Zhava slid to a stop. The figure was dressed in black, with a hood over his head. (Her head?) He did not move but simply stood there, blocking the path.

"I see you," Zhava said, trying to keep her voice from shaking. "Who are you?"

The figure stared at her from within the hood.

"I'm meeting my friend," Zhava said. "She's out here too."

The figure's head turned as if scanning the darkened trees surrounding them.

"Perhaps you've seen her?" she asked. If she could convince this person that she was not alone, perhaps he would leave. Zhava wasn't sure she believed that, but she had to try something.

The figure turned his head back to her, raised one finger into the air, and pointed at Zhava.

A burst of wind escaped the trees at her side, and claws gripped Zhava's shoulders. She screamed at the pain, and she was lifted into the air. Another burst of wind, and a rush of wings beat before her face. The claws dug deeper into her shoulders, and she saw the trail race past her feet. She looked up, and a bird – the largest bird she had ever seen – flapped through the night air, carrying her away in its grip.

Zhava yelled again, and swung the sword in a looping arch above her head. The blade sliced through the bird's feathered leg, and the creature let loose a piercing cry. The talons released their hold, and Zhava fell to the ground, rolling through the dirt.

Remembering Io Suleenuo's fight training, Zhava used her momentum to roll right back up to a standing position – but then slipped in the dirt, lost her balance, and landed on her butt with a jolt that made her teeth ache.

The man in the dark robes strode down the path, darkly laughing at her.

Somewhere in the rolling and standing and falling, she had lost her sword. Io Kua had told her not to use her Abilities, but this was life and death. She flung her hands out before her and sent a gust of wind down the trail.

The man bowed his head as the wind whipped at his robes, but it did little to slow his advance. Zhava stumbled to her feet and flicked her wrist, calling a dozen flames to her hand. She drew back her arm to throw them at the man in the robes, but something pounded into her from behind and knocked her to the ground. She heard the beating of the bird's large, powerful wings as it soared back up from the circle of the Sparring Grounds, and the robed man laughed again, this time much louder.

Zhava shook her head, trying to clear the spots floating before her eyes. Her body ached, and her arms and legs did not want to move. She coughed, and dirt and blood scattered before her face.

The man's boots crunched on the rocks near her. He pressed his knee into her back and leaned down, forcing the air from her lungs. She gasped and tried to drag in a breath.

"I'm disappointed, Zhava," the man said.

She coughed again. Her chest ached from the pressure of his knee in the middle of her back.

"You showed so much more promise than this. You have an Ability not seen…since legend. But you can't harness that power."

Her vision blurred, and she flailed at the dirt and rocks around her. She tried to reach for the man, but she swished her hand through empty dirt.

"You're just too powerful," the man whispered. "You're all too powerful…and too weak to harness that power. Then shall the world be purged of the meekly powerful, and only then shall the rightful heirs inherit the land."

She had no idea what the man was babbling, but she would not be hurt by him. She would not killed by him. He had surprised her, and he had some trained bird. She had so much more than that.

She shut her eyes and called forth every flame she possibly could. She invited them all to herself, to within her, to enwrap her body from the inside out – and then she shoved them away.

The air exploded around Zhava. The man was flung far away as the flames burst forth from Zhava's body. She rolled over and gasped a ragged, painful breath – then shut her eyes at the blindingly bright light of the little flames dancing through the Sparring Grounds. They were scattered across the ring, clinging to the branches and leaves and rocks, and riding the air as they glided back to the ground.

Zhava rolled over and pushed herself up – and spotted her Felton sword lying at the edge of the Sparring Grounds. She staggered over and retrieved it from the ground, then turned to look for the man in the black robes again. She held a hand before her eyes to shield herself from the flames, but the ring was empty. The man seemed to have fled. Or vanished.

She turned in a slow circle as the last of her little flames gently drifted on the air. The ground was pulsing with the joyous dancing of hundreds of flames, and she began to smell the distinct odor of burning wood. She gave a quick whistle, and the flames that were clinging to the trees let loose their hold and began dropping down.

"Zhava," yelled a woman's voice.

She spun to the sound, her sword raised before her. Then she saw the woman on the other side of the Sparring Grounds – Plishka.

"Get down!" Plishka yelled as she ran forward. In one swift move, Plishka ran into Zhava, pushed aside the sword, and tackled her to the ground.

Zhava gasped as the air was once more shoved from her lungs. The rocks dug into her back and shoulders, and her head throbbed as she struck the ground.

"You're not safe," Plishka said. "He's still out there."

"Who is he?"

Plishka's eyes grew wide, and her body tensed.  She clenched Zhava's arms in a death-grip, and her mouth opened to speak – and then a powerful wind blasted at the ground, and Plishka was yanked into the air, carried high as the bird's sharp talons gripped her, and its wings beat furiously.

"No!" Zhava yelled.  She struggled up from the ground, swinging her sword wildly before her – and watched Plishka disappear high into the night sky.

# CHAPTER 14

Within moments, the Sparring Ground's clearing was filled with soldiers, their swords drawn and their torches held high. They surrounded Zhava and made her drop her sword and kneel to the ground, her hands held high above her head. Several soldiers threw blankets on the ground to put out her little flames, and others kicked dirt or stomped on the remaining embers until they died. When Zhava tried to speak, she got a sword pressed to her throat and a glare from the soldier in charge. They stationed themselves around the edge of the clearing, and several groups of soldiers ventured deeper into the woods to scout the area.

A group of four Ios soon joined the soldiers in the Sparring Grounds, taking in the scene. One met with the soldier in charge, but the other three went straight to Zhava. They looked imposing in their black and red robes and scowls on their faces.

"Speak," one man said.

"They took Plishka," she blurted. Her heart raced, and a chill ran down her. These four Ios, none of whom she knew, held her life at this moment. All they knew was that something had happened in the woods, flames were scattered everywhere – and Zhava was in the center of it all. They could kill her, and they would get into trouble with no one.

"Plishka?" the man asked, turning to another Io.

"Second-year Initiate," that woman said. "Uneven temperament. Uneven abilities, but impressive when she can bring them to surface."

The man turned back to Zhava. "Who took her?"

"I don't know. A giant bird."

The man's eyebrows rose at that, and Zhava realized how stupid it sounded to him. He hadn't been here. He hadn't seen the bird attacking her, hadn't watched it carry off Plishka.

"And a man!" she said. "A man in black robes. I couldn't see his face. He was controlling the bird. He attacked me – well, the bird attacked me, but then he attacked me, and then the bird attacked me again. That was after I used my flames on him." She cringed. She was babbling – she sounded like Barae.

"Why were you out here at night? No one is allowed off Hibaro grounds after sunset without an escort."

"Plishka sent me a note to meet her out here. I mean, I thought it was Plishka. The note wasn't signed, but–"

"Why did you sneak past the guards?"

"What guards?"

The Ios glanced at each other, frowning, and then the first man continued. "Three soldiers are stationed along this path every night to guard this way in and out of the Hibaro. Why did you sneak past them?"

"I...didn't see any guards." How could she have missed guards? She hadn't been trying to sneak anywhere – she had, in fact, been shuffling her feet through the dirt to make noise and scare away any large animals. If there had been guards, she would have seen them. They would have heard her. "There were no guards," she said, shaking her head.

The Io turned and yelled to the soldiers, "Sargeant!"

A soldier near the edge of the clearing rushed over and gave a quick salute. His armor gleamed in the firelight of the torches and lanterns spread throughout the Sparring Grounds. "Yes, Io."

"Report."

"Sir, my squad was on patrol. Three of us, myself included, were stationed at the trailhead, I had four walking perimeter, and the remaining three had taken lookout positions throughout the forest." He glanced at Zhava and frowned, then turned back to the Io. "I'm sorry, but none of us saw her. I don't know how she sneaked past, but we will investigate the woods at dawn. She may have used the same route that Io Kua reported her using upon arrival...I just don't know – yet."

Zhava stared at the soldier. That wasn't what happened at all. No one had been on the trail – the trail had been empty.

"Thank you," the Io said. He dismissed the soldier with a wave of his hand, then turned to the other two Ios. "Lock her up. Inform Io Kua what has happened here, and then dispatch a messenger to Io Liori. She'll want to know what a waste this Initiate has been."

"Wait," Zhava said. "That's not-"

The Io clamped a hand across her mouth. He squeezed, his fingers digging in to her cheeks, and then he leaned in close, his eyes narrowing on her. "It's time for you to shut up now," he whispered. "The High Priest will deal with you." He flicked his hand away.

The other two Ios gripped Zhava's arms and dragged her up from the ground. They yanked her along, her arms burning from their grips and her feet shuffling through the dirt, and the Sergeant and two of his soldiers fell in beside the Ios to act as escorts. Zhava tried to keep pace with them, but they were pulling her too quickly, and she stumbled along beside them. Some soldiers stood at attention, others were using their torches or lanterns to search the surrounding woods, and several were chatting with each other or watching the Ios rush her off. She heard bits of conversation as people were debating what happened.

"Half the trees were on fire by the time we arrived."

"There was no blood? How?"

"Did she turn invisible?"

"Where's her sword? I set it right here."

Her sword! She turned to look at the man who said that, but she saw only the back of his gleaming helmet before she was led down a bend in the trail, and she lost her view of the Sparring Grounds and the bustling activity. The conversations and the lights were quickly swallowed by the night, but the Ios kept their grip on Zhava's arms. Two of the soldiers scanned the tree line, their lanterns held high, while the third kept pace behind Zhava and regularly shoved her in the back to keep her moving. Within moments, they emerged from the trailhead and into a crowd of people at the edge of the Hibaro grounds. She saw dozens of older students milling around the soldiers, but everyone kept their distance from the Ios and soldiers marching Zhava through the grounds. That didn't stop people from talking loudly, however, and Zhava realized how bad the rumors were becoming – and how quickly they were spreading.

"They caught the killer?"

"Who did she kill?"

"She looked like trouble the moment she arrived."

They led her to double doors set into the ground, lifted the doors from their mounting brackets, and pressed her forward down a steeply descending staircase. At the foot of the stairs, lanterns were spaced unevenly down a rough-hewn hallway, their heat and smoke drifting on the still air. Heavy doors with bands of metal lined each side, and the Ios led her along while the soldiers stood back at the stairs. The Ios reached an open door, roughly shoved her inside, then slammed the door shut behind her. The bolt echoed hollowly through the dark space. A skinny, metal panel in the door's center slid open, allowing a sliver of light to enter the prison room, and the Ios walked away. The silence that followed was almost deafening in its stillness.

Zhava shivered, not from the cold – if anything, the dark room was stiflingly warm – but from fear. Fear of what would happen next. Fear of what Io Kua would think – what he would say to her. They would tell him what they suspected, that she had killed a fellow student, and he would turn his back on her. He would refuse to listen to her, or if he listened, he would refuse to believe. He hadn't wanted to be her Mentor, he hadn't wanted to remain at the Hibaro to train her.

She sat on the floor and scooted back through the dirt until she came to the rough, stone wall. She curled into a tight ball and stared at the sliver of light coming through the sliding hole in the door. For some reason, she wasn't scared of the man in the woods, or of his trained bird. No one knew who the killer was, but she had seen him, and he was just a man. A powerful man. A well trained man who could brush aside her Abilities as if they were cloth. But he was no more to be feared than any other man she had met. He had Abilities, certainly, but he also had weakness. He relied on that giant bird to distract someone and to carry off people, but she had used her little flames to push him off of herself, and she had heard him cry out in pain when he fell. He must have hurt something when the flames pushed him away, possibly his leg or his ankle.

People were scared of him for killing people – and now they thought she was the one doing the killing – but they were only scared because no one had seen him and lived to tell of it. She had lived.

She held her hand out before her and called one of her flames. It spun to life in her palm and danced before her. She smiled. She had only lived because of these little ones. They had almost lit the forest on fire, but they had beaten back her attacker. She had lived...because of them. She shut her eyes and let the dancing firelight flicker through her closed lids. And she smiled. Papa had sold her away for a few bags of coins. Mama had run screaming from home because Zhava wouldn't go off and be married to Ooleng. Io Kua, Io Suleenuo, and Priest Qi – they had all begun training her, and she had used that training to fight off her attacker. Sister Tegara would be proud. Even Io Liori might be pleased, though she seemed a hard woman to please. And Priestess Marmaran. Oh, Priestess Marmaran would be smiling the happiest of smiles right now to know how well Zhava had done...

...except that Plishka was still gone. Was still dead.

Zhava's smiled faded, and the little flame slowed his dancing. He twirled once more in her palm, then sat, his fire flickering in the cold sadness.

Plishka hadn't been nice in the Tower, but she had tried to save Zhava in the woods. That was so much like her. Mean one moment, and then caring the next. Zhava had never quite understood Plishka...and now she never would.

"Oh, child," a woman whispered through the darkness.

"Marmaran," Zhava whispered back. "Did I do well?"

"My child."

"Did I do well?" She opened her eyes, but beyond the little circle of flame in the palm of her hand the room remained black.

"You've much to learn, my child."

"But I did well." She wiped a tear from her eye. Why would Priestess Marmaran not say it?

A door slammed outside in the hallway, and Zhava jerked herself completely awake. She shut her hand on the little flame as voices echoed – several voices.

"We will see her now," a woman said – and Zhava's heart leapt at the voice. Sister Tegara.

"But High Priest Viekoosh has not said–"

"She is an Initiate in my charge, and I will meet with her. We will be allowed inside."

"I can – maybe. One at a time only though."

"Acceptable."

The voices were right outside the door, and she could see through the narrow slot that lights and shadows flicked back and forth in the hallway. A set of keys jingled, one was inserted into the lock, and the bolt twisted free. The door swung open on its heavy hinges, and two guards blocked the prison entry, one facing into the cell and with his hand on his sword, the other looking at Sister Tegara and holding a small sandpiece. He flipped it over, the sand draining from the top and into the bottom glass bubble.

"This long," the guard said, pointing to the sandpiece. "One turn."

Sister Tegara turned to glance behind her and said, "Go."

Barae rushed into the room, her arms open wide, and ran straight toward Zhava.

Zhava sat up, and they wrapped their arms around each other.

The door slammed shut, sealing them in the darkened space. Barae held on tight, and Zhava felt the girl's tears against her face.

"Thank the Gods you're safe," Barae whispered.

"Thank you for coming."

"I heard about the fight – I mean, everyone's heard about the fight, but no one knows what happened, and people are saying the most awful things about you, and I know those things aren't true. They can't be true. I know I only just met you, but I feel like I know you better than I know my own brothers, or my father, and I just can't believe – I mean, they said Plishka is dead. They said you killed her, but you never would have done something that horrible. I went to Plishka's room, and she wasn't there, but that doesn't mean anything because Plishka is hardly ever in her room, and–"

"Barae," Zhava said, squeezing her tight.

"Yes? I'm here for you. What? Anything, just tell me."

Zhava took a breath. She didn't want to say this, but Barae had to know. She had to hear it from Zhava, and not from anyone else. "Plishka is dead."

Barae tensed. She squeezed Zhava tighter, and she buried her face in Zhava's neck. "You…didn't-"

"No," Zhava said with a quick shake of her head. "I didn't do it. There was a man in the woods. A man with a large bird. That bird carried off Plishka, and then the man got away."

The guard pounded on the door, and both Zhava and Barae jerked at the sudden noise.

"I knew you were innocent," Barae said.

The door swung open, and the guard yelled, "Out!"

Zhava and Barae stood, still embracing in the dark cell.

"Whatever you need," Barae said, "just say it. I'll get it for you – I'll do it."

Zhava smiled. "You've already done it," she said. "You came."

"Now!" the guard said, stepping forward. He grabbed Barae's arm and yanked her away. "I said to get out."

Barae started to say something more, but the guard spun her away, and she yelped in pain. Sister Tegara slipped around the two of them and strode through the darkened cell.

"Only one turn for you, too," the second guard said, and he slammed the door shut.

Sister Tegara wrapped her arms around Zhava, gave her a quick hug, and then stepped away.

"You are well?" she asked. "They have not mistreated you?"

"I am well," Zhava said with a quick bow – though she doubted Tegara saw it in the dark. "Thank you."

"And you told your story to Barae?"

"I did."

"Is there anything more I should know?"

Zhava thought back to the fight in the woods. She had told Barae about the man and his bird, and she had explained how the bird carried off Plishka. What else was there? "No, Ma'am."

"Good." Tegara stepped forward, right before Zhava, and she began to whisper. "Now listen carefully. High Priest Viekoosh himself plans to call for you first thing in the morning. You are to give your testimony to him – do not leave out anything. If he is to help you, you must be truthful with him. Trust me, High Priest Viekoosh is the best leader the Hibaro has had in more than a dozen seasons. He will help you."

"Yes, Ma'am."

"Very good. You must also know that Io Kua met with me as I was on my way here. He had to leave the Hibaro immediately, but he said he would return as quickly as he could with someone who could help – one of the King's own Salients."

Zhava could think of nothing to say. Kua had told her a Salient was coming to the Hibaro – but why bring her sooner?

"Together, she and Viekoosh will discover what truly happened."

The guard pounded on the door. "Time," he yelled.

"Have faith," Sister Tegara said.

"Yes, Ma'am."

The door swung open, and the guard said, "Out. Now, before I have to drag you out too."

Sister Tegara turned in the harsh glare of the lantern light, and said, "Place one hand on me, soldier, and you will be dead where you stand."

The soldier cleared his throat and took a step back. "Just...um, saying, Ma'am. Your time's up."

Sister Tegara strode from the cell. In the hallway, she turned and gave a quick smile to Zhava before the guard pulled the door shut again. The iron bolt clanked tight, and the guards and the two women walked away, their footsteps fading.

Zhava slid to the floor, pulled her legs up against her chest, and buried her face between her knees. It would be all right, she told herself. It would be all right.

"Oh, child," Priestess Marmaran whispered into the darkness. "His corruption began long ago. Remain diligent, for worse is yet to come."

Zhava shifted uncomfortably. She much preferred her friends' encouragement over Priestess Marmaran's warning.

# CHAPTER 15

Zhava awoke the next morning shivering, stiff, and aching in her hips, arms, and legs. The cell's floor was packed-hard earth, and the stone walls seemed to leach away any bit of warmth that might be in the room. She huddled even tighter on the floor and called forth a bundle of little flames. They danced before her, and she waved her arms through the air to dispel the chill. Within moments, they had warmed the room enough for her to slowly stretch, stand, and begin to work out the kinks from her aching body.

She had no time to get comfortable, though, as the guards bustled down the hallway, and she waved away the flames. The key slid in the door, the bolt clanked as it slid out of place, and the door released a heavy moan as it swung open.

"Out," the guard said.

She left the cell. The guard shoved her in the back, and she walked swiftly forward. Without another word, they left the long hallway and went outside to the pre-dawn glow. Three more soldiers joined the procession as they walked the near-empty Hibaro grounds, entered the Tower, and climbed the stairs all the way to the top floor and the little foyer outside High Priest Viekosh's private room.

The guards opened the doors, pushed her forward, and shoved her into the single chair, which sat in the center of the room. High Priest Viekoosh sat behind that expansive desk of his, leaning back in his chair and resting his chin in the palm of one hand. He leisurely tapped one finger against his cheek as he stared at Zhava.

"Sir," one of the guards said with a salute.

"Dismissed," Viekoosh said.

"Sir?"

"Dismissed." He waved a hand through the air without even looking at them.

"Yes, Sir. We'll be just outside, Sir."

"This won't take long."

The soldiers saluted again, backed out of the room, and gently shut the door behind them.

High Priest Viekoosh smiled at Zhava as he sat in his chair and stared at her.

She smiled back. Then she glanced at the floor. Then back to the High Priest, who was still smiling at her, then she looked out the open doors behind him and to the morning glow shining on the balcony beyond. She turned to stare at the books on the shelves. At the floor again. Back to him, and he was still smiling at her.

"Sir?" she asked.

"You think you're not in trouble?"

Her smile began to fade.

"You left the Hibaro campus grounds."

"Yes, Sir, but-"

"You snuck past the guards."

"No, Sir, I didn't-"

"You met someone in the woods-"

"Please, Sir, that's not-"

"-who killed a fellow Initiate-"

"-the way it happened, Sir."

"-and then you were caught before you could escape."

She stared at him. A chill ran down her spine. He had already decided her fate.

"I should throw you back in prison for the rest of your life," he whispered. "You were Liori's little pet...and see what you've become."

A tear ran down Zhava's cheek. Sister Tegara had believed her; Barae had been there for her. How could she make High Priest Viekoosh understand? Make him see the truth?

"All that power," he continued. "And for what? You're meek, and it's all…wasted."

"Sir, you don't understand-"

"I do. I really do. And that's why I won't be throwing you into prison today."

Zhava gasped, and she hadn't even realized she'd been holding her breath.

"No, it won't be prison. I'm going to return you to Ooleng."

She sat there, her mouth open as she tried to think of any response.

"That was his name, yes? Ooleng? Your betrothed from across the Purneese Mountains? I read it in Io Liori's report, that you were about to be married when she intervened. That Ooleng came from a family of mountain traders, that the whole family was there to collect you and take you back over the Purneese. That Priestess Marmaran had been instructing you on how to be a good and propoer wife. Yes?"

She slowly nodded. Ooleng? After all she had done? After all she had learned? To be cast back to Ooleng? It didn't seem fair. It wasn't right.

"So there we are." He nodded and leaned forward, steepling his fingers on the desk. "The reports are clear about what you've done."

"But, Sir-"

He slammed his hand on the desk, and Zhava jerked back in her chair. She dropped her gaze to the floor and sat there with her hands in her lap.

"Do not interrupt me again," he said with a snarl. "I've been patient with you up to now, but I am done with that. I am done with you. I know what happened in the woods last night – I've read the reports. I've interviewed every soldier out there. You should be thankful I'm letting you live."

Zhava wanted to cry out. She wanted to scream with everything inside her that he had it wrong, that the soldiers were mistaken, that she had been fighting for her life out there.

"It is a mercy for me to send you away, to allow you to live out the rest of your days with your husband and his family – and you should thank me for that!"

Zhava clenched her jaw. No matter what happened, she would never thank anyone for sending her off to be Ooleng's wife.

"The guards will escort you back to that little village of yours, and they will find a guide to take you the rest of the way into the Purneese. That is all."

He sat back in his chair again and stared at her some more.

"Well?" he asked. "Have you nothing to say?"

Through blurry, tear-streaked eyes, she glanced up at him. What could she say? What would he hear that would persuade him to change his mind? To understand the truth?

"I didn't think so," he finally muttered. "I spare your life – though you should rot in a cell or be thrown to the wild beasts – and you can't even show enough decency for a proper 'Thank you.' A show of respect before you're allowed to return home...in disgrace, but with your life. What you did...." He shook his head.

Zhava squeezed her eyes shut. It was over. The life she had dreamed for one brief moment could be hers...and it was over. She hadn't wanted to hear Priestess Marmaran's warning last night that the worst was still to come, but it had been true.

"Very well," High Priest Viekoosh said with a sigh. "I'm sending you away now. Guards."

She sat in her chair, numb, and clenched her fists to her eyes. This was far worse than if she had simply left with Ooleng that first morning. To be saved from a life of servitude and shown another way to live – a way to make something more of herself, a way to have friends who loved her and wanted the best for her...only to be cast back out into that other life again. It was more cruel this way, and she wondered which of the Gods she had offended to be so cursed.

"Guards!" Viekoosh yelled again, and Zhava started at the yell.

The doors swung open, but no one entered the room. There was a thud as something struck the heavy desk, and High Priest Viekoosh cursed in pain. Zhava opened her eyes to see him standing behind his desk and rubbing at his leg, his face pinched and his mouth stretched tight.

"Salient," Viekoosh muttered as he unsteadily pushed back his chair. "Welcome."

Zhava turned to see an old woman with a cane slowly hobble into the room. She was dressed in flowing, brown robes with a hood flopped behind her head. She swiped at her face and – just as Zhava had done – made the dirt and grime fall away. One eye was clouded over, but the other one looked bright and alert, the blue/gray shining knowingly from between the lines and wrinkles.

"Welcome," Viekoosh repeated as he gently put pressure on his foot and limped from behind the desk.

"Is this the girl?" the Salient asked as she walked past Zhava seated in the chair.

"Yes, Salient Noomira," came another voice – a friendly voice. The voice of Zhava's Mentor, Io Kua. She turned and smiled at him, relief flooding through her.

High Priest Viekoosh clenched his jaw as he glanced at Kua standing in the doorway, then he turned to Salient Noomira and said, "I wasn't expecting you until much later tonight."

"Obviously," she said. She stamped the cane against the floor with a loud crack that made everyone in the room jump. "High Priest, you are dismissed."

"Yes, Salient." He edged out from behind the desk and limped out, taking a moment to glare at Zhava as he went.

"Io Kua," the Salient said, "you may leave also."

"Yes, Salient." He bowed.

"But remain just outside. See that we are not disturbed. This will take a long time."

"Of course, Salient."

Zhava wiped away the tears on the sleeve of her shirt. Io Kua winked at her as he turned to leave, then slowly shut the doors behind him.

The woman shuffled behind the desk and flopped into the large chair with a heavy sigh. She was far too small for that chair, and she looked like a child sitting in it. She studied Zhava for a moment, then braced the cane against the desk and leaned forward.

"Are you in love with Io Kua?" she asked.

"What? No, Sir," Zhava blurted. She sat back in her chair and crossed her arms. How dare this woman think that – how dare she speak the thought aloud.

"Good," she said. She nodded and glanced at the few papers and scrolls scattered across High Priest Viekoosh's desk. "His urgency at bringing me here, it made me wonder at certain...motivations, possible reasons. I do not like to be rushed. I do not like to rush, and this young Io, with such a fire in his belly, he rushed me here."

"I'm sorry," Zhava said.

"Hah! That is funny. You are sorry. Yes, we will see just how sorry you are. I spoke with the guards. I spoke with your friend Barae. And, of course, Io Kua spoke with me most of the way here, though his words were disjointed and uninformed. He seemed to have the least of importance to say, yet he was the one most passionate to bring me here. To meet you. To investigate this incident." She stared at Zhava.

Zhava shifted in her chair. Should she say something more? Should she apologize for putting this woman through so much discomfort?

"The truth," the woman finally said. "Did you kill Plishka?"

"No. I–"

"But you did not like her."

"No, I liked her. I mean...I didn't dislike her. It was really hard to be friends–"

"What do you know of Salients?"

Zhava did not like being interrupted, and she wanted to be able to finish saying one thing before she had to say something else. She pursed her lips. She could keep talking about Plishka, or she could answer this latest question.

"Very little," she said, deciding to go where this woman took the conversation. "Io Liori said she's a Salient–"

"She is First of the King's Third Salient, yes."

"Um...yes. So she's–"

"I understand. You know nothing." She leaned back, and the bulk of the chair's stained wood seemed to swallow the small woman. "Come around. Come here."

Zhava went around the large desk, and Salient Noomira shifted in the chair to face her. This close, the woman's one clouded eye looked menacing, especially paired next to the intense, icy gaze of her good, blue/gray eye.

"Those who are of the Third Salient, such as your Io Liori, are warriors of the battlefield – the best warriors in the land. The Second Salient are warriors of the forum. Their weapons are rhetoric and reason, and we employ them when it is best to avoid the battlefield. People are trained for many seasons before they are allowed into the ranks of either the Second or Third Salient." She sat up a little straighter. "I, however, am Second of the King's First Salient. The First Salient cannot be trained – we are born. We are the warriors of the mind."

Zhava shifted slightly back from Salient Noomira. She wasn't sure what a warrior of the mind did, but it didn't sound good.

"We investigate the truth. We uncover the lies. We expose the crimes that people seek to hide. That is why Io Kua brought me here with such urgency – and that is why I must do this." She flung herself forward and gripped Zhava's head–

–*and Zhava found herself standing in the dark outside the Tower. The sky was clear, and a chill had begun to roll in. The quarter-moon was rising in the sky, painting the ground and the nearby trees in a blue-white glow. Zhava tried to move, but she couldn't. She stood stiff as a rock, her body in mid-stride.*

"No!" she screamed, and her voice echoed through the darkness.

"Quietly," Salient Noomira said. *She stepped up to Zhava and looked around. Though the voice was unmistakably the Salient, her body was young and healthy, her blond hair long and braided down her back, and her brown robes flowing elegantly behind her. She turned to Zhava with two good eyes, studying Zhava as if she were a wild animal in a field.* –This is your memory, but I am in control. We shall see what you really know. So, why are you here, just outside the Tower?–

"The note," Zhava said. "I got Plishka's note."

Salient Noomira leaned down to study Zhava's hands. "Yes, now I see it. And who gave you this note?"

"Brother Tymare."

"Oh." She stood up straight and smiled. "I have not seen Brother Tymare in several seasons."

Salient Noomira waved a hand in the air, and Zhava felt herself pulled backward. Still facing forward, she reached back and caught the door to the Tower just before it had shut. She walked backward, the door swinging at her as she stepped through the door frame, back through the tables of people studying. She turned around and faced Brother Tymare, his smile beaming on his face – and then she stopped.

Salient Noomira stepped forward and looked at the slip of paper in Zhava's hand.

"Valuable," she said. "Why waste such valuable paper on a note such as this? 'I want that book. Bring it to the Sparring Grounds.' Interesting."

Salient Noomira waved a hand through the air, and Zhava was pulled forward again. She folded the paper. Brother Tymare wished her a good night. She walked back outside, turned, and started down the path to the Sparring Grounds.

"Where are the guards?" Salient Noomira asked.

Zhava stopped, frozen again in mid-stride. She hated being out of control, and she fought to move, to step forward or backward. To do anything!

"The more you struggle," Noomira said as she stepped forward, "the more exhausted you will become. I know this is hard, but do not fight me." She stepped off the path and into the treeline. She waved her arms through the air, and a soldier, standing still as a statue, glowed a bright yellow. He was crouching behind a tree and watching Zhava.

"Who is that?" Zhava asked, suddenly afraid. She wasn't sure why, but the thought of a soldier secretly watching her made her even more frightened than what Salient Noomira was doing to her.

"One of the guards. Hiding." She turned and walked toward the other side of the trail. She waved her arms through the air again, and another soldier shown bright yellow, this one leaning in the crook of an old tree and watching Zhava.

"How are you doing this?" Zhava asked. "How did you see those men?"

"I did not see them," she whispered. "You saw them. You saw everything, but you failed to notice. That is why I am here, to notice. To record. To investigate and uncover the truth. And there is a truth being kept well hidden. We will continue."

They walked on through the woods. Salient Noomira found three more soldiers hiding along the pathway, two in the brush and another stationed with a bow high in a tree. They reached the clearing, Zhava called out to Plishka, she read the note again, and then she turned to go back to the Hibaro. The man in the black robes stepped onto the path, his body glowing yellow like the hidden guards, and everything froze again. Zhava shivered as she stared at the man. She had been scared when he first appeared, and for good reason. He had meant to surprise her, to frighten her.

Salient Noomira walked slowly forward. She cocked her head to the side as she approached the frozen man. She leaned in close to his face. She sniffed his robes. "This one is dangerous," she said. "And proud. He wanted this moment with you. Why? What are you to him?"

She put her hand in the air and slowly rotated a finger. The moment went on far longer than Zhava cared to relive. Slowly, ever so slowly, she spoke to the man, told him about a friend waiting in the woods, asked him if he had seen her. With an agonizingly slow turn, the shadowed man looked into the woods, and Salient Noomira stopped rotating her finger. She looked into the woods. She stepped into the woods. She raised her arms and looked around. Finally, she returned to the path.

"What is he doing?" she whispered. "Who is out there with him?"

She raised her hand again, and the giant, glowing bird slowly emerged from the trees. Again, Noomira stopped the memory. She walked up to the bird, her eyebrows raised and her mouth open.

"A sengret?" she said.

"What is it?"

"A bird out of legend. They were hunted to extinction in the mountains long ago, long before any of us was ever born. These birds would actually hunt us down and steal our children, taking them as food for their young at the nest." She turned back to the shadowed man. "And he has found one? Trained one? But...how?"

Salient Noomira allowed the memory to continue, and Zhava ached at what was to come. She sliced at the bird's leg, fell to the ground, rolled and lost her balance. She used her Ability with the wind, but the robed man brushed it aside.

*She began calling her flames, but the bird knocked her to the ground again, and the man knelt on her back. Her spoke to her, he called her by name.*

"Yes, this was personal for him," Salient Noomira muttered. "Why?"

*The robed man began speaking of power, of how she had too much power, of how they all had too much power.*

*"You're all too powerful," the robed man said. "And too weak to harness that power. Then shall the world be purged of the meekly powerful, and only then shall the rightful heirs inherit the land."*

"He quotes Coredor," Salient Noomira said. "That could be useful."

*Zhava pulled her flames to her, let them loose upon the Sparring Grounds, and the robed man went flying off of her. She rolled over, and* Salient Noomira stopped the memory again. *Zhava lay painfully upon the ground, her back aching and her chest desperate for a breath of air.* Instead, however, Noomira stood gaping at the forest around them.

*Zhava's little flames were everywhere. They were scattered on the wind, they were flying into the trees, they were racing along the ground – several even clung to the robed man's leg as he tumbled through the air and back into the woods.*

Salient Noomira turned to stare at Zhava. "Who taught you this?"

"No one."

"Not Priestess Marmaran?"

"I hid this from her. She did not know." That thought hurt. If Priestess Marmaran was alive now, Zhava would proudly show off her little flames, and Marmaran would probably laugh and smile and praise Zhava for such a wonderful Ability.

Salient Noomira stepped closer and studied Zhava, then waved a hand through the air to let the memory continue. *The man stumbled away and into the treeline while Zhava retrieved her sword. She turned back to the circle and looked around. Plishka burst from the treeline, yelled Zhava's name, and knocked her to the ground.*

*"Get down. You're not safe. He's still out there!"*

*"Who is he?" Zhava asked.*

*The sengret dove into the clearing, wrapped its talons around Plishka's body, and rose into the sky.*

"No!" Zhava yelled. Reliving the memory like this was somehow worse than the first time. She knew what would happen, but she was powerless to stop it. At least the first time she had fought to do something. This time she could do nothing but watch, her body reliving the unchanging actions, her mouth saying the unchanging words.

The soldiers ran down the path and surrounded Zhava. Several of them went off into the woods to search while the Ios stepped up to Zhava. As the Io man in charge opened his mouth to speak, the memory stopped again.

"I've seen enough of this," Noomira said, her hand waving in the air. "The note you received. Why did you believe Plishka sent it?"

"She knocked the books to the floor. I found the one she missed, the one about Coredor."

"Take me to that memory," she said, and she snapped her fingers.

Instantly, they were in the second floor of the Tower collections. Zhava lay on the floor cradling her elbow. Plishka stood above her, the blue sparks lighting the air and disintegrating the sconce rod.

"Another unique ability," Noomira muttered, her eyes squinting at Plishka. "Interesting that you two should meet. Truly a shame that one of you died."

Plishka yelled at Zhava, scooped up her books, and stormed from the room. Noomira walked over to the wall and glanced at the little book on the floor, which Zhava had not even noticed the first time she lived this event. The old man helped Zhava stand. Zhava went downstairs, got another sconce rod, went outside to light it, went back upstairs, lit the remaining ceiling sconces, and then found the book lying on the floor.

"Plishka is not here," Noomira said, stopping the memory again.

"No. She had left."

Noomira walked around the tables of the second floor collections room, glancing down the rows of shelves. "Everyone has left. This room is now empty."

Zhava hadn't even noticed the room was empty when she'd lit the remaining sconces. She had a job to do, and she was focused on doing it. Brother Tymare would expect the sconces lit whether anyone was using the room or not. He was adamant that the collections room be ready for anyone to use at any time.

"So who saw you retrieve that book? Who knew you did that?" Noomira asked. She waved her hand in the air, the memory continued, and Zhava leaned out the window. Noomira stopped the memory. "What are you doing now?"

"I thought Plishka might still be nearby."

Noomira stepped up behind Zhava and looked over her shoulder. The grounds beneath the Tower were empty. A light wind was blowing a couple leaves across the ground. The treeline was dark, several branches swaying in the breeze.

"There," Noomira said, pointing.

A yellow glow formed just behind one tree. The robed man was leaning out and staring at Zhava in the tower. Though she couldn't move within the memory, she felt a shiver of fear at seeing the man there. How long had he been watching her? Why was he watching her?

"He followed you," Noomira said, stepping back from the window. "Why? Who are you, and why does he care so much about you?"

"I'm nobody," Zhava said, still staring at the glowing man outside. She wished the Salient would release this memory to continue. She didn't like standing there, leaning out the window as he watched her, studied her.

"Take me to your home," Salient Noomira said with a snap of her fingers.

Instantly, Zhava was back home and standing in the kitchen. Mama was at the cookstove and preparing a meal.

"No," Noomira said, and snapped her fingers again.

Zhava ran through a muddy field, a cloth bundle dangling from her hand. Papa stood in the field, wiping his forehead as he watched her carry the mid-day meal to him.

"No." Another snap of the fingers.

She peaked around the curtain and watched her three brothers playing a game of dice in her home's center courtyard.

"No." Finger-snap.

Zhava's vision blurred. The room was bright, and the lights hurt her eyes. There was crying in the room, a person was crying. But it was more than one person; it was two people, and one of them was a child, an infant. The shrill cry stung at Zhava's ears, and she shook her head. She reached up with one fist and stabbed at her eyes, trying to clear them, and she realized the cry was coming from her own mouth. That she was the screaming infant. She was being held in someone's arms, and she was crying. She was unhappy and she was scared and *she didn't like the bright light and she wanted her mother to comfort her...but her mother was crying. Her mother held her tightly, and she was crying. Zhava didn't like her mother crying, but she didn't know what to do, she didn't know what was wrong. Something was wrong, and Zhava just wanted it all to stop. She wanted to go back to her nice warm blanket and be held. She wanted to be wrapped up in her mother's arms and be held and carried and have someone coo at her and come near and...*

*...her mother seemed to know what she wanted because her mother leaned in close. She leaned down, and her mother's face became more than a large shape hovering above her. Her mother gently brushed at the little shock of hair on Zhava's forehead, and she cooed at Zhava, even through the tears her mother cooed at her and rocked her and told her everything would be all right, that it was all for the best and that Zhava would be safe and to know that Mama loved her. And then Mama came even nearer. She bent down to snuggle with Zhava, to embrace her tightly, and Zhava felt so much better. She still cried, but she loved the embrace. She loved her Mama's warmth and her Mama's gentle touch and her Mama's soft kiss upon her brow. And as Mama leaned back, Zhava turned to stare into those loving eyes...and she realized this woman was not her Mama.*

"There it is," Salient Noomira said.

*The face above Zhava came into sharper focus for a tiny moment, and she saw the woman more clearly. She felt it, deep down within her, that this was her Mama, but this woman looked nothing like the woman who raised her. She knew it within her very being that this woman had been with her since long before she was born, that she had heard this woman singing to her in the swimming darkness, but this woman was not the same Mama who had raised her. Who was she? Who was this woman who birthed Zhava?*

"That is the memory I wanted," Noomira whispered. "Oh yes, things are much clearer now."

# CHAPTER 16

Zhava slipped to the floor. She saw the room for just a moment before it all seemed to slide away, then slip upside-down, and the next thing she realized she was lying with her face pressed to the polished wood and staring into the distance. Her stomach lurched within her, and she pressed one hand firmly against her mouth, trying to stop everything from coming back up. She coughed, and her vision began blurring at the edges, a fuzzy blackness slowly folding inward.

"Io Kua," Salient Noomira called, and her voice seemed to echo through Zhava's mind.

The sound of the doors swinging open was like the sound of water dumping over her head, and Zhava shut her eyes. She tried to take a deep breath, but her stomach rebelled against it, and she fought again to keep from vomiting.

"The supplies," Noomira said. "Get out a warm blanket and some water."

Even with her eyes shut, Zhava felt the room spinning again. Footsteps thundered through the wooden floor. Noomira banged her cane against the desk, and Zhava thought her ears would explode from the noise. People began talking, what sounded like hundreds of people in the tiny space of this dark, noisy room, and all Zhava could think was that she wanted it all to end.

A blanket was spread across her, and Zhava opened her eyes to see Io Kua kneeling at her side. He reached one hand beneath her head and slowly, gently slipped a woolen cloth beneath to prop her up.

"It's normal," Kua whispered. "I've seen this before, and it will pass momentarily – although, you were both gone a really long time."

She squinted past him, her eyes blinking rapidly, and looked out the doors and onto the patio beyond. It was filled with bright sunshine that hurt to see, and she quickly rolled her head away. Kua leaned forward, blocking out the rest of the light. He pressed a cup to her lips, and she gratefully sipped at the cool water.

"The dizziness should have passed by now," he whispered.

She nodded. The room had stopped spinning.

"The nausea will take a little longer."

"How long?" she asked between sips.

"Soon," he said. "You'll feel better soon."

She shook her head, and her stomach twitched at the movement. She shut her eyes and let the wave of nausea pass her by, then asked, "How long were we gone?"

"Oh." He turned to glance out the open doors, then back to her and smiled. "It's well past midday. I sent a message to your friend, Barae, to come and take you to your evening meal."

"Thank you." She turned from his face to the ceiling and then the wall of books. The room had stopped its spinning. She coughed, and her stomach did not rebel at the movement, so she sat up and looked around. Io Kua was kneeling beside her, and Salient Noomira was writing on a parchment spread across the desk. She didn't know if all the people she'd heard had really been there and gone, or if she had simply imagined the conversations. She reached for the desk, but her hand shook.

"Do you want to stand?" Kua asked.

But the memory came back to her in an instant – of that other woman, of her birth mama, the woman who had been crying over her as an infant.

"Who was she?" Zhava asked.

Noomira waved a hand through the air and continued writing.

"Salient Noomira, you must tell me," Zhava said. She struggled to sit up, leaning into Kua's helping hands.

"I mustn't do anything," Noomira muttered. "Except we have a conspiracy to stop and a killer to catch. You are dismissed."

"No!" Zhava wrenched her hand from Kua's grip, leaned against the desk, and struggled to stand up straight. "You saw that woman. You know who she is."

"Kua," Salient Noomira said with a sigh. "Get her out of here."

"I apologize for her behavior," Kua said with a quick bow. "She is exhausted and distraught." He wrapped his arms around her shoulders and gripped her tightly, turning her from the desk and leading her away.

Anger flared within Zhava. She wasn't some unruly child to be taken away. Salient Noomira had uncovered something important – there was a truth to be learned. She had to know more about her past. She had to know the identity of the woman who had held her as an infant. Without even realizing she was doing it, she began calling forth her flames, willing them to herself and instructing them to –

"I know what you're doing," Salient Noomira said. She glanced up with her one good eye. "I feel the power answering your call."

Zhava ducked her head and fought to control her temper. Kua glanced back and forth between the two women.

"Focus," Noomira said. "We have a killer to catch. All other considerations – including the identity of your mother – must come later."

"You will not forget?" Zhava turned and stared at Noomira, waited to see how she would react – and she saw anger rise in the hard set of the woman's jaw.

"I am Second of the King's First Salient. I do not forget."

\*\*\*

When Io Kua led Zhava from the office, Barae and Posef were waiting for her. She hugged them both, then they helped her navigate the nine flights of stairs back down. Zhava was exhausted by the time they reached the bottom and went outside, and she sat in the grass and leaned against the side of the building for a long time, simply breathing and enjoying the late-afternoon sun and gentle breeze. Posef ran off to do something – Zhava didn't pay attention to where or what – while Barae sat beside her on the ground and held her hand. Surprisingly, Barae remained mostly quiet, choosing instead to gently squeeze Zhava's hand at regular intervals, a silent show of love and support from one friend to another.

When Posef returned some time later, he was carrying a large, closed bucket with a handle, three small bowls, and three spoons. He grinned.

"Hungry?" he asked.

Zhava hadn't realized how hungry she was until Posef sat and spooned out a large bowl of soup and set it in her lap. She devoured the steaming soup before Barae and Posef had even begun eating theirs, and then she sat back and gripped her stomach. The broth was hot, and the barley and chicken were filling. She had definitely eaten too quickly.

"Were you scared?" Posef asked between bites.

"High Priest Viekoosh was going to send me back home to marry," Zhava whispered.

"What?" Barae said, chinking her spoon against the side of her bowl. "Why? You didn't do anything."

"I don't know." She shook her head. That had been scary, when he wouldn't listen to her, when he had already made up his mind what to do with her. She shivered.

"Io Kua brought that old woman to talk to you," Barae said. "Who was she?"

"Salient Noomira."

Posef's eyes grew huge, and he stared at Zhava. "She's here? And you met her?"

Zhava nodded. "She went inside my mind. It was...awful."

"I've heard about her – she's amazing," Posef said, grinning as he set down his bowl. "She's Second of the King's First Salient. Did you know that?"

"Yes," Zhava said with another nod. "I met her."

"Did you know the King has only three First Salients? They can't be trained. They have to be born, and a new one is usually only born once every dozen seasons. Except now we haven't had a new First Salient born in almost 20 seasons, and Salient Noomira is so old that nobody knows how much longer she'll be around to help the King."

Zhava shut her eyes and leaned back against the stone wall of the Tower. Barae took her hand again and squeezed, and Zhava smiled at the contact. Posef kept talking, but she gave him only a bit of her attention as she rested in the late afternoon sun. She felt better after the food and some time to recover. She didn't know how Salient Noomira could do that and not be affected by it. Zhava felt as if she'd been dragged through the sand behind a camel.

"Zhava?" Barae said, squeezing her hand again. "It's time to wake up."

Zhava opened her eyes. She couldn't believe it – the sun was just setting. "What?" she asked, shifting uncomfortably against the stone wall. "I...fell asleep?" Posef was gone. The Hibaro grounds were nearly empty, and a loud buzz of conversations emanated from the dining hall. She yawned. "I wasn't trying to sleep. I didn't realize I fell asleep."

"You were exhausted." Barae smiled and stood up. She offered Zhava a hand. "Let's get you home."

Zhava stood, and the two women ambled across the Hibaro grounds. Zhava's head no longer hurt, but her body tingled all over, and the chill of the evening air made the hairs on arms stand on end. She crossed her arms and shivered.

"You fell asleep just as Posef started talking about Salient Noomira."

"I hope he wasn't offended."

"Hah! He didn't even notice. He talked about her for a really long time. She solved a murder somewhere. She found some guy the King wanted brought to him. She traveled to the highlands and discovered the truth about some middin that had collapsed. He talked so long that his soup got cold, and that's when I told him it was probably best to leave us alone so you could rest."

"That was very kind of you, but you didn't have to stay."

"Sister Tegara gave me special dispensation for the day. Io Kua told her the Salient was interviewing you, so Tegara said to get you whatever you needed. You looked like you needed rest, so I stayed and let you rest."

Zhava smiled and leaned into Barae. "You're wonderful," she whispered. "I've never had a friend like you."

Barae wove her arm around Zhava's, and the two of them walked together, arm-in-arm and in silence the rest of the way to the Initiate

House. People were going about their business across the Hibaro grounds, and no one looked at Zhava. She wasn't sure if that was because they thought she was a killer or because they knew she was innocent...or because they simply did not give her any attention as she went along with her friend. Whatever the reason, she was glad people were ignoring her again, especially when just last night they had been saying the worst possible things about her. She couldn't believe anyone actually thought she would hurt Plishka. But, many people were scared. People seemed more willing to believe crazy stories when they were scared, especially if those stories made them feel better. It was crazy to believe that Zhava was the killer who had been taking people from the Hibaro the past several moons when she had only just arrived a couple weeks earlier – but as crazy as that sounded, everyone just wanted the killer caught.

By the time they arrived at the front door of the Initiate House, the sun was nearly set, and many people were preparing for rest. They walked through the long hallway and the bustling of a few people still getting work done, and they stopped outside Barae's door.

"Thank you for being with me today," Zhava said with a shiver.

"It's going to be all right," Barae said. She leaned forward and gave Zhava a big hug. "From what Posef said, Salient Noomira will figure it all out. Just rest."

Zhava smiled and wished her friend a good night, then went upstairs to her own room. She fumbled in her skirt pockets for the key, but she couldn't find it. She had no idea where she might have dropped it. Her hand wrapped around a small scroll tied to the inside of her pocket, and she pulled it out. It was Plishka's scroll, the one she had dropped in the Tower. Zhava felt a tear edge at the corner of her eye, and she blinked it away. Plishka may have been hard to know, but there were times when she had been nice. And in the end, she had given her life to protect Zhava. That was what she would remember, that last act of kindness.

She clutched the little scroll tightly and reached for the door handle. It opened, and she was thankful someone had thought to leave it for her. The room was dark with the shutters closed, so she left the door swung open and moved slowly forward, remembering the little table that had cracked her in the leg. She edged around it and toward the shutters, and the light in the room began to dim – the door was swinging shut again. She turned around just as it latched into place, and a shadow darted across the room, pounded into her, and slammed her against the wall.

Zhava started to scream, but someone clamped a hand across her mouth. The shadow pressed against her, pinning her in place, and the shadow leaned in near Zhava's face.

"I should kill you now for what you did," the shadow whispered – and it was the voice of a woman.

Zhava was too stunned to do anything more. The shadow killer was a woman? But...Salient Noomira had said the killer was a man.

The shadow's other arm came forward, and a small blade glittered in the air. The shadow pressed the blade to Zhava's throat.

"I thought you were her friend – her friend!" the shadow hissed.

Blue sparks began sputtering from the hand that held the short sword. They crackled between the woman's knuckles, wound their way between her fingers, and arched across the back of her hand. The blue lightning flashed brilliantly in the dark room, and Zhava recognized the sword – it was Zhava's own Felton sword, the one Kua had given her.

"I give you one chance," the shadow woman said, leaning back. "Give me the name of the man in the woods, and tell me where I can find him."

The blue lightning flashed between them, lighting up the shadow woman's face as she eased her hand away from Zhava's mouth – and Zhava gasped.

"Plishka, you're...alive?"

# CHAPTER 17

"Tell me!" Plishka hissed. "His name – who is he?"

"I don't know. He never took off his hood."

Plishka raised her hand, edging the sword closer to Zhava's throat, and she squinted into Zhava's eyes. "You called my name in the woods. Why?"

Zhava quickly explained about the note, the hidden guards, the man waiting for her – how it had all been a trap to lure her out there by herself.

"And last night?" Plishka asked. "You never returned here. Where were you?"

So she quickly told about the prison cell, Salient Noomira, and then how Posef and Barae had brought her dinner and helped her back to her room. Plishka's shoulders slumped, and she lowered the sword, staring at the floor. Zhava carefully edged out of her grip, called a little flame to her hand, and let it loose to run to the oil lamp sitting on the table. He climbed up to the wick and set it afire, then he disappeared in a wisp of smoke. The room brightened as the lamp's light glowed brightly on the table.

"What was that thing?" Plishka asked, pointing where the flame had been.

"A friend. My only friend for a while, besides Priestess Marmaran."

Plishka tossed the sword to the bed and collapsed to the floor without another word. She stared at her hands as the lightning slowly ebbed away. She was dressed in a woolen coat that bunched around her on the floor. Small branches and a few leaves were stuck to the cloak, and Zhava saw more twigs, dirt, and leaves scattered around her small room.

"What about you?" Zhava asked. "How did you escape?"

"I didn't." She hiccupped and turned her face toward Zhava. Tears were streaming down her cheeks.

Zhava reached for a towel from the table and knelt at Plishka's side. She handed it over, and Plishka wiped the tears and dirt from her face.

"That...bird never took me. It took my sister."

Zhava sat beside her, stunned. She tried to process, tried to understand. She had only ever known Plishka, and no one had said anything about Plishka having a sister.

"Vinaara," Plishka said. "It means 'second joy.'" She wiped at her face again and put her head up, staring at the wall. "And that's what she is – a joy. She is the most loving, giving person I have ever met, and she makes me so angry with that incessant joy of hers. And she's everyone's friend." She suddenly turned to Zhava. "She was your friend, and she didn't even know you. You arrived, and all Vinaara could say was, 'Zhava is really nice' and 'Zhava is really brave' and 'Zhava and I got along great.' I wanted to hit you before I even met you."

"But...." Zhava squeezed her eyes shut, trying to understand. "Vinaara is...?"

"My sister – my twin. She was born just moments after me." She smiled as she told the story. "My mother didn't know we were twins. The midwife didn't know. Vinaara had fooled everyone. But she was born so tiny, my mother said. I was strong and healthy, and I grew immediately, but Vinaara almost didn't make it to her first moon. Mother said she coughed and cried through the nights, and she wouldn't put on any weight. Mother said that every night for six moons she knelt at the cradle and said a Leaving Prayer over Vinaara, expecting her to be gone by morning, but every night Vinaara stayed with us. She had a will to live, and that came on stronger as the seasons went by. When she got older, she ran everywhere and climbed everything and did anything anyone ever asked her to do no matter how hard it was." She sighed and swiped at another tear threatening to roll down her cheek, pursed her lips, and continued. "And the Hibaro wouldn't take her. They wouldn't even accept her as a Candidate." That was said with a bite of anger. "She never displayed any Abilities at all...ever. That was me." She waved her hand through the air and let the blue sparks dance across her knuckles. "They have to see something inside you, within your eyes, or see you do something extraordinary, before they'll even allow you on the Hibaro grounds. I'm blessed by the Gods, but Vinaara...she's just Vinaara."

"So why was she here? She had a job, and she was being trained with me – or was that you?"

"No. Her," Plishka said, turning and staring at Zhava. "I would do anything for her. There was nothing for her at home – I couldn't just leave her there."

"But...your mother and father? What did they say?"

"Oh, you don't know. They died a couple seasons back. Vinaara and I were homeless and begging for food in the village square when one of the Hibaro priests found us."

Zhava gasped. She had heard of the hard life that some people experienced when they were forced to a life of begging, but she had never before met someone who had done it.

"We found a small cave here, down by the stream, and we took turns living at the Hibaro and then living in the cave," Plishka continued, watching the blue lightning dance across her hand. "I would do the philosophies and attend the training sessions that required my Abilities, and she would do the body training, all the running and fighting and whatever else she could do that didn't require any of my Abilities. If one of us was surprised by a teacher, if someone asked her to produce lightning, or if someone asked me to run the track 30 times, then we would become suddenly ill." She chuckled. "We are more likely to get sick or to have short-term memory gaps than anyone else on this campus."

Zhava stared at the lightning as Plishka rolled her fingers and twisted her wrist. It was beautiful as it crackled and popped across her skin.

"It's really quite unfair, actually," Plishka whispered. "Vinaara worked twice as hard here as I did, but nobody cared about that – none of the priests or the Ios or the soldiers. All they cared about was my lightning."

"That's not true," Zhava said. "Salient Noomira said it was sad you died because...." Zhava's voice trailed off as the memory fully returned. Salient Noomira had not expressed any remorse that Plishka was gone, only that it was a loss of someone with great powers.

In the silence, Plishka gave a slight smile – a sad smile that didn't extend to her eyes. "You don't have to say it. I know."

What could Zhava say? Plishka already knew the truth. A "unique Ability" was all the Salient had said about Plishka when she unleashed her lightning on the sconce rod in the tower. And when Plishka – actually, it was Plishka's sister, Vinaara – was taken by the sengret in the woods, the Salient had simply said, "I've seen enough of this." Zhava thought back to those three Ios who had questioned her, and she remembered the one man did not even know who Plishka was. He had to ask the other Ios, and one of them said, "Second-year Initiate. Uneven temperament. Uneven Abilities, but she's impressive when she can bring that lightning to surface." They valued Plishka for her Ability, certainly, but they did not seem to value her for much else. What could she say that would make Plishka feel any better?

Zhava rolled the little parchment in her hand and held it out. "I still have this," she said.

Plishka chuckled as she took it. She slid off the tie binding it together and slowly unrolled it. "'Coredor and the Women of Saed,'" Plishka whispered. "Do you know it?"

Zhava shook her head. She knew little of Coredor except that he was a terrible God who had tried once – unsuccessfully, of course – to trick Preizhavan into marrying him.

"It's a terrible story – at least for women like us, the ones with Abilities. Here, read it." She handed over the little scroll again, and Zhava began to read:

*It was about that time that the oceans spat out onto the ground on the Isle of Saed a new life, a baby boy named Tu. Tu arrived fully formed upon the beach, and he immediately set about counting the very sands he found there, for he* determined that the sands upon the shore should be the number of his days, and he wished to live a productive and long life.

But the God Coredor, that rogue of mischief and play, spied young Tu upon the beach counting the sands of his days, and he thought of how he might trick the young boy. While Tu was crawling along the beach and counting the sands of his days, Coredor whispered to the Rascal Fish playing among the shadows, "That young boy thinks those grains of sand are bits of jewels upon the beach, and once he has counted up his riches, he will cart them all away – and then you won't have any more sandy shallows in which to play."

At the thought of a little boy stealing all the sand of their shallows, the Rascal Fish grew angry, as only a disturbed Rascal Fish could do. They asked Coredor, "What can we do? How should we stop him?"

"Oh, there is no stopping him," Coredor said. "The only thing you can do is delay him. Keep him counting for as long as you can, and then you will keep your sand."

This sounded good to the Rascal Fish, and they began shifting the sand. As the tide rose, they gathered the sand along the beach, and as the tide retreated, they washed the sand in their mouths and scattered it farther along the beach. As they remained hiding beneath the waves, the little boy Tu never saw them, and he never realized that they were moving the grains of sand around him. He continued counting the sands of his days, believing that each grain was a new grain he had never before seen, freshly polished as they were from within the mouths of the Rascal Fish. For two dozen seasons this went on, and the boy Tu grew into a fine, young man, full of energy and strength from his long time working on the beach.

It was about this time that a young woman named Re was walking along the beach, and she saw Tu bent over and counting the sands of his days. Re was one of the daughters of men, and as the men of that age had not yet grown into their fullness of time, she, too, was tiny and weak and unable to take care of herself for very long. When she saw Tu, however, she was both scared and intrigued by his strength, for she had never before seen a man like him, one gifted to the shores by the Gods. However, Re had the Ability, and she could see immediately into the waves that the Rascal Fish were swimming beneath the tide and shifting the sands upon the shore, all the while making Tu's task impossible to complete. She laughed aloud, and Tu heard her, and he stopped his counting to look upon her standing on the beach.

*As Tu had never before seen a woman, for so focused had he been upon his task that he had never before seen anyone, when he looked upon her standing on the beach and watching him work, he immediately fell in love with her.*

*"Do you not see what the Rascal Fish are doing?" she asked, and she pointed into the ocean.*

*The young man Tu, when he turned his gaze upon the waves and saw the Rascal Fish shifting the sands of his days upon the beach, he grew angry. He spoke loudly, and he cursed those fish right there. He said to them, "Long have you toiled to lengthen my days, but so too have you made them impossible to complete. As such, your task shall be without end. From this day forward, you will work the beaches of the world, tilling the sand with each passing wave and depositing it into a new location. But just as there is no end to the sand within the ocean, so too shall there be no end to the labor you are to endure. Furthermore, you shall from this day forward remain invisible to all but the most fervent seekers, forever toiling within the surf but never being seen by anyone who could acknowledge your labor or thank you for the work you do or give you relief from the task you can never complete." Immediately, the Rascal Fish disappeared from sight, and they have been washing and moving the sand upon the beaches of the world ever since, never being noticed or even acknowledged for the tiresome work they do both day and night.*

*The young man Tu thanked the young woman Re for revealing the truth to him, and he kissed her, and he went off with her to her village of men, and the two of them were joined as a couple. Over the next several years, they had several dozen children, all young girls who possessed the Abilities of their mother and the strength and vigor of their father, and both Tu and Re were happy living on the Isle of Saed.*

*At about that time, however, the God Coredor remembered the task he had set for the Rascal Fish, and he wished to see how much torment and agony they had produced for the boy Tu. When he went searching for the Rascal Fish in the evening surf, however, he could not find them, nor could he find Tu upon the beach where he had left him. He searched the Isle of Saed far and wide, and he happened upon the village where Tu and Re were living with their family and their children. Coredor was astounded at discovering Tu had the strength to escape the God's scheme and to curse the Rascal Fish, and when he learned that Re had used her Ability to see the Rascal Fish in the ocean surf, he grew angry. However, when he* saw the daughters on the Isle of Saed, the daughters of Tu and Re, the God Coredor also became afraid.

He said to himself, "These daughters are as beautiful as Re and as strong as Tu – and they have the Gods' own Ability. These children must not be allowed into the world, or they shall multiply and grow even stronger. Someday they might even challenge the Gods themselves."

So Coredor set about scheming how he might stop the daughters of Saed, the children of Tu and Re, from spreading across the world. As he was walking around the village and considering what should be done, he came upon a group of their children, now young women actually, who were working in the stream to clean the family's clothes, beating out the tops and the bottoms of the clothes upon the rocks and letting the stream carry away the dirt. The young women had made a game of their labor, and they were laughing and splashing through the water and chasing each other as only the best of sisters may do.

Coredor hid behind the rushes and cursed the children, saying, "No longer shall your labor be easy and full of joy, but it shall be hard. The work you do shall bring you no joy, and when joy is to be found in the smallest of toil, then shall that labor increase tenfold."

But the God of the stream, Umri, heard this curse upon the young women who were making a game of their labors within his very waters, and he rose up before Coredor. He held his hand out to Coredor and said, "Stop. Why do you make this curse upon the children of Tu and Re?"

"Do you not understand?" the God Coredor said. "Those daughters have the beauty of Re and the strength of Tu – and they have the Gods' own Ability. Surely if we allow them to multiply and to cover the world, they shall become too strong even for the Gods."

"I cannot allow you to take all of their joy," the God Umri said. "As such, I shall bless the children of Tu and Re with an equal measure of success in this life and in the next for every moment of joy you withhold from their labor."

"No!" the God Coredor yelled, and his yelling rattled the reeds and the bushes within the stream's waters. "They are all too powerful!"

"But they are too weak to harness that power," the God Umri declared, and he blessed the daughters of Tu and Re and all of their children forevermore to the same measure that the God Coredor had cursed them.

*The God Coredor grew even angrier at this. He walked along the island until he came upon another group of Tu and Re's children. They were congratulating the eldest daughter, Iure, who was far along in her pregnancy and due to give birth at any moment. The God Coredor hid behind the rocks of this festive gathering, and he cursed the daughters of the Isle of Saed, the children of Tu and Re. He said, "From this day forth shall the daughters of Re experience great pain – and sometimes even death – in childbirth. Their hearts shall yearn for the children they bring forth into the world, but they shall fear for their own lives, always wondering if they will be trading their own life for that of their child."*

*At this, two Goddesses arose at the God Coredor's side. They were Erinian, the Goddess of beauty, and Preizhavan, the Goddess of bounty.*

*"Why do you make this curse upon the daughters of Re?" the Goddesses demanded.*

*"Can you not see?" the God Coredor demanded. "The daughters shall bring forth children of their own who shall inherit the beauty of their mother Re and the strength of their father Tu, and they shall all be born with the Gods' own Ability. Soon they shall band together, and they will threaten even the Gods. We must prevent that."*

*The Goddess Erinian, said, "Your curse is a hard burden upon the daughters of Re on the Isle of Saed – the daughters whom I love. As such, I shall cast a curse upon the sons of the men who walk upon the world. They shall be blinded by the beauty of the daughters of Re that they see before them such that they shall be struck dumb around the women of men, those women who do not carry the Gods' own Ability. In the presence of those women shall the sons of men be unable to think, and they shall act the fools, and the daughters of men will be repulsed by the dumbfounded sons of the men who walk the world such that they will not want to walk with them nor speak with them nor certainly ever fall in love with them until such time as those men fully humiliate themselves before the feet of those daughters of men."*

*"Furthermore," the Goddess Preizhavan said, "when those daughters of Re find their one love, they will carry ten-fold more children within them than any of the daughters of men, such that they shall know the joy of a house full of delighted children long before they reach your cursed end of their days."*

*"No!" yelled the God Coredor. "You cannot curse the children of men, or how shall they multiply upon the world? And you cannot bless the children of Tu*

and Re as you have done. They will wield their beauty before those unwilling to resist, and they shall turn their strength upon the weak until none but those with the Ability shall remain. The Gods must not allow the powerful to rise up from the ashes of such destruction, for then shall those children of Tu and Re bear that destruction upon us all."

But the Goddesses Erinian and Preizhavan would listen to no more of the God Coredor's anger, and they left him alone. So he walked even farther until he came upon a third group of Tu and Re's children, these young women lying upon a hillside and watching the evening sun set. He stood up before them, and he said, "You shall be set upon with swords by the sons of the men of this world. You shall use your father Tu's strength against them, but they shall overwhelm you by numbers. You shall bring forth your Ability upon the land, but the sons of the men of this world will rush over you as a tidal wave shall wash upon this very Isle of Saed."

It was this last curse that finally brought forth the Ruler of the Gods Himself, Vek, who appeared before the God Coredor and said, "Stop. Long have I been patient with you and your foolish curses upon these women of Saed, these daughters of Tu and Re. No more. You say that the sons of the men of this world shall overwhelm these daughters of Saed. I say that those sons of the men of this world shall live their lives in chaos and disorder. They shall band together as one, and then strife shall set them apart. They shall travel the world far and wide, and they shall begin speaking their own languages among themselves, and they shall not understand each other when once again they meet. They shall take offense at the unintelligible ramblings of their fellow men, and they shall set upon each other with their swords and with their clubs long before they ever turn those same swords and clubs upon the daughters of Saed, upon the children of Tu and Re and upon their children's children and on down through the ages. This shall come to pass such that the sons of the men of this world will never gather together to set upon these children of Tu and Re. So shall it end."

"No!" the God Coredor yelled. "They are all too powerful! They are too weak to harness that power, but they shall grow with each generation, and then the Gods will see what shall become of this generation. For then the world shall be purged of the meekly powerful, of those who feign their obedience to us, of those who would speak of devotion in one moment and of blasphemy the next. The world must be purged of the meekly powerful, and only then shall the rightful heirs inherit the land."

But Vek, the Ruler of the Gods, would hear no more of this, and he banished Coredor from ever again harming the women of Saed.

Zhava set the scroll aside and shivered. Not from the chill, for the room had grown quite warm with the light of the lamp and the closed shutters. She shivered from the story she had just read. Priestess Marmaran had told her many stories of the Gods, and Zhava had even kept a few of those close to her heart. She had only ever heard two stories of the God Coredor, and she had not liked either one. The first, which she read because of her love of the Goddess Preizhavan, was a horrible story of Coredor trying to trick Preizhavan into marrying him. He almost succeeded in his plan, but Preizhavan saw through his disguise at the last moment, and she chased him all the way down the mountain and out into the sea before she let him slip away in disgrace.

The second story was one that Priestess Marmaran had told before bedtime one night, of Coredor eating wood nymphs along a stream. He gorged himself on them until he could eat no more, but he did not know that the wood nymphs could not die. They danced inside his belly and made him so sick that he finally vomited them up again. Zhava did not like either of those stories, and she thought Coredor was a mean God who spent His time bullying and tricking everyone around him.

She turned to Plishka and said, "That's an awful story."

"Of course it's awful," Plishka muttered with a shrug. "It's Coredor."

"So why is this story so important?"

"I don't know." Plishka rubbed at her eyes, squeezing them shut and struggling to hold back more tears. "Vinaara said to collect the stories. She wanted me to read them all as quickly as I could, and then I was to bring them to her at the cave. She had some idea that everything started with Coredor, that the people who disappeared from the Hibaro were being punished by Coredor. Vinaara was – is – so smart."

Zhava picked up the scroll again and unrolled it in her lap. Something had to be here, she thought. Vinaara had wanted the stories of Coredor for some reason, because she believed they were important. She started reading again from the beginning, more slowly this time as she tried to think as Vinaara would think. That was hard, however, when she had only known Vinaara as "Plishka," and she had never realized that Plishka was two people, and neither of the sisters had ever spoken to her for very long. The most Vinarra had ever spoken to her was that day on the track, when Zhava was struggling with her injuries.

"Have you read this?" Zhava asked, offering the scroll to Plishka.

"I know the story, but I didn't have time to read this scroll." She took it and stared at the words on the page. "You kept interrupting me, remember? You had a sconce to light."

Zhava ducked her head, but saw the beginnings of a smile on Plishka's face. Plishka apparently hadn't meant the comment to hurt – she actually seemed to be teasing, which was a weird thing from Plishka.

"Then read it now," Zhava said. She stood and walked to the closed shutters. She slipped open the latch and spread the shutters wide, taking in a breath of cool, night air.

Plishka began reading aloud, and that startled Zhava. She hadn't expected that, but Plishka had a good voice for reading. She changed her voice each time another person in the story spoke, and that made Zhava smile. The little boy Tu was a squeaking 5-year-old. The young woman Re was actually Plishka's own voice – an interesting choice. Coredor was appropriately snarling and mean. Erinian's voice was whispy as a dream, and Preizhavan's was deep and purring – Zhava rather liked that voice for her favorite Goddess. Vek, the Ruler of the Gods, was quietly powerful, confident in his own authority. As Plishka reached the end of the story, she read Coredor's final speech to Vek in that snarling, vengeful voice, and Zhava realized that voice was completely wrong for him.

"Stop," she said, turning around.

"Why?" Plishka asked. "You know what Vinaara wanted?"

"No, but...." How could she explain? She had heard those words of Coredor, spoken by the shadow man in the woods, and now the voice Plishka had chosen did not seem right at all. Coredor should sound more like...whom? "Read that in Vek's voice," she said.

"That's not right," Plishka replied, shaking her head. "Vek is powerful and wise – he's the ruler of the Gods. Coredor is just...mean."

"Please do it," Zhava said, shutting her eyes.

Plishka sighed, but she did as Zhava asked. In the voice of Vek, that confident and deep voice, she read, "They are all too powerful. They are too weak to harness that power, but they shall grow with each generation, and then the Gods will see what shall become of this generation. For then the world shall be purged of the meekly powerful, of those who feign–"

"Yes," Zhava whispered. "That's the voice of the shadow man." But there was another voice she heard, and Zhava clenched her eyes tight and tried to recall that second voice. Someone else had said those very same words, and the memory was just there, just barely out of reach. Salient Noomira would be able to retrieve it, Zhava thought. Salient Noomira would dive into Zhava's mind as if it were a crystal sea, and she would swim through those memories until she found–

"All that power," the man said. "And for what? You're meek, and it's all...wasted."

Zhava stumbled and slipped to the floor with a gasp.

"Zhava!" Plishka tossed aside the scroll and clambered over, reaching out a tentative, supporting hand.

"I'm all right," Zhava said, shaking her head. She was sitting on the floor, her back to the wall beneath the window and her mouth dry. Now that the memory had returned, she couldn't believe she hadn't noticed before. But she couldn't be right. If she was right....

"What is it?" Plishka asked. "What happened?"

The words Plishka had read...Zhava had heard them spoken, but not once – she had heard them twice. She had heard that man's voice in the woods, and she had heard those same words again, spoken by–

"No," Zhava said, squeezing her eyes shut. "I'm wrong. I know I'm wrong."

"What are you talking about?" Plishka said, anger now tingeing her words. "Tell me."

Zhava kept her eyes shut tight and whispered, "High Priest Viekoosh said those words to me."

Silence. Zhava sat on the floor, her eyes still shut, and listened to the silence stretch out between her and Plishka. Zhava went over everything again in her mind, a second time, a third time. The man in the woods had brushed aside her Abilities as easily as swatting a bug, so the shadow man had to be someone powerful – High Priest Viekoosh was very powerful. The shadow man had quoted Coredor to her – and High Priest had...used most of those same words. But had he actually quoted Coredor? He had not exactly quoted the God, but he had certainly said something very much like what Coredor said. He talked about "power," and he talked about the "meek." But...was that enough to say that the shadow man and High Priest Viekoosh were the same person?

No, Zhava thought. That could not be right. Many people talked about power. They talked about the meek. She could not think of any of her friends who had ever talked about the meek, but other people certainly did, people such as...well, actually, no one came to mind who spoke of the meek. But that did not mean the shadow man was High Priest Viekoosh. Viekoosh was in charge of the entire Hibaro, and people would not trust him if he betrayed that trust, if he hurt them.

But the voices. Were the voices really similar enough? Could she say that the shadow man in the woods really sounded like High Priest Viekoosh?

She had to be wrong. She had to be! She opened her eyes.

Plishka was staring intently at the floor, her eyes hard and her fists clenched. "You're sure?" she asked.

"Plishka, no. No! I just thought it sounded like him, for just a moment I thought that, but I can't be sure. The memory is too far gone, too much like smoke. I cannot hold onto it."

Pliska looked up, her jaw tense. "That Salient you talked about, though. Salient Noomira? You said she went through your memories and found those soldiers hiding in the forest. She could hold that memory for you. She could see if it's High Priest Viekoosh."

"Probably." Actually, after watching how Salient Noomira walked through memories, Zhava rather doubted that the old woman could know for sure if the shadow man and High Priest Viekoosh were the same person. After all, the Salient couldn't discover anything that Zhava hadn't already, somehow, sensed. Her own eyes had seen the soldiers hiding, though she hadn't really noticed them. Her eyes had also seen the shadow man outside the Tower window and watching her, but again, she hadn't really noticed him there. Never, in any of her memories, had she seen the face beneath the hood the shadow man wore. If she had seen that detail, Salient Noomira would have seen it too.

"Let's go," Plishka said, abruptly standing, smoothing her woolen coat and flicking a leaf off the sleeve. She flipped up the hood on the coat to hide her own face, then reached down and helped Zhava stand.

Zhava wasn't sure she liked the idea of returning to the Tower, especially so late at night, to have Salient Noomira dig through her memories again. Plishka, however, seemed determined. She picked up the Felton sword from the bed and shoved it into Zhava's hands, tossed a shawl at Zhava, and even blew out the flame on the oil lamp. She reached for the door handle, then turned back.

"I know I don't actually say this enough...or, probably ever, but...thank you," Plishka whispered. "If we can find my sister...."

Zhava thought of that final bit of memory Salient Noomira had uncovered, the memory of her real mother crying over her when she was an infant, and Zhava knew exactly what Plishka was feeling. That memory...Zhava would do anything to uncover the identity of her mother. "You're welcome," she said.

They left the room. Plishka kept the hood up and her head down so her face stayed hidden as they walked. They slipped quickly down the narrow stairs, then down the hall of the first floor. They could hear people talking in the common room, but no one was wandering the hallways, and they were able to leave quietly from the building and into the chilled night. Outside, however, soldiers were marching everywhere, and several of them glanced at the two women walking the path so late. One soldier squinted, then turned and strode toward them.

"I'm sick," Plishka whispered into Zhava's ear. She stumbled on the walkway, and Zhava barely caught her in time to keep her from falling into the dirt.

The soldier stopped before them, his hand out to block their path. "Names?" he said.

"I'm Zhava," Zhava said. Plishka made a retching noise from beneath the hood of her coat, and she leaned over into the dirt, coughing and sputtering as if she would vomit at any moment. "And this is...Vinaara," Zhava continued.

"Vinaara?" the soldier said, glancing at the back of Plishka's coat. "I don't know that name."

"She's just a Candidate," Zhava said. "She asked for my help learning the Codex of Preizhavan, but then she got sick. We're on our way to-"

Plishka launched into another coughing fit and sputtered, "Please – just...."

"Fine," the soldier said, waving a hand. "Be on your way."

Zhava quickly thanked him, then snaked an arm around Plishka's back and helped her walk. Plishka continued the coughing and hacking until they rounded the next building and out of sight of that soldier.

"Why did we do that?" Zhava whispered. "We shouldn't have lied to him. He seemed nice, and he might have helped us."

"Zhava," Plishka said, turning and giving her a confused look. "I'm supposed to be dead, remember?"

Zhava turned away, embarassed that she hadn't thought of that. They walked briskly to the nearly-deserted Tower and then inside the first-floor reading room. Plishka stayed by the door, pretending to be very interested in a book left open at a table while Zhava went to Brother Tymare's desk. As usual, he was sitting behind stacks of books and reading.

"Is Salient Noomira still upstairs?" she asked him.

"Hmmm...I think so."

"You never saw her leave?" Brother Tymare might hide behind his books all day, but he still seemed to observe everything that went on inside the Tower. If anyone had come or gone from the main floor, he would have noticed it.

"Hmmm...no, I never saw her leave."

"Thank you." She started to walk away, then thought of another question and turned back. "And High Priest Viekoosh? Is he up there?"

"No. He left early this morning, and...hmmm...he's been gone all day."

"Thanks." She rushed back to Plishka, and they began the long climb up the nine flights of stairs to High Priest Viekoosh's office. By the fifth floor, they were both getting winded. By the sixth, Zhava had broken into a sweat. Between the early morning climb to meet High Priest Viekoosh, and then Salient Noomira going through her memories, the discovery that Plishka was still alive, and now rushing back up the Tower stairs – Zhava had done more physical activity and experienced more emotional trouble in this one day than she could count in a dozen days back home. At the seventh-floor landing, they stopped for a moment to rest.

"Why did they have to build this thing so tall?" Plishka said with a gasp.

Zhava just shook her head and squeezed her eyes shut. As she stood there trying not to gulp in breaths of air, she realized she was hearing far more noise echoing up from beneath them than she should for this late hour. People were yelling, and she could hear the pounding steps of people running. She looked down.

"What is all that noise?" Plishka asked. She flipped back her hood and looked down the narrow flight of stairs.

The scent drifted on the breeze from below, and Zhava's heart clenched. Fire! She opened her mouth to say the word, but a rumble suddenly echoed from far below. The floors shook. The wall beside them cracked, and the wooden beams began to warp. They braced themselves to keep from falling. Zhava turned to Plishka, and they both gasped. Something beneath them had exploded.

"We have to help the Salient," Plishka said. She spun and ran up the next set of steps two at a time, Zhava right behind her. They climbed as quickly as they could, the building shuddering around them. People in their private rooms began to rush down the stairs, and Plishka and Zhava had to dart around them. Wooden stair joints popped. Plaster shattered from the walls. They reached the ninth floor landing, and the dark, polished floor was warped as if it was made of cloth. Up here, they could feel the building begin to sway as the lower-level supports buckled beneath the weight. Zhava had no idea how they would get back down once they found the Salient, but that problem would have to wait.

The doors to High Priest Viekoosh's office were already open. They saw the large desk in the middle of the room, but they did not see the Salient. They rushed inside, calling her name.

"Salient Noomira!" Zhava yelled. "Are you here?"

"Salient?" Plishka said, cupping her hands to her mouth.

The room shuddered, and the desk slid aside. Zhava saw Salient Noomira lying on the floor, a line of blood running down her head.

"Salient!" Zhava said. She was about to rush forward, but a black-feathered head and an orange beak popped up from behind the desk.

Plishka skidded to a halt, her eyes wide. "What is that?" she said.

The sengret fluffed its feathers and stood up taller, and that's when Zhava saw that its dark breast feathers were streaked in blood – Salient Noomira's blood. She tried to think what she could do, but nothing came to mind. The giant bird, the sengret, had...killed her? But how had it even gotten into the room? How had no one seen it? Noomira was a Salient...she should have been able to defend herself.

Plishka cried out in pain, and Zhava turned. She was lying on the floor, a spot of blood on the back of her head, and a soldier standing over her. He swung a short club into his hand, then turned to Zhava and smiled. "You're next," he said.

But before Zhava could move, a man's arm wrapped around her from behind, pinning her arms at her sides. Another hand came from behind her head and shoved a cloth against her mouth and nose. She struggled to reach up and free herself, but the man's grip was strong, and she couldn't get her arms loose.

"Just breathe," the man whispered into her ear.

She began calling forth her flames, willing them to herself...and to...aid her...as she felt...herself growing...so...very...tired.

"That's it," the man said with a chuckle. "Breathe it all in, and go to sleep."

The darkness closed in around her just as High Priest Viekoosh's smiling face came into view, and then she fell asleep.

# CHAPTER 18

It was the crying that Zhava heard first. The sobs of someone far away echoed through the darkness to her. She struggled to sit up, but the darkness was complete, and she couldn't find her hands or her feet or even the floor beneath her. She rubbed at her eyes, and she found that they were open, but the darkness swallowed up everything around her so that it didn't matter. Everything but the sobs, the long wails that echoed from a great distance.

"I'm here," Zhava called, and the darkness seemed to swallow her words as easily as it swallowed her sight.

With a stumble, she started walking. The crying echoed all around her, so she had no way of knowing if she was going toward it or walking away from it. The cries were definitely coming from a woman, though she did not sound in pain. The cries were deeper, more anguished. This was a woman who had suffered something deep, emotional, and those feelings were bursting from within.

"I'm coming," Zhava yelled – and she slammed into a wall so hard she bounced off, collapsed to the ground, and saw bright spots bounce before her eyes. She held her pounding head as she lay still and tried to get her thoughts to come back to her. She should have known better than to run through the darkness.

"My child?" the crying woman said.

Zhava struggled against the pain to open her eyes. Was this another memory? Was this her mother again? Who was the crying woman, and how did she know Zhava?

"Oh, my child, it is you again," the crying woman said.

A dim light began to glow, a moving shape appeared on the other side of the wall, and Zhava realized she could see the woman through that wall. The woman was unformed, though, fuzzy around the edges as if she was not all there – or as if Zhava was seeing through a clouded window. With that little bit of light, however, she tentatively stood and pressed her palms to the wall.

"I'm here," Zhava said.

"Oh, my child." The woman hobbled forward, and Zhava recognized her even with the dim light and through the murky glass.

"Priestess Marmaran."

The old woman stepped to the glass and placed her palms on the other side, mirroring Zhava. Her form was still fuzzy, as if the wall itself was distorting her. "I wish you hadn't come," Marmaran said.

"I don't know where I am." Zhava looked around, but everything beyond their circle of dim light was solid black. "Is this the Hibaro?"

"Zhava, listen to me." Priestess Marmaran knelt on the other side, carefully keeping her hands pressed firmly against the glass. "Child, you are in grave danger, and I am prevented from crossing to you."

"Prevented? But...how?"

"Listen to me. I am alone, for the first time ever – utterly alone. Cut off from you, cut off from the world, but I am not important. You are. You must escape. You must run away, get back to the Hibaro."

"I don't know how," Zhava said. The darkness was beginning to scare her more as they talked. What could be preventing Priestess Marmaran from going anywhere? She was a spirit – couldn't spirits simply float away?

"Oh, my child," Priestess Marmaran said. "I will miss you so much. I wish you could stay, and I know you will hate me for this, but...." She slowly stood up, and she removed first one hand from the glass wall and then the other.

"No," Zhava cried. She pounded at the wall. "Do not leave me here."

"My child," she said, "I would never leave you. It is, however, time for you to leave me." She spread her arms wide, swung them together, and a thundering crack resounded through the darkness, splitting the glass wall before them—

—and Zhava jerked awake. She lay in a pool of water on a stone floor. Her body ached, and she shivered from the frigid water misting down from above and soaking her clothes, her hair, her skin. She wiped at her eyes to clear away the water, and a heavy chain clanked at her side. The chain was attached to a band at her left wrist, the other end clamped to a ring that was set into the rock wall.

"You're awake," a woman said.

Zhava turned to the voice, and she saw Plishka on the other side of the small cave, a chain around her wrist and tied to the opposite wall. Her hair was streaked red with blood and water, and she was huddling against the wall.

"You're alive," Zhava said. "The last thing I remember, you were lying on the floor by that soldier."

"Yes, we were both stupid," Plishka said. She gently rubbed at the back of her head and winced at the pain. "They snuck up behind us when we were distracted. That guard knocked me with that club of his, and Viekoosh stuck some cloth to your mouth and you fell asleep."

And that was when Zhava remembered the entire scene in High Priest Viekoosh's office. The sengret behind the desk, blood on its beak and down its feathers, and Salient Noomira dead on the floor. The explosions in the building, and smoke in the Tower.

"What happened with the fire?" Zhava asked. She wiped at the water on her face and looked up. A little stream ran down the walls and into the small cave, bouncing off the rocks and splashing both her and Plishka in a frigid mist. It pooled at their feet, then ran down the center of the cave and into the distance.

"What I saw," Plishka said, "was…awful. You should thank the Gods you were asleep. You and I were thrown into a net together, and that giant bird carried us away. We flew above the Hibaro, and I could see people down there fighting. There were fires *everywhere*. Soldiers were fighting soldiers, the Ios were out there too, but there were just too many soldiers for them to stop. And the birds – there were five or six of those giant birds, and they were each carrying a net full of something out of the

Hibaro. I saw one other person in a net, but the others were full of small crates." She lowered her head and sniffled.

Zhava looked around again. The cave was actually rather small, and the light came from a single lantern set on a rock several paces away. She tested the chain around her wrist, but she couldn't go very far from the wet wall. "Where are we?" she asked.

"Just off the desert plateau," Plishka said. "Somewhere atop the leading edge of the Purneese Mountains."

"The Purneese?" Zhava gasped. "But that's...." She quickly calculated in her head. "That's at least four or five days from the Hibaro – longer on foot. How long was I asleep?"

"Only a short time. It was sunrise when we arrived. Those giant birds fly fast."

"They're sengret."

"Well, they're fast. And hungry and dangerous."

Zhava shivered in the cold water. She held out her hand and called for a flame. It flickered in her palm, then disappeared in a wisp of smoke as the falling water doused it. She called it again, but the same thing happened. She stepped away from the wall, stretched out the chain as tight as it would go, and extended her other arm. Again she called to the flame, but she was still too near the water's spray, and the little flame fizzled out in her palm.

"Viekoosh was smart," Plishka said, "to put us in here."

"Then use your lightning on these chains. Get us out of here."

Plishka turned and stared at her. "Have you never seen what lightning does to water?"

Zhava shook her head. She had seen thunderstorms, of course, but those were fast, dramatic things just on the edge of the desert. She and her family had to worry about rushes of flood water, but they seldom even thought about the lightning flashing in the sky. If it hit a tree, it could start a fire, but that rarely happened.

"You do not want me tossing lightning in this room," Plishka said. "I threw some lightning into a pond once when I was younger. Half the water ended up on shore, and I killed every fish in there."

Steps echoed in the small cave, and they both turned to stare down the tunnel. Bootsteps and the clanking of metal bounced off the cave walls and made it sound as if a hundred people were marching toward them. When the three soldiers stepped around the corner, it was almost a relief to Zhava that it was so few. A moment later, however, High Priest Viekoosh limped around the soldiers and stepped into the dim glow of the lantern light. He glanced at Zhava, and his eyes grew wide for just a moment, apparently surprised to see her standing. He quickly looked to Plishka, then back to Zhava, this time without any surprise.

"You're awake," he said. "That's – good." He clasped his hands behind his back, flicking the black robes away as he did, and carefully stepped forward onto the wet rock, favoring his one, injured leg. "I suppose, Zhava, that I really should thank you."

She took a step back but did not reply. She had trusted this man, the High Priest of the Hibaro, and he had betrayed her. He had betrayed everyone. If he wanted to thank her for something, it could not be for anything good.

"If not for you," he continued, "I have no idea how I would have acquired my supplies."

She didn't know what he meant, but she remained silent.

"Not curious?" He smiled, turned to Plishka who was still shivering against the wall, then back to Zhava. "You don't want to know how I used you to get more...eggs?"

He obviously wanted a reply, so she decided to give him nothing. She leaned back against the cold, wet wall and stared at the floor.

"Ah," he said, his smile growing. "So the fight has finally gone out of you, has it? I wondered what it might take, but as Coredor says, everyone has a breaking point. And you haven't even learned the half of it." He chuckled.

"What eggs?" Plishka said.

Zhava turned and glared at her. This was what the High Priest wanted, for them to respond to him, and Plishka should have stayed quiet.

"The sengret," Viekoosh said, still staring at Zhava. "They're very hard to breed, especially in captivity, but the newborns are surprisingly easy to nurture. The key is to be there when they hatch. They imprint, you know, on the first animal they see." He stepped back and dipped his head in a slight bow. "I'm a natural mother."

Zhava rolled her eyes.

"But you," Viekoosh said. "You, I am very glad to say, are going on one more very long journey. But this time, I will never see you again."

She tensed at that. What was he going to do? Kill her? That didn't make any sense. If he wanted to kill her, he could have done that back at the Hibaro. He could have simply left her in his office to die in the Tower fires.

"And this," he said, and he pulled a bottle from beneath his robes. "This is one special charm I shall treasure for the rest of my days."

She squinted into the bottle. The glass was frosted and dark, and a thin crack ran from the base to the neck where a thick cork had been shoved into it and tightly tied down. Viekoosh shook the little bottle, and something chinked against the sides of the glass. It was a another bottle, a little brown bottle made of –

Zhava gasped and reached to her neck. The little pottery bottle with Priestess Marmaran's remains – it was gone.

"Thank you so much," Viekoosh whispered.

"That's mine!" Zhava yelled, and she lunged at him.

He jumped away, just out of reach, and Zhava was yanked back by the chain around her wrist. She twisted and slipped on the wet stones, then collapsed onto the floor, her shoulder wrenched and aching.

The soldiers laughed, and Viekoosh quickly stowed the frosted bottle. He balanced himself against the cave wall and gingerly placed his weight back on his injured leg.

"Zhava," he said with a wave, "live a long, miserable life, and do it very far from me." He turned and slowly walked away, the soldiers following behind.

"No," Zhava screamed. She stood again and tugged at the chain, struggling to break it free of the rock. "Bring that back to me."

The echoing footsteps faded. Zhava stared into the flickering shadows at the edge of the lantern light.

"What was that thing?" Plishka asked.

"My teacher," Zhava said. She turned back to the chain and the metal ring and swiped at the water running down her face. She grabbed the ring and pulled. The ring didn't come loose – it didn't even bend. She braced a foot against the wall and pulled again, harder this time. Again, it didn't move. It certainly didn't break.

"So what did your teacher teach you?" Plishka said through chattering teeth.

"She taught me the ways of the Kandor," Zhava said as she struggled at the metal ring. "She was teaching me to meditate, and to control my emotions–"

"That worked well." Plishka laughed.

"–and she was teaching me to move stones," Zhava said with a grunt at the chain. Then she stopped and stared at the ring. It was metal, and its base was metal, but that base had a pin that was sunk into the stone wall behind it. She shouldn't be working on the metal, she realized. She should be working on the rock holding the pin.

"Someone's coming," Plishka hissed.

Zhava turned. More footsteps. Again, it sounded as if several people were coming, but now Zhava could better tell the echoes in the cave. She shut her eyes and listened. She counted only one set of steps.

"Viekoosh!" she yelled. "Give me back that–"

The man came around the corner, and Zhava's voice cracked. It wasn't Viekoosh. This man was dressed in brown robes, and red and green rings glittered on his fingers in the lantern light. His dark hair was tied with a red ribbon in a bun atop his head, and his eyes seemed just a little too near to each other, as if the skin of his face had been squeezed tight. He flashed a big, toothy grin at Zhava as he stepped carefully, delicately, along the wet stone, and when he spoke, it was in a Purneesite dialect that Zhava had not heard since the day she left her home.

"My wife," Ooleng said. "At last, you have been returned to me."

# CHAPTER 19

Zhava stepped back, her mouth gaping open, as she stared at Ooleng on the other side of the cave. He shouldn't be here. She had left him behind when she left her home. Yes, she had thought about him, and she had even had a dream that he had been a good man, a good husband – but she had rejected that dream. She had chosen to leave that dream when she returned to Priestess Marmaran. How could he be here, now? And how did he know High Priest Viekoosh?

But she remembered what the High Priest had said, right before Salient Noomira interrupted him. He had said that he was returning her to Ooleng, that he would send her away to be Ooleng's wife. Even though Salient Noomira had stopped it from happening then, Viekoosh seemed to have found another way to make it happen.

"You are even more beautiful than I remember," Ooleng said. He delicately stepped across the wet rocks, careful to keep his slipper shoes out of the puddles.

Zhava looked down at herself. Her clothes were soaked, she had mud caked to her feet and ankles, her arms were purple from standing beneath the splashing water, and her hair was caked to the top of her head. How could this possibly be "beautiful"?

"I know you have been through much," Ooleng continued. "The Priest told me about the terrible things you had to do. They forced you to fight." He gestured to the sword at his hip – Zhava's own sword. "They made you learn their philosophies of fighting. How your head must have hurt." He chuckled brightly at that.

"Who is he?" Plishka said.

Ooleng glanced down at Plishka who was still huddled in a ball against the far wall. Much more of the water was hitting her, and she looked as if she could hardly move from the cold spray.

"That one, however," Ooleng said. "Clean her up a little, and she might make an acceptable servant."

"Ooleng," Zhava said. "Please, you have to let us go. That Priest, he's hurting people."

"Only his own people," he said with a nod. "Those Remmliits, yes. But you do not need to concern yourself with them anymore. Now that we are to be married, you will no longer be a Remmliit like him. You will join our clan; you will be a Purneesite like me, and like my father and brothers. Like my mother. And our children will be Purneesite. Let the Remmliits fight and tear at each other. What will that be to us?"

"No," Zhava said with a quick shake of her head. "I am a Remmliit, and I want to return to the Hibaro. I want to return to Io Kua and continue my training-"

The slap came so suddenly to Zhava's face that she stood in place, stunned. Her cheek tingled, and her jaw ached. Tears sprang from her eyes, but not tears of sadness – they were tears of surprise. Tears of anger. Her body began shaking at the raw emotion that welled up within her.

"That is enough of that talk," Ooleng whispered. "You will never again speak of the Hibaro or your time there. You will never again speak a man's name that is not my own, or one of my brothers' names. You will marry me, and we will have our children, and we will continue my father's business. This is your life now. You will accept it."

He stepped forward again, and Zhava took another step back – and pressed against the cold, rock wall behind her. She reached up and gripped the metal hook that held the end of the chain to her wrist. She had nowhere to go, nowhere to run or hide from this man who was trying to claim the rest of her life, the rest of her world.

"It may seem difficult at first," Ooleng said as he leaned forward, preparing to give her a kiss. "But you will come to love me. This I know."

The rage flashed up within Zhava, and she reached out with every last bit of energy, reached out to her Abilities. She brushed her will within the stones behind her, became one with the shapes and textures and pressure of the rocks layered upon each other, the slow, gradual movements of them upon the world, she sought out the wound that had been inflicted upon it by the placement of the metal spike, by the pounding of that sharp object inside the smooth skin of the rocks...

...and the stone wall let that metal spike slip free.

Zhava yanked hard on the chain and pulled the ring and the pin from the wall. She swung her arm around Ooleng's shoulders and wrapped the chain across his back, then yanked up on it, hard. The metal rings bit into his back and sliced it open, spinning him around as he screamed out in pain.

Io Suleenuo's fighting training sprang to mind, and Zhava dropped to the ground, swung her foot around, and kicked Ooleng's legs out from under him. He flipped in the air, water spraying off his slippers, and his hair flying loose, and then he landed with a crack of his head on the wet floor.

Zhava jumped up, used the momentum to spin the chain around her hand, straddled Ooleng's body, and brought back her metal-wrapped fist, ready to strike if he moved again.

He lay still on the rocks beneath her, a gash across his right temple and to the back of his head. A thin line of blood began washing through the water beneath him.

"Did you kill him?" Plishka asked. She was standing again, hugging her arms at her sides and visibly shaking.

Zhava wasn't sure what she had done. Io Suleenuo had taught her only a few ways to take down an enemy, and the weapons teacher had been vague on the effects of a move like that. Zhava leaned down and placed her hand against Ooleng's chest. It rose and fell in short, uneven breaths.

"He lives," she said, and she didn't know how she felt about that. She had known Io Suleenuo was teaching her to fight, but she had never thought about the reality of actually killing another person. Part of her was glad she hadn't done it, but another part of her desperately wished she had.

She left Ooleng bleeding in the pool of water and went to Plishka's side. She wrapped a hand around the metal ring stuck in that wall and gently brushed her will into the stones. The rocks loosened, and Zhava yanked that pin free. Plishka stumbled forward, and Zhava caught her, eased them both out of the spray of the little waterfall and toward the lantern set on a small rock in the narrow passageway. Plishka's teeth were chattering, and now that the excitement was over, Zhava could feel the cold beginning to freeze up her own joints and muscles. She called to her flames, and a dozen of them sprang to life at her side. They piled atop each other, and another dozen appeared, climbed on the shoulders of the first dozen, and so on until a wall of little flaming men stood emblazoned before Zhava and Plishka. The heat was bliss after standing in the cold spray of the water.

"So...who was he?" Plishka said through chattering teeth.

"He wanted to marry me."

Plishka laughed. "You said no?"

Zhava unwrapped the chain from her hand and studied the cold metal of the lock at her wrist. It was a simple key mechanism that joined the two pieces that folded open and closed. Except she didn't have the key. She looked at Ooleng's body. She could go over and search him, but she was finally warm sitting in the glow of the wall of fire. She called another flame to her, and he flickered to life in her hand.

"Burn it out," she said, pointing to the lock. The flame ran down her hand and wrist and jumped into the metal chamber. She twisted the lock so it faced the floor, and soon the metal began to glow. The heat quickly grew intense against her wrist, and a few drops of liquid metal spilled from the keyhole and onto the ground. The mechanism popped, and Zhava twisted it off her wrist and tossed it aside.

"Great trick," Plishka said, her eyes wide. She had finally stopped shivering. She held out her arm, and Zhava sent another of her flames into the lock around Plishka's wrist.

She might not care about a key, but Ooleng certainly had something Zhava wanted back. She stepped carefully on the slippery rocks and bent over his body. The water pooling around him had turned a light pink from the gash on his head. She felt his chest, and his breaths were still quick and shallow. She didn't care if he lived or died, as long he didn't wake up before they could escape. She reached for the buckle at his waist, snapped it open, and slid the belt and scabbard – and her Felton sword – from around him. She wrapped it around herself and smiled. She might not be very good with that sword, but it was hers. She was thrilled to get it back.

"What do we do now?" Plishka asked. She was playing with the loose chain, studying the metal and testing the ring that had held everything pinned to the stone wall. "We have no idea how many more people are out there."

Zhava had already thought of that. She called a couple more of her flames, whispered to them, "I want to hear what Viekoosh is saying," and then set one on the ground. It went running off toward the entrance, and the other one climbed Zhava's arm and perched itself on her shoulder.

Plishka just watched. Within moments, the flame on Zhava's shoulder began whispering in her ear, repeating the words the first one heard from the cave entrance:

"Where did that boy get off to now?" the flame said. That was likely Ooleng's father, and Zhava realized that she had never actually learned the man's name. What did they expect her to do, simply call him "Papa" for the rest of her married life, as if he was her father too?

"Are you listening?" the flame said. "We have our supplies stowed, and we are ready to leave." That could be anyone speaking those words, Zhava thought. Someone in charge, a soldier or an Io perhaps.

"Yes, Viekoosh, I heard you."

Zhava nodded. So High Priest Viekoosh had contacted Ooleng's family – this meeting was no accident. But why? What was he doing?

"You there," the flame said. "Have you seen my son?"

"I'm sorry, but I don't know your son."

"Did anyone see where my son went?"

Zhava sighed. Ooleng had apparently snuck away to visit her in the cave. His absence was a problem.

"Enough. If we find your son, can we conclude our business? Good. Servant, go check on the girls; he probably snuck off to be with them."

Zhava stood and waved her hand at the flames. They dispersed and vanished in little puffs of smoke.

"What's going on?" Plishka asked, sitting up straight with a little shiver.

"Someone's coming."

"What? We have to hide."

Zhava looked around. Her eyes had trouble adjusting to the sudden darkness without all of her flames to light the way, but she couldn't see any corners in which to hide. It was nothing more than a narrow passageway carved out by years of flowing water. Worse, Ooleng's body would be obvious the moment the servant came near.

"No, we're done hiding," Zhava said. She pulled her sword from the scabbard and pointed at the chain Plishka held in her hand. "Use that for your lightning, and crouch over there." She stood against the wall on one side of the tunnel while Plishka knelt against the other. Plishka held one end of the chain in one hand and the other in her other hand, a huge grin spreading across her face.

Within moments, they could hear the sounds of boots tromping down the cave.

"Ooleng!" the servant called. "Are you in here?"

The man came around the corner, and for a moment he was brightly lit by the lantern on the rock. He raised his hand to block the light and squinted down the tunnel.

Zhava stepped out from her hiding spot so the man could clearly see her standing next to Ooleng's body.

He slowed and reached for his sword. "What happened here?" he drawled, squinting from Zhava to Ooleng.

Plishka reached out and swung the chain at the man's ankle. It wrapped around his boot, and she flashed a bolt of lightning through the metal. The lightning traveled through the chain, up the man's leg and through his body. He tensed and jerked, then collapsed and fell with a spray of water into the pool next to Ooleng.

He was a large man, and Zhava and Plishka worked together to roll him over in the spreading muck of cold water and mud and Ooleng's blood. Then they searched him for weapons. Plishka plucked the man's sword from his grip, but Zhava was thrilled to find a belt filled with short, shiny knives – throwing knives just like the ones Io Suleenuo used in their practice sessions. She unbuckled that belt, then wrapped it around her waist. Between her own sword belt and now the knife belt, it felt a little hard to breathe. However, she wouldn't give up her own sword again, and the knives might be useful during their escape.

"Look at all these," Plishka said. She yanked a set of keys off a loop on the servant's trousers. Three keys were strung to a small, metal hook. They chinked together as she shook them.

"Keep them," Zhava said. "They might open a door or something to get out of here."

Armed and far more confident than they had felt earlier, they crouched and began slinking back through the tunnel. Zhava sent one of her little flames ahead again, and a second flame perched on her shoulder. They conveyed the conversation as Viekoosh and Ooleng's father negotiated for another delivery. Viekoosh seemed to want more...of something, probably those eggs, but Ooleng's father refused to deliver without payment. Viekoosh was unsure how much longer before he could get a new shipment. He had been exposed and could not return to the Hibaro – *Good*, Zhava thought – and it might be several moons before he could resupply.

All of their talk, however, assured Zhava that no one was paying attention to the little tunnel where she and Plishka were supposed to be chained to the wall. They reached the entrance and peaked around the corner. Their tunnel was one of many that all branched out from a large, central chamber. She could see Viekoosh and three men talking farther back in the main chamber, three soldiers standing by the far wall and talking with each other, and two Ios who were admiring the sengret. Six of the birds were perched in a group with hoods tied over their heads. Immediately to Zhava's left, and between them and the gaping cave entrance were three large, wooden crates. As no one in the chamber seemed to be looking in their direction, Zhava and Plishka darted into the shadow of those tall crates.

They could see the dim light of the cave entrance. The shadows outside were long, and the light was a dull orange. If they had arrived at sunrise as Plishka said, then this was probably now sunset. They shifted in the cramped space between the crates and the cave wall, then leaned in close to whisper to each other.

"It looks clear," Plishka said.

"I'll send a flame ahead to check."

"No. If we run now, we can get out before anyone sees us."

"But what is outside? More soldiers? We could run straight into them. My flame would tell me."

"Hello?" a small voice said.

Zhava and Plishka tensed.

"Who are you?" the voice whispered.

It was a high-pitched, thin voice, and it came from just the other side of the crate's wall.

"Hello?" Zhava said, leaning near the back wall of the wooden crate. She studied the box more closely now. It was large but solid, made of finely crafted boards that had been banded together with metal plates at the seams and corners. It looked like it could hold a great weight, maybe even as much as a couple camels.

"Are you here to get us all out?" the voice asked.

"Who are you?" Plishka said.

"Candidate Siena."

Zhava and Plishka stared at each other. A Candidate? From the voice, she sounded like a young girl. What was she doing here, inside this crate?

"I've only been here for a couple moons, but some of the others have been here much longer," Siena said.

Plishka leaned forward and whispered to Zhava, "I remember hearing about Siena. She got lost outside the Hibaro. The woods were searched, and someone finally found a bloodied, torn shirt. High Priest Viekoosh said she was attacked by wild animals."

Zhava thought about Viekoosh negotiating with Ooleng's father. He had said he wouldn't be able to get "new supplies" since leaving the Hibaro....

"He's been selling the students," she said. "But why?"

"Oh, I know," Siena said through the wall. "The Purneesites are giving him eggs for those birds. They're giving him five today, which is amazing because they only gave him one egg for all three of us. But he said he wants dozens of eggs. He's breeding a whole flock of those giant birds and dedicating them to the God Coredor."

# CHAPTER 20

"We need to get them out of here," Zhava said.

Plishka nodded. "But how?"

They edged back the way they'd come and peered out from behind the wooden crate. The three soldiers were now standing with the Ios and the sengret, tying a net around a small box. The Ios were pulling on overcoats, and one was untying the blindfold from a sengret's head.

Zhava turned to study the other end of the cave. Viekoosh and Ooleng's father were smiling and talking with each other while a servant, dressed in the same riding clothes as Ooleng's father, was tying a cord around a rolled scroll. Viekoosh would be leaving soon, and he would probably be taking those Ios and soldiers with him. Once they were gone, the only ones left would be Ooleng's family, his father, the two servants inside the cave, and whatever other servants might be wandering around. They could try something now, or they could....

"We wait for them to leave," Zhava whispered.

Plishka nodded.

Zhava was about to back away when she saw Viekoosh pull out a dark bottle from the inside folds of his robes. He peered within it and gently shook the bottle, and Zhava's jaw clenched. Priestess Marmaran. How could she leave her beloved Marmaran with that evil man?

"Don't do it," Plishka whispered. She tugged on the back of Zhava's shirt, gently easing her back into the shadows. Once they were well hidden again, Plishka said, "I know your teacher was important to you, but we can't fight two Ios and those soldiers and the High Priest. We were lucky with Ooleng and that one servant."

Zhava squeezed her eyes shut. Plishka was right. They were Initiates, just learning their craft. Ooleng was too stupid to think Zhava couldn't defend herself, and they had caught that servant by surprise. In a fair fight, though, neither Plishka nor Zhava would fair well against any one of the people waiting out there. It hurt to think it, but Zhava knew she had to let Marmaran go. Someday – maybe – she would get back that necklace and those remains of her beloved teacher.

One of the sengret let out a loud caw.

They pressed themselves against the back of the wooden crate and peered out toward the darkening sky. A tall, woven basket with an arching handle was perched at the cave entrance, one of the Ios kneeling within the round basin. A sengret launched itself from the floor, gripped the basket's handle, and flew from the cave and into the sky. It was an amazing and beautiful sight, even if the sengret were vicious animals. They bobbed into the night sky, the sengret carrying the basket and the Io far away.

A second basket was pushed to the cave entrance, and the second Io climbed inside. Another sengret gave a great caw, flapped into the air, gripped the basket, and flew out of the cave, following the first.

"Have you ever seen anything like that?" Plishka whispered.

Zhava just shook her head. It was an amazing sight. She had seen only the one sengret in the forest the night she was attacked, and they were powerful animals. Those men were heavy, especially with their gear and the weight of the basket, but the sengret flew off with them as if they weighed nothing.

Another basket, this one for a soldier. Within moments, a sengret gripped that basket and flew away.

The two remaining soldiers stepped forward, one pushing another tall basket while the second delicately set a small chest within it. *Likely the eggs*, Zhava thought. Viekoosh stepped forward, leaned into the basket and adjusted the little chest, then climbed in himself. He beckoned the soldiers to him and began saying something. Zhava thought about sending her flames to listen to that conversation, but she didn't want to risk being seen.

From behind her, Plishka suddenly shrieked. Zhava spun around.

"Got you," a man, one of Ooleng's servants, shouted. He yanked back on Plishka's shirt and pulled her out from behind the wooden crate. She landed hard on the ground beneath him.

"Hey," Zhava yelled.

The man's head snapped up to her. Before he could do anything else, though, Plishka grabbed him by his leg and sent a bolt of lightning into him. His body jolted, and he fell backward with a spasm.

Zhava rushed out from behind the crate and knelt at Plishka's side. "Are you hurt?"

"How did he see me?"

Zhava pulled her up, and they stood in the center of the cavern, staring at the puzzled faces surrounding them. It felt as if time stopped as everyone stared, wide-eyed, at everyone else. Ooleng's papa and remaining servant were open-mouthed behind them at the rear of the cavern. Viekoosh stood in the carrying basket at the cave's entrance, his body twisted so he could see them and anger flaring in his eyes. The last soldier was reaching up to remove the blindfold from a sengret along the far wall, but he had stopped in mid-motion to stare at Plishka and Zhava and the commotion with the servant.

A jumbled chorus of loud voices broke that still moment as the children locked inside the crates began jumping and crying to be released.

"Go," Plishka yelled. She shoved Zhava forward, then darted toward the back of the cave.

Zhava took a couple stumbling steps, then got her balance and ran straight toward High Priest Viekoosh in his basket. The Priest turned around, something like a small reed in his mouth, and puffed out his cheeks. For just a moment, it looked to Zhava as if he blew a whistle, but she didn't care. She was determined to stop him from getting away. The basket was woven strands of rope and strips of wood, so it would easily burn. She called her flames to her. She wrapped herself in them as she ran, calling them to pile atop her, to wrap her body in fire, to ride along with her as she rushed at Viekoosh and his basket. The little flames were yelling their excitement in her ears as they grinned wildly at the prospect of being released – but then they all shrieked in alarm.

Zhava dove for the ground just as a sword flashed above her head. The little flames splashed around her and tumbled across the ground, and Zhava drew her sword in a swift roll that brought her back up and facing the soldier who had nearly struck her.

"A Felton?" the soldier chuckled, taking a step back to eye Zhava and her weapon. He waved his sword through the air – a sword that was at least three times as long as hers. "You're fighting me with a Felton? This will be like swatting a gnat."

Zhava ducked as a sengret flapped above her, heading toward Viekoosh's basket. She gestured at the flames and sent them running across the ground, trying to reach the basket and set it afire.

"Little girl," the soldier said as he advanced with a smile, "I'm putting you back in your cage."

He swung, and Zhava jumped away, nearly losing her footing on the wet rocks. She glanced away long enough to see that Viekoosh had easily brushed aside most of her little flames already.

Another swing from the soldier's sword, and Zhava stumbled again, caught her balance, and just managed to deflect the blow with her sword. Her fingers tingled from the jolt of metal against metal. This man was strong.

The sengret took hold of the handle on Viekoosh's basket, and he grinned at Zhava as it was lifted from the ground.

"No," she yelled.

The soldier leaped at her, and she used one of Io Suleenuo's fighting tricks. She ducked beneath the man's swing, twisted her wrist, brought back her sword arm, and slashed out with the sword's pomel instead of the blade. She cracked the little ball of metal into the soldier's knee, heard a satisfying pop, and rolled away in one swift move. The soldier shrieked at the pain, hunched over, and stumbled on the slick rocks. He fell face-forward into the dirt and skidded, his cries of pain echoing through the cavern.

Zhava reached out with her Abilities, sensed the rocks and dirt beneath the soldier, and shook them all loose as quickly as she could. The man's body vibrated atop the stones, and he began skidding along in the dirt, his cries of pain vibrating as the debris carried him along. Then Zhava reached out to the air, whipped the currents into a quick frenzy, and blasted them at the soldier's side. In an instant, the wind and the stones shot him across the ground, out the entrance to the cave, and into the air beyond. For just a moment, the soldier hung suspended against the dark, a look of terror on his face – and then he dropped out of sight, his shrieks of pain punctuated by the crashes as he bounced and rolled out of sight and down the mountain side.

Zhava jumped back up and called her little flames to herself again. She went to the mouth of the cave and scanned the dusky sky for the birds and their baskets. Spotting the nearest one, she plucked three of the throwing knives from her belt, wrapped the shiny blades in grinning flames, and flicked them through the air in quick succession, a tiny burst of wind propelling them along. The first one flew right past and disappeared into the night, but the second and third lodged themselves into the woven basket.

Viekoosh turned and doused the flames with a flick of his hand, then tossed one of the blades back.

Zhava ducked aside, but not quickly enough. The blade sank deep into her left shoulder, and she cried out at the sharp, piercing pain. She would not let him get away, though. She could not. With a burst of will, she called dozens of flames to her right hand, rolled them into a ball as big as a grain sack, and let them fly. Again, she loosed just one burst of air, and that propelled them forward.

Viekoosh flicked his arm, and the ball of flames burst apart, scattering bits of fire across the sky and around the basket to fall onto the scrubby ground below.

Anger welled up within Zhava, and she called another legion of flames to herself. Before she could do anything with them, however, the water spilling out from the cave's mouth dammed up before her and splashed back at her, dousing her from head to feet. The flames died in puffs of steam around her, and the cold water stunned her for just a moment. She stood there, her mouth open and the water running off of her and back to the ground before her.

She turned back to the sky. Viekoosh was getting away.

"No!" she screamed. She flicked the water off her arms and grabbed hold of every current off air passing by the cave. She wove them before her, spinning them, churning them, gathering them into a cyclone rotating violently before her. She shoved the storm away from her, straight at Viekoosh and the sengret. The storm quickly overtook them, and Zhava shoved the entire mass of air into the ground, carrying the sengret, the basket, and Viekoosh with them.

The explosion resounded across the mountain, and the force of the blast knocked Zhava off her feet and sent her flying backward into the cave. She landed hard, skidded across the ground, and ricocheted off several small stones before sliding to a halt in one of the trickles of water.

"Are you okay?" Plishka yelled.

Zhava staggered back up, nearly lost her balance, then glanced around to get her bearings. She had been blasted halfway back through the cave. Nearly a dozen faces peered wide-eyed at her from behind the slotted doors of the wooden crates. The children were using a ring of keys to open their prison doors. Plishka stood far back and over the unconscious body of one of the servants, lightning crackling from her fingertips, as Ooleng's father knelt before her. And the remaining sengret, the blindfold still over its eyes, twitched nervously and fluffed its feathers near the cave's side wall.

"Keep the children safe," Zhava yelled. "I have to stop Viekoosh." She stumbled forward and peered outside. The cave entrance stood far above the nearest rock outcropping, but rough-hewn stairs had been cut away from one side, and she quickly climbed down those rocks. The night air chilled her wet body. She called her flames and wrapped them about herself, the water quickly evaporating off in puffs of steam and heat. When she reached level ground, she sprinted away, darting through the scrub brush and brambly bushes that littered the mountainside. In no time, she reached the area where her blast of wind had struck the ground. The short grass had been flattened to the dirt, and the bushes had been snapped off and squashed beneath the wind. A few little fires littered the area, remnants of the fireballs she had tried to throw.

The basket was a tangle of wooden strips scattered outward, and Zhava saw streaks of blood that led away from the center of the blast. She called more flames to herself, lighting the surrounding area as bright as the noonday sun, and stepped carefully across the basket's wreckage. An egg lay smashed upon the ground, and a short, thin tube of wood, that little whistle Viekoosh had used, was mixed with the broken shell. She picked it up, wiped it off on the hem of shirt, and stowed it in one of the loops of her throwing-knife belt. She walked forward, raising her right arm above her head and preparing to defend herself from the High Priest.

The flames' light spilled across the dead sengret, its body broken across a series of small stones jutting from the ground. She walked on, but the blood trail ended soon after that. She tossed several of her flames into the air to shine upon the ground, but she did not see High Priest Viekoosh anywhere.

"No," she muttered. She circled back and walked in another direction. Again, nothing. "You can't get away. You can't." Back to the sengret again, then off in another direction. Nothing. "Viekoosh," she screamed into the night. The flames across her body roared their own anger, mingling their crackling voices with her own. "Viekoosh!" She flung her arms wide, and the flames burst out from her, scattering in all directions. They landed far and wide from her, setting the grass and brambles ablaze. She yelled his name again and again, but nobody responded. For all she knew, he could be just over the next rise of hill, but he obviously was not coming back to face her.

Zhava collected several of the flames, but she left most of them behind to burn up the area. She staggered back up the hill, stunned at her loss. She hadn't been able to stop Viekoosh, and he had escaped with most of the sengret eggs. She hadn't been able to retrieve her necklace with Priestess Marmaran's remains. The two Ios and the other two soldiers had gotten away, carried off by the first few sengret. She wasn't sure what else she could do, but her efforts so far had gotten her nowhere. She despaired that she might never even find her way back to the Hibaro, assuming she and Plishka could get down this mountainside and find a familiar path.

She climbed the rough stairs back up to the mouth of the cave. The moment she stepped inside, almost a dozen children rushed forward and grabbed her, nearly knocking her to the ground. They wrapped themselves around her and hugged her until she could barely breathe, thanking her and cheering her and babbling at her about the incredible fight against the High Priest. She returned their affection, and, though she might not have felt it only a few moments before, a smile of genuine happiness came upon her.

They walked in a shuffling group to the rear of the cave where Plishka stood guard before Ooleng's father. The man was standing now, though he was still backed against the cave wall. The remaining servant lay still upon the ground, his chest slowly rising and falling.

"Zhava," Plishka said, her eyes wide as she pointed at Zhava's shoulder. "We need to take care of that."

She looked down. The throwing knife, now scorched and burned from the flames that had been dancing across her body, still protruded from shoulder, streaks of blood running from it and down her arm. Now that she saw the injury, she realized the pain had been with her all the way down to the wreckage of the basket and back again. Plishka was right; they would have to do something about that. But first....

"What about him," Zhava asked, pointing at Ooleng's father.

"He said we can have his horses," Plishka said. She gestured back toward the mouth of the cave. "He told me where they're tied up. Seemed a fair exchange for his life."

"Maybe," Zhava muttered. She stepped forward and stared into the man's eyes. She had never really looked at him up close like this when he had visited her Papa's farm. His eyes were sunk deep in the aged wrinkles of his brow and cheeks. His black hair was messed and stringy, and it hung flattened against the sides of his head. He was breathing heavily, and his brown and white robes fluttered as he fidgeted with his hands. "What's your name?"

"I will not give you that kind of power over me," he spat. "Take the horses. Be gone with you – the lot of you."

Zhava flicked her wrist, and a bundle of flames sprang to life in her hand. She had no more patience, and her anger was boiling up within her. "Tell me your name."

"Lojuen," he muttered, glancing at her flaming hand. "It's Lojuen."

Zhava nodded. She knew just enough Purneesite to recognize "lo" meant "honored," and "juen" meant "prince." "Tell me, honored prince," she said, "what was your bargain with the Remliit High Priest of the Hibaro? How many eggs for these children?" She pointed behind her, to the dirty faces watching from a distance.

"One egg for every four children," Lojuen said. "And another five for the pair of you, a gift to my son." He gestured at Zhava and Plishka.

"And what was your plan for the children?" Zhava continued.

"The desert market, of course. Children make some of the best household servants, a tidy profit for the family."

Zhava shut her eyes. There were 11 children behind her. That was 11 children that had been taken from the Hibaro and flown up to this mountainside to be bartered away and sent into slavery...for the price of a handful of sengret eggs.

"I want to leave," one of the children whispered.

Zhava opened her eyes and stared at Lojuen. She wanted to kill this man. She clenched her jaw and thought of all the things she and Plishka could do to him. Lightning. Flames. Buried inside the very rocks of this hidden cave.

Plishka leaned forward and whispered, "The children have seen enough. We should leave."

She was right. As hard as it was to admit, the children had seen enough of the fighting and the violence and the worst possible things in their time held captive in those crates. It did seem best to take them away from here as quickly as possible.

"One egg for every four children?" Zhava asked Lojuen. "Plus another five for the two of us?"

He nodded, glancing between her and Plishka.

"So here's the new deal." She stepped back, pulling Plishka along with her. The children needed no direction; they shuffled quickly away. Zhava called flames to her. They appeared in her hands, one after the other, and she gently tossed them to the ground. They pooled at her feet, dancing and tumbling over each other and spreading across the damp ground. Steam began rippling through the air as they dried off the wet stones. Zhava kept calling them, kept dropping them, kept stepping backward and laying a carpet of fire across the cavern floor. Within moments, the flames had spread in a half-circle around Lojuen and the unconscious servant, effectively capturing them in that corner of the little cavern.

Next she turned her attention to the unconscious servant just outside the little cave where she and Plishka had been held prisoner. She dropped dozens – hundreds – of the little flames from her palms and let them run and dance and leap to that edge of the cave until they had surrounded that spot as well. Lojuen was surrounded by one wave of flaming men, and the servant and the cave with the unconscious Ooleng were surrounded by another.

"Eight days," Zhava called over her shoulder as she walked away. "One day for each egg. And if you try to escape, you will get burned."

"You cannot do this," Lojuen yelled, his words echoing through the expanse. "We had a bargain – my life for those horses."

"The sengret comes with us," Zhava said to Plishka. She held out the reed whistle. "I think this controls it."

"Do you hear me?" Lojuen said, his voice wild. "You will pay for this, woman. You will pay for your treachery. You and all the other women cursed by Coredor!"

Zhava stopped. She had heard enough of this God and the curses he had placed on the daughters of Tu and Re, and all the other children like her, the ones with Abilities. Viekoosh and his people followed this terrible God, and apparently so did Lojuen, and probably even his son Ooleng. She called one more flame to herself, one more dancing man into the palm of her hand, and she leaned forward and whispered to him. "Tell all your little friends: Double the time. Keep these men your prisoners for 16 days." She set him on the ground, and he ran to the sea of flames flickering in the large cavern, and then she and Plishka led the children out the mouth of the cave and away from Lojuen's wild ranting.

# CHAPTER 21

Two servants were guarding the horses, but several flashes of Plishka's lightning made those men run screaming into the night. There were six horses and three wagons, all of which were flatbeds apparently ready to cart away the wooden crates. They tied the sengret into the back of one wagon, then searched the remaining campsite. They found bedrolls enough for half a dozen men and a couple bags of food. It was mostly dried meats, but the hungry children didn't care; it was more food than they'd had in several nights. They climbed into the backs of the wagons, bundled themselves against the chill, and settled in with strips of dried deer meat. Zhava and Plishka munched small strips of meat as they tended to the horses, saddling them and hitching them to the wagons. Neither had much experience with horses, but the saddles and harnesses were near enough to what Zhava had used with the farm animals growing up that with only a little trial and error she figured out how most of it was secured. Halfway through the process, one young boy climbed out of the wagon and offered to help. He said he could speak to the animals, and the work seemed to go more quickly with him whispering into the horses' ears.

They set off slowly down the trail with Zhava and her flames at the front to light their way and Plishka and her lightning guarding the rear of the procession. Three of the children volunteered to keep the reins of the wagons, but the rest were quickly asleep or trying to rest in the backs of the wagons. They traveled like that until the moon was high in the sky, then stopped to rest, assuming they were far enough from the cliffside cave that no one would pursue them. Late the next morning they ate more of the dried meats, found a stream for water, and set off again. During the day, Zhava and Plishka sat on the wagons and scanned the trail for problems, but nothing happened. They met no one else, and no one seemed to be following behind. The boy who claimed to speak with animals spent most of his time riding in the last wagon with the sengret, apparently fascinated by the enormous bird. He had removed the bird's blindfold, and it jerked and bobbed its head and wings with each bump of the road, but the boy seemed able to make the bird remain in the wagon.

For two more days they followed the trail, their supplies beginning to run low and their taste for dried meats waning fast. By the middle of the third day down the mountain, Zhava finally recognized some rock formations in the distance. She sighted from the rocks and down to the plains in the distance, and she guessed they were no more than a couple days from her family's farm. Had she been alone on a camel, she could have covered the distance in one long day, but the wagons and the children slowed them down. Plishka took some of the children out hunting and returned with three rabbits. Some water from the stream, some seasonings from the food bag, and they had a rather bland meal of rabbit soup that evening. It was a welcome change.

The next two days were more of the same, and Zhava began to relax as they neared her family's farm. By the evening of the second day, she thought she could actually see the edge of her Papa's grazing field and some of his cattle. She was anxious to be so near her home and her family again. She had not been able to say good-bye to her Mama, and her Papa had simply stood in the yard and watched her and Priestess Marmaran depart. She had no idea how well they would welcome her return...or if they even would. For the children, however, she had to try, and she counted on their presence to smooth over any problems. No matter Papa or Mama's feelings toward her, they would never turn away weary travelers so desperate for food and shelter.

By late morning of the next day, they reached the edge of her Papa's farmstead. She could tell that the grass was bitten down short, so the cattle or the sheep had been grazing here recently, perhaps only a couple days before they arrived. They cut across the flat land, and it wasn't long before a servant came running toward them from far away, his dirty robes billowing behind him. They did not recognize each other, but Zhava assured the man she was the farmer's daughter sent to the Hibaro, and he agreed to relay the message. He ran ahead to inform the household.

They met the long trail that wound its way up the middle of the land, and Zhava's heart began to race. She was returning home. When she left with Priestess Marmaran and Io Liori and Io Kua, she had never thought to return. She had never even considered that she might want to return, and seeing it all again now, she was even less sure how she felt. It felt good to be back to a place she knew, a place where she had lived and grown to be a young woman. But...she was no longer the same person she had been when she lived here. She had done so many new things she never expected to do – never knew she was even capable of accomplishing.

They followed that trail up to the side of Zhava's home, and the same servant ran to tend to their horses and wagons. Zhava squeezed Plishka's hand, asked her to remain with the children, then went on alone up to the side door of the house that led from the well and on up to the kitchen. The door was open, and heat and the blissful smells of a beef stew wafted over her. She shut her eyes and breathed it all in. The room was empty, but her mind filled in the gaps for the moment. Her brothers arguing in the yard. Papa coming into the kitchen and sneaking a taste of the stew when Mama was pretending not to see. Marmaran sitting on the wooden bench at the side table and making little Zhava recite her evening lessons from the Kandor. Those were good memories.

She opened her eyes. Mama stood in the center of the kitchen, staring at her in silence. She looked somehow older, more tired than she had been when Zhava was still living here.

"So," Mama said, glancing up and down Zhava's torn and dirty clothes. "You're back."

"Yes, Mama."

"Well, I guess that's good," she said with a sigh. She pointed at the sink. "Those dishes from the midday meal, they need doing. Get to it." She turned and walked back upstairs.

Zhava took a step forward, then stopped. No, she thought. She was not here to do dishes. She was not here this time as a daughter. She was here this time as a representative of the Hibaro, an Initiate who had risked her life to fend off an evil man and rescue a group of Candidates who had been taken against their will. She was here this time to request safe lodging for the charges in her care. She was here, not as a daughter, but as one among a group of people traveling through and just trying to get back...home.

She turned and walked away.

Plishka and the servant had unloaded the children from the first two wagons, and the boy who could speak to animals, Weclin, was making calming, cooing noises to the sengret in the back of the final wagon. The servant led the children a few at a time to the nearby stream where they could wash themselves. Zhava considered joining them, but then noticed two men walking through the far field and toward the activity. She knew the shorter man immediately – her Papa – and she walked to him. The field was uneven and tramped down from the grazing, and Zhava walked it slowly so she did not stumble or fall. Her Papa saw her approaching, and he clapped the second man on the shoulder – the hired farmhand, Zhava now recognized – and the man walked away toward the little shack where he lived at the edge of the fields. Papa continued toward Zhava.

They met in the middle of the grazing field, and Papa stopped a bit away from Zhava, his hands on his hips as he looked her up and down.

"You're a fine mess," he said with a low chuckle. He reached out, gripped her shoulders – she winced as he grabbed her injured, left shoulder – and pulled her in close.

Zhava was so startled at the hug that she didn't even respond at first, but then she tentatively reached around him and returned the affection. He broke his grip before she, and he stepped back, glancing at the ground and straightening the belt at his waist. He cleared his throat and began ambling on toward the house.

"Who are these folk?" he asked, waving at the activity around the wagons.

"Children from the Hibaro. They were being sold as slaves up in the mountains, but we helped them escape."

"Did you now? That's good. Really good." He glanced over at her. "And that shoulder of yours? What happened there?"

So he had noticed. She said in a lower voice, "That's...a knife wound."

"Hm." They walked in silence for several moments, and then he said, "We'll have Rakeuvan tend to that knife wound for you. He can work miracles, that man."

"I remember. Thank you."

He waved his hand through the air, brushing aside her thanks. "How long will you be staying?"

"Not long," she said, hoping to assure him with that answer that they would not be a burden to the family. "We should return to the Hibaro as soon as possible. They probably think we're all dead."

"Sounds like quite a tale," Papa said. "You'll have to share it with us over the evening meal. And do not feel you must rush away; we can tend to your horses and the children for as long as you need. A day or two...three if need be."

They had reached the wagons, and Papa's eyes grew wide as he watched Weclin lead the sengret into an empty room of the workshop, but he said nothing about the sight. Instead he began greeting the children and learning their names. Mama soon came out to the wagons to do the same, but she avoided Zhava's gaze. By the time the children had washed much of the grime and dust down the stream and dried off, the sun was nearly set. Mama and the servant walked to the rear of the house, back in through the kitchen, while Papa led the children and Plishka and Zhava through the home's front door and into the center courtyard. Torches had been lit along the walls, casting bright light and dancing shadows across the colorful flowers and tall, scraggly trees that grew within. A bright linen had been laid out on the ground, covered in figs and grapes, and bowls were set out for the beef stew that would be brought out soon. Zhava sat at the edge of the courtyard and ate her stew as she watched Papa. He chatted and laughed and listened intently to all the children babbling around him. Even Mama smiled and talked to the children as she directed the servant to distribute the rest of the bowls and serve the food. It was such a beautiful sight; it felt almost...loving.

The conversation began turning toward the fight in the mountain cave, to how Zhava and Plishka had helped the children escape. How Zhava had fought the evil High Priest. How Plishka had thrown lightning against the walls to scare the evil Purneesite traders – Lojuen and Ooleng and their servants, though the children did not know those names for their story. Papa glanced back at Zhava several times during the more exciting parts of the story, his eyebrows furrowed. He seemed to study her, and he looked at her differently, seemed to be evaluating her somehow.

She decided to leave before the story of the fight reached its explosive conclusion. She had lived it; she didn't need to hear the chidren's telling of it. And, really, Papa's studious gaze unnerved her. She didn't know if he was proud or puzzled or angry or what. Better to be away, to let him decide his feelings on his own.

Slowly, trying hard not to distract the children, she walked along the edge of the courtyard and toward the heavy blanket separating it and the kitchen. She hadn't seen Mama for a long while, which probably meant she was tending to some outside work with one of the servants. Zhava didn't care; she wasn't looking for her Mama.

The kitchen was humid, but the chill of the night was beginning to pull some of the heat out the rear door. Two oil lamps were burning, one near the sink – where, Zhava noticed, someone else had washed those dishes from the noonday meal – and the second at the little table near the door. The table where she and Marmaran would practice her Abilities and recite lessons from the Kandor. She smiled at the memory and tried hard not to think of where Priestess Marmaran's bones and spirit might now be held.

She took the lamp off the table and climbed the steep, narrow stairs to the upper floor. When she had left with Io Liori, she had left everything behind. She now realized that might have been a mistake. Those little wood carvings from the side table of her bedroom would be a nice, personal touch back in her Initiate room – and she could show them to her friends, Barae and Posef and Plishka. That felt good, to say that she had friends. The door to her room was closed, and she slid aside the bolt and pushed it open – then stopped and stared into the dark room, the oil lamp's flickering flame casting bouncing shadows across the walls.

Her little bed on the floor was gone. The table was gone. In their places now stood a small pile of clothes, a sack of cotton, and a spinning wheel and chair. The shutters were closed and latched tight. Bits of thread and patches of cloth lay scattered across the floor.

Zhava just stared into the room that used to be her bedroom, too stunned to even move.

"What are you doing?"

She turned to see Mama climbing the stairs, an oil lamp in her hand.

"My...room?" Zhava said.

Mama walked over, yanked the door shut, and slid the bolt back into place. "You left. We needed a sewing room."

"And my things? My clothes? My carvings?"

"We threw them away. You obviously didn't care enough to take them with you."

They stared at each other in the dark hallway, the two little flames of the lamps flickering between them, and Zhava's anger began to rise. Did Mama really despise her so much that she would wipe away all memories of her? Did Papa care so little for his only daughter – adopted daughter, she had come to realize – that he would allow this to happen? It had been unlikely that she would return from the Hibaro very soon, but to simply throw away her belongings? To toss them aside...as easily as they tossed her aside? Daughters weren't like sons, but that did not mean they weren't people. That did not mean they did not have feelings. Lives. Affection, even love, for the treasures of their youth.

Zhava realized there was nothing here for her...except the answer to one last, burning question.

"Who is my mother?"

Mama stepped back and squinted at Zhava in the dim light. "Your mother? I am your mother."

"I know the truth, Mama," Zhava said, glancing down. This was harder to do than she thought it would be, but she was determined now that she would learn the answer to this question. "You are not the mother who birthed me. Who was she?"

"You ungrateful little urchin," Mama spat.

Zhava jerked at the sudden outburst.

"You have lived with us all these years, and you want to know who dropped you off?" Mama continued, her voice rising to a yell. "Who dumped you on our doorstep? What do you think, that they'll take you in now? Welcome you as the daughter they abandoned? After all these years?"

The intensity of Mama's yelling surprised Zhava, and it made her even angrier. She clenched her fist, feeling that this argument was unfair. Mama knew the truth, and she was holding back, using the answer as a cruel way of tormenting Zhava.

"Your mother didn't want you then, and she certainly would not want you now. Any woman who can dump a child – a baby – on someone's doorstep. That woman is not worth the respect you would grant your worst enemy."

"Tell me her name," Zhava yelled back, trying to get her words spoken over Mama's increasingly harsh screams.

"I will never tell you that name. I am your Mama – me!"

"Tell me."

"I nursed you!"

"What was her name?"

"I cared for you!"

"Just tell me!"

"I tried to teach you–"

"Her name!"

"–but you have never listened! You rebellious little–"

"You are not my mother!"

Mama's hand shot up with such ferocity, and Zhava's training took over without even a thought. She blocked the strike with one arm.

"You ungrateful–" Mama began.

Zhava twisted her arm, knocked Mama's hand aside, stepped back for better balance, and turned to strike out – prepared to fight just as she'd done against that soldier in the cave.

"Stop!" a voice boomed through the narrow hallway.

Zhava swung her arm wide, swiping just above Mama's head but not connecting with anything more than the top curls of graying hair. She turned to see Papa standing at the top of the steps, an oil lamp in one hand and a child gripping his other hand. The little boy's eyes were wide as he peeked out from behind Papa's robes and glanced between Zhava and Mama.

Mama burst into tears immediately and wiped at her eyes. "You should have heard the things – just the most awful things."

Zhava stared at Mama, stunned. Who was the one yelling about being ungrateful? That certainly had not been Zhava.

Papa stepped to the top landing and pulled the wide-eyed boy forward. "This little one spilled his supper," he said to Mama.

Zhava could see the orange broth stains across the boy's thin shirt. He turned away, trying to hide the spill from Zhava.

"I'll deal with her," Papa said, glancing at Zhava, "while you tend to this little one."

"Thank you," Mama said with a whimper. She took the boy's hand, and the two of them hurried down the stairs. Their steps retreated through the kitchen and outside. Zhava wasn't sure where she planned to take the boy. The washroom was up here, right next to Zhava's room – now the sewing room – and the kitchen held still more washing supplies. But outside...to the well? Although it really didn't matter, so long as Mama went away and stopped her yelling.

"Walk with me," Papa said. He turned and stomped down the stairs.

Zhava followed. They went through the dark kitchen and out into the night's chilled air. Zhava set her lamp on the back step, wrapped her arms about her chest, and followed Papa through the yard. They walked slowly, purposefully, in silence for a while. They passed the small stables where the horses and the sengret had been put up for the night. They walked around the fenced-in yard where a dozen camels were arrayed, most of them asleep, but one that eyed them as they walked past. Papa had not owned a dozen camels when she lived here. Two camels only, and those both to haul goods to town.

They climbed the path of the little rise that led to the near pastures. At this time of night, the cattle would have all bedded down, and as they reached the top, Zhava could see them on the hillsides as far as the rising moon would shine. It was a beautiful sight, the cattle resting beneath a starlit sky, and she took in a deep breath and shut her eyes. Out here, in the silence and the dark, away from her screaming Mama and the anger of not knowing who she was or where she really came from...she could almost forget.

"We expanded the herds," Papa said. His voice was soft. Not quite a whisper, but certainly more gentle than Zhava expected after what he'd witnessed at the house. After what that little boy had been forced to see.

"I noticed," she replied, matching his tone.

"That Io paid very well when she took you away."

"I saw that, too." Yes, she remembered Papa standing in the yard, the bags of gold at his feet.

He turned and studied her, glanced at her from head to feet. "You have grown so much."

"I have not grown. I have been gone just the one moon."

"But now you have grown. Those children know it. Your friend, Plishka, she knows it, too. She will follow you, and that is a heavy burden." He turned back to stare at the fields, then shuffled away a little and sat in the grass. He looked up and watched the stars sparkle.

Zhava joined him. She wasn't sure what to say. She didn't know if he thought it was a good or a bad thing that she had "grown so much." She wasn't even sure he was right.

"Who told you about your mother?" he said, his voice much quieter this time.

"Salient Noomira."

"A Salient," he spat. "Witches, all of them."

Zhava did not reply. Salient Noomira had seemed nice, at least nicer than some of the other people she had met. Certainly nicer than the evil High Priest.

"Your Mama cannot tell you the name of your birth mother. She does not know it."

Zhava sighed. She turned to the ground and started playing with the blades of grass, tugging on them, breaking off a few of them and scattering them in the night's gentle breeze.

"And you?" she asked.

"I did not meet her either."

Then no one was left who would know, she thought. Salient Noomira had been killed, and no one else at the Hibaro had said anything about Zhava having a different mother. How would she ever learn the truth?

"Five men brought you to our home that evening."

Zhava stopped tugging on the grass and listened.

"I remember that night clearly. Your Mama and I had sent the boys on an errand to town, and we did not expect them back until the morning. A simple errand for the boys. Those five men came to the front door later into the evening, and they said they had been watching our farm, they had noticed we had no daughters, and they said they could offer us a daughter. Mama and I were suspicious of those men immediately. Where had the child come from? Who was the child's mother? They wouldn't say. All they would say was that the King would reward us someday for being loyal subjects in this small matter. And then the one, a man named Viekoosh-"

Zhava tensed.

"-pulled aside his traveling cloak for just a moment, and he let us see the Priest robes he wore beneath them. The others did the same – they were all men of the King – and then they handed us the baby, you, and your Mama held you for the first time. I believe she loved you that first moment; I could see it in her eyes. You were sleeping, wrapped in several blankets against the night air, and Mama carefully pulled aside those blankets from your face, and she smiled. It was the largest smile I had seen her give to anyone...in so long. I could not remember the last time she smiled like that. I agreed to join in the men's service at that very moment. We would adopt this baby, keep the secret as they said to do. The men pulled out a small bag of gold right then, handed it over to me, and said to tell no one what had happened that night – especially not you. We agreed, of course, and the five men left."

He stopped speaking, and Zhava glanced up at him. His jaw was clenched, and he was wiping his eyes with the edge of his shirt sleeve. He was fighting back tears, she realized, but she had no idea why.

"I – I went upstairs. It was just a moment, no longer. Just to get some more blankets. But when I returned, two of those men had come back. I will never forget those two, Viekoosh and Kretsch were their names. They had come into the courtyard, and they were with your Mama.

She was still holding you, but...but she was looking at one of the men. She was turned and looking at Kretsch. She was staring into his eyes as if she was asleep while she was awake, and he...he was holding her head in his hands, and he was staring back at her. The other man, Viekoosh, he was laughing at the whole thing, as if it was all some sort of joke to him. I demanded that they leave, but they wouldn't go. They said they had one more thing to do before they could leave the baby – before they could leave you with me and your Mama. They said I had to make a choice, that they couldn't trust me to keep the secret of their visit to myself unless I first made a choice. Unless I saw for myself how bad things could go for us if anyone ever discovered the truth of your delivery to us that night. The one who was staring at Mama, the one called Kretsch, he was an Apprentice Salient of the King's First Order, and he was going through Mama's mind. He was going through her memories, and he was giving her new ones, replacing...replacing some of the ones that belonged in there with new ones of his own making. New ones that would tell a completely different story. But first I had to make...a choice."

Zhava reached over and took Papa's hand. He didn't move away, but he didn't turn to her either.

"I'm sorry, Zhava," he whispered. "I have never told you this – I could never tell you this, or our lives would have been made so much worse, those men said so. Your life would have been so much worse. Unbearable. He said to me that I had to make a choice. I had to decide if you...had been abandoned on our doorstep by some unknown woman, or if you had been the daughter of another woman. My daughter...from another woman. He said that one of those memories was going into your Mama, but the choice of which memory was mine to make. I had to decide. If you had been abandoned on our doorstep, then I would have insisted on keeping you. Your Mama would hate you for the rest of your life, but...but she would remain...loving to me. She would stay by my side because of the love I showed to an abandoned child. She would always love me. If I chose the other, however. If I chose that you were the daughter of another woman. If your Mama believed I had cheated on her with another woman, then I would lose her love forever. She would despise me...but she would love you all the more. She would never blame you for what I had done. She would adopt you as her own, and she would give you all of the love that she had for me. That was my choice. That was what Viekoosh and Kretsch said I had to do. I had to make my decision right there, in that courtyard, in that very moment. Decide who she would love, and – and I am so sorry, Zhava. They made me choose right then, and I chose...I chose...."

She leaned forward, and she wrapped her arms around him. He bent his head and wiped at more tears as his body shook silently. If anything, that frightened Zhava even more. In all her years at home, she could not remember her Papa ever crying. The pain he felt over this action, the regret he felt from this choice he was forced to make, must be so severe if he would shed so many tears with her.

"I'm sorry, too," Zhava whispered.

He gripped her arm and pulled her close, and they sat like that for the longest time, hugging each other, comforting each other, and giving each other all the love that they had never been able to share as a whole, complete family.

# CHAPTER 22

They stayed at the farmstead another two nights. Several of the children had grown weak from their time held captive in the cave, and Mama took it as her duty to give them the food and rest they needed to get better. Zhava watched Mama closely when they were with the Candidate children, and she could see that love Papa talked about with every smile and kind gesture Mama showed to them, and somehow that made the pain so much worse. She had already known High Priest Viekoosh had become an evil man as he followed the God Coredor, but she had no idea who this "Apprentice Salient Kretsch" was who had poisoned Mama's mind – though his name felt somehow familiar, as if she had heard it once before and simply could not place it.

The Candidate boy who could speak with animals, Weclin, used all of his time to work with the sengret. He spent nearly the entire first day with the bird in the stables, then led it out to the yard for all to see during the early morning of their second day. He told them all how smart the sengret was and how they had reached an "understanding" with each other. He removed the bird's hood and let it soar into the sky. It circled the farmstead several times, then dove for the ground and snatched a rabbit from a nearby field. It returned to the yard and began tearing into its meal, and that was when most of the children dispersed with equal cries of fascination and disgust. Only Weclin ventured near the sengret as it ate, and even he kept a wary distance from the carnage. Papa, however, was most intrigued by the giant bird, and he spent much of the morning questioning Weclin about it.

By that evening's meal, everyone knew it was time to be leaving, but it was far more of a joyous affair with the unexpected arrival of one of Zhava's brothers, Caleb. Zhava was sure her three brothers had all been informed of her arrival, but Caleb, being closest in age to her and still living single in his little house in the valley, had always been most fond of her. He sat with her and Plishka at the meal, and he listened as they told him of their adventures in the cave, though as the evening wore on he seemed to listen far more intently to Plishka than he did to his little sister. After the sun set, he said he had to return to tend to his own home, but he made a point of telling Plishka he would see her once more before she left.

The children finally felt rested, with full bellies, and they all agreed they were ready to continue on to the Hibaro the next morning. Zhava's shoulder had been tended several times by one of the family's servants, Rakeuvan, and it had nearly stopped hurting. She was looking forward to Sister Tegara administering her healing touch upon it...assuming Sister Tegara still lived. She pushed aside that sobering thought and focused on the evening's preparations.

As Papa had said, Plishka seemed to be at Zhava's side most of the time. Though a little older than Zhava, Plishka deferred to her on most things about their return journey, including what items they should bring with them, what time they should leave, who should ride in which wagon, and even the rotation of watches along the trail. Again, Papa was correct that this level of responsibility seemed quite a burden to Zhava. She wasn't sure she liked being solely responsible for all the decisions she was being asked to make.

At dawn on the third day, Zhava directed the children onto the wagons. Weclin guided the sengret, its hood removed, to fly up onto the third wagon, and then he took his place next to the bird. That seating arrangement made Zhava nervous, but Weclin insisted, several times, that he and the sengret had reached an understanding with each other. She allowed them to ride together only after Weclin agreed to harness the bird to a sideboard. She would watch them closely, and if the sengret harmed Weclin in any way, she would cut off the bird's head.

Papa and Mama and a couple of the servants joined them all in the yard to wish them well on their journey back to the Hibaro. Zhava's brother Caleb showed up with several packages of dried meats and fruits to distribute to the children, and one special package he presented to Plishka – only after Zhava became busy helping some children climb into a wagon.

When the children and the supplies were finally loaded, Zhava went up to her parents.

"Safe travels," Papa said with a stiff bow.

Zhava reached forward and hugged him. He gave her a quick hug in return, then pushed her away with a glance at Mama.

Mama said nothing as she stared into the distance.

"Thank you for letting us stay," Zhava said. "The children are doing so much better."

"You watch those children," Mama said, pointing at the wagons. "I don't know what got into your head thinking you could be a mother to all of them – you can barely take care of yourself."

"Yes, Mama," Zhava said. She clenched her jaw at the insult as she gave Mama a quick bow. She kept remembering Papa's words of the other night, that Mama had been forced to act this way, that this was because of two evil men who followed the God Coredor and thought it funny to ruin people's lives. Though she knew those things in her mind, it didn't make the sting of the words any easier to endure.

"You've been lazy most of your life," Mama said, "but now you have to step up. You have responsibilities to those little ones. They're in your charge."

"Yes, Mama," she repeated, again with a quick bow, and she turned to walk away before anything else could be said.

She and Plishka – and Caleb – checked over the wagons one last time. With everything in place, they mounted the lead wagon, first Plishka to take the reins and then Zhava to act as lookout, and turned to wave goodbye. The children all yelled their thanks, and even the sengret gave a loud caw. Plishka snapped the reins, and they trundled off down the main road from the farmstead and on their way back to the Hibaro. Zhava gave one final wave, but neither Mama nor Papa returned it. She turned in the wooden seat and listened to the wagon wheels thumping and crunching across the ground and the horses' bridles chinking together.

"Did you see this?" Plishka asked. She held open the little package Caleb had given her. It contained six long strips of dried meat, several handfuls of dates and figs – and a bunch of blue Lagav Meadow flowers.

Zhava's eyes went wide. "My brother gave you those?"

Plishka grunted but said nothing.

Zhava turned back. Caleb was standing at the edge of the road and watching them ride away. He waved, and Zhava waved back before turning around again.

"You can smile about those flowers," Zhava said, "but I can tell you some awful stories from when we were children."

Plishka did not reply, instead handing over another package, this one much smaller and bundled in burlap, tied with a length of oily rope.

"What's this?" Zhava asked.

"It's from your father. He said to give it you only after we'd left the farmstead. Apparently it would make your mother angry?"

She fiddled with the little knot at the top of the bundle, wiping the grease on the underside of the wooden board on which they sat, then slowly, carefully unfolded the rough cloth. She could feel several small items rattling around inside, and she was careful that none of them fell out. As she pulled the last of the burlap folds aside, she gasped.

Plishka glanced over. "What are those?"

Zhava picked up first one and then another and then another. The bag contained the little wooden carvings from her bedside table, the ones Mama had said had been thrown away. The camel she had carved with its two humps. The long, thin stretch of wood that she had carved into a tiny boat – she could still remember it floating in the puddles after the spring rains. A bit of bark she had carved into the face of an old man, just because she thought it was funny. And, most precious to her, a tiny bit of wood she had slowly etched into the curved, wrinkled face of her teacher, Priestess Marmaran.

"He kept them," Zhava whispered. She wiped a tear from her eye and quickly folded up the little carvings back into their burlap wrappings. She hugged the bag to her chest and shut her eyes. She didn't know what they would find when they returned to the Hibaro, how many might still be alive and how many had died in the fires and the fighting that Plishka had witnessed.  She had no idea why she had been given away as a baby at that little farmstead, or the name of her real mother.  She knew, though nothing had been said these several days, that Plishka wanted nothing more than to venture back into the mountains and find her lost sister.  And, most important to herself, Zhava wanted to stop High Priest Viekoosh from his evil plans, and retrieve the necklace with her Priestess Marmaran's remains.  All of those pieces of her life were calling out for her attention, but at this moment, in the peace and rhythm of their horses slowly pulling them back to the Hibaro – and with the love that had come from the simple gesture of her Papa giving back to her these little treasures of her childhood – she knew that she could face all of those trials whenever they came.

Made in the USA
Middletown, DE
25 September 2019